W9-BDT-792

It was almost like a scene from a farce!

Elissa felt herself blush with embarrassment. She stood helplessly at the stove, with Stacey at one door of the kitchen, Logan at the other. "This isn't what it looks like," she said, "believe me...."

There was pure skepticism in the look Stacey sent her, and who could blame her? A strange young woman, clad only in a fancy peignoir, in Logan's kitchen, preparing his breakfast.

But Logan didn't seem overly upset that his fiancée was misconstruing the entire situation; it was simple enough to him. In the Outback one always helped a stranger.

Stacey's voice was cold. "Logan, I'm waiting for an explanation." Then, as Elissa tried to speak, "Not you. Logan has to tell me who you are!"

OTHER
Harlequin Romances
by ESSIE SUMMERS

Many of these titles are available at your local bookseller
or through the Harlequin Reader Service.

For a free catalogue listing all available Harlequin Romances,
send your name and address to:

HARLEQUIN READER SERVICE,
M.P.O. Box 707, Niagara Falls, N.Y. 14302
Canadian address: Stratford, Ontario, Canada N5A 6W2

or use coupon at back of book.

The Lake of the Kingfisher

by

ESSIE SUMMERS

Harlequin Books

TORONTO • LONDON • NEW YORK • AMSTERDAM
SYDNEY • HAMBURG • PARIS

Original hardcover edition published in 1978
by Mills & Boon Limited

ISBN 0-373-02239-5

Harlequin edition published February 1979

Dedicated to the three grandchildren

Elizabeth brought us,

Murray, Jennifer and Kathryn Jack;

and of course to that adorable,

accident-prone canine, Benjamin.

———◆●◆———

Copyright © 1978 by Essie Summers.
Philippine copyright 1978. Australian copyright 1978.

All rights reserved. Except for use in any review, the reproduction or utilization
of this work in whole or in part in any form by any electronic, mechanical or
other means, now known or hereafter invented, including xerography,
photocopying and recording, or in any information storage or retrieval system,
is forbidden without the permission of the publisher. All the characters in this
book have no existence outside the imagination of the author and have no
relation whatsoever to anyone bearing the same name or names. They are not
even distantly inspired by any individual known or unknown to the author, and
all the incidents are pure invention.

The Harlequin trademark, consisting of the word HARLEQUIN and the
portrayal of a Harlequin, is registered in the United States Patent
Office and in the Canada Trade Marks Office.

Printed in U.S.A.

CHAPTER ONE

ELISSA MONTGOMERY stared blankly at Rupert Airlie. 'Go right to New Zealand to redecorate Airlie House for you? You must be joking! It would be so much cheaper to engage a firm there. The firm Victoria worked for, for instance.'

Rupert Airlie chuckled. 'Put it down to a whim, Elissa. I'm old enough now to be indulged in such things.'

'Don't give me that. I may have called you Uncle Rupert ten years ago, but when you suddenly turned up in England, I was amazed to find you so young. But even a whim has to have some reason behind it, so . . .?'

'Because I don't want a stranger doing it, lass. You knew and loved Airlie House and the Glen and the lake when your mother was governess to my children. I think you were even keener than Judith and Elspeth to listen to the stories of the early days, so you have a feeling for it. You wouldn't banish things that ought to be retained for posterity, or put way-out styles into a one-hundred-year-old dwelling. When you took me through that Georgian house you restored in the next village I made up my mind. I've set my heart on it, girl. When you said you had three months' leave to pay a surprise visit to your mother in Canada, and that Victoria Doig was going to take your place here, I felt it was providential. I got hold of Victoria on the quiet and found out she could do it for an indefinite period if need be.

'If you'd fly out to Ludwigtown for a few weeks, then I'd pay your fare there and back, with a stop-over on the way back to see Meg. Canada is practically on the way. I take it she wants to stay as long as possible with her sister?'

'Yes. It's helping Aunt Jean to adjust to her sudden loss better, and her daughter will be taking up a position in her home town later. But it will cost you the earth, Rupert.'

His blue eyes lit up. 'So you *will* consider it? I was only terrified you were so set on this long holiday in Canada that you wouldn't. Canada is a glorious country—I know from my visits to Douglas.'

Elissa's blue-green eyes went reflective. 'Could it be any more beautiful than New Zealand? And specially Central Otago. Most of all, Airlie House, the Glen, the lake?'

Rupert knew enough to hold his peace right then, to allow this coppery-headed girl in front of him to conjure up in the eye of her mind, the loved remembrances of some of the years of her childhood ... Moana-Kotare, the Lake of the Kingfisher, so-called not only because of the kingfishers that nested in its banks but because its snow-fed waters held all the shimmering blues and greens of the *kotare*'s plumage. Snowy-shawled peaks mirrored themselves in its waters, dark-green pines set a serrated border on the Ludwig side, but at the Glen Airlie inlet native forests clothed the indented shoreline save where in solitary bays, settlers of long ago had planted willow and poplar saplings, oak and larch and birch, to bring a touch of autumn into an evergreen land.

Elissa would never forget the utter desolation that had descended upon her when her mother had so suddenly decided to return to England and to her own kin. Understandable, had she done just that in her first grief at losing her husband so young. Angus Montgomery had been a New Zealander with no near relations of his own. Their small farm had been sold up, mortgages repaid, and the balance gave Marguerite Montgomery a nest-egg for her daughter's future. For the present she had taken a position as governess to a widower on a remote lake homestead. It had meant their keep, a roof over their heads, security.

But evidently only for a time had it satisfied Mother. She hadn't even given the fourteen-year-old Elissa time to take the launch over to Glen Airlie to say goodbye to loved scenes, to her puppy, the cats, to Elspeth and Judy. 'Goodbyes can be very sad when you're young, darling,' she'd said. 'Better to be up and off, and to remember them as untinged with sadness.' Elissa had, by then, been attending

High School in Ludwigtown, and had boarded at Cloudy Hill, with old Trudi Klausner.

All the delights of Glen Airlie had been bottled up in Elissa, because Mother had never seemed to want to talk about those years. So it had remained an idyllic memory, of an inlet on a lake, a gracious homestead, a scented garden ... a place where, in those days, not even a road ran by, so that its solitudes were undefiled. A secret place, a dream, that Elissa had always treasured.

But now it was being offered to her on a platter ... this chance to revisit that remembered paradise. But was it ever wise to try to recapture such delights? Time and again people visited some spot that in their childhood had been beloved over all, only to find themselves disenchanted. Better to remember Airlie House as it had been, with its gabled roof, the little diamond-paned windows sparkling in the sun, its inglenook where the children had listened to Rupert's tales of the hardships the pioneers had faced, carving out sheep-runs from cruelly dramatic country, their only pleasures the beauty of their surroundings, the little jetty jutting out into the kingfisher-blue waters, their one link with the distant world; the bellbirds singing above the cascades, friendly fantails fluttering about their heads in their forays into the tangy, secret forest, the trout swimming in the clear green pools of the Wai-o-Atarangi, the Waters of the Shadow; the shoreline of their side of the lake, holding promise of exciting explorations in bays and other arms of the lake, the back of beyond some called it, gloriously remote, loved, lonely, lovely.

Certainly a road led to Glen Airlie now, a rough, steep, dangerous road that stopped there. It had ended the worst of their isolation, Rupert said, but had it also despoiled it? She looked at Rupert, patiently watching the expressions flitting across her face. 'Is it as lovely as I remember it?'

He understood. 'Just as lovely. So little is changed, and though work needs to be done to Airlie House now, I want it more restored than modernised. After Donsie left I'd a good enough housekeeper, who knew all about preserves and linen and spit and polish, but lacked a love of old things. But the MacCorquodales are different. Mrs Mac feels an Early Colonial house like Airlie deserves something better. She said it needed a professional. You've heard me mention my manager, Logan MacCorquodale?'

She nodded. 'Well, if they approve, I wouldn't be meeting opposition there. But you've got a long visit ahead of you with Douglas in Canada, Rupert. I'd want you on the spot to advise, to consult with, to work out ways and means.'

He said, 'In these days of speedy air-travel, nowhere is far from anywhere else in time ... I could spend at least six weeks with Doug and family and then fly home. That would give you time to get the feel of the place, so that nothing need to be done with a sense of urgency. Besides, if you take off for Canada first, I've a notion your mother might put you off the idea.'

Elissa looked at him sharply, a query line between her russet brows. He said hurriedly, 'I mean she might want you to spend longer with her over there.'

'I doubt it. She's always trying to push me out of the nest. Unsuccessfully too. I'm quite happy to share a home with my mother still.'

Rupert cocked a brow at her. 'She wants you married? No hero on the horizon yet?'

'No, none. Anyway, I don't suppose she'll stay on much longer than three months. If I consider it ... I said *if* ... it's just as well it should be a surprise visit, so she won't be disappointed. It's a wonder I didn't succumb to the temptation to tell her ... as a child I could never keep a secret. I seem to have reformed.'

Rupert had a wry twist to his mouth, she thought. He shrugged. 'I wouldn't call that reform. Who likes secretive people? Most prefer people who are open, above-board.'

Elissa wondered if he was thinking of Douglas, who, once he got away to Varsity, had gone wild, something that turned his father's blond hair to silver during the years Elissa had been at Glen Airlie. It had seemed odd when Rupert himself was such a winsome, strong character. He was still a handsome giant of a man, upright, moving lithely. But his face was sadder in repose than she had remembered it.

It hadn't been easy to rear three children by himself. Douglas had been a charmer, brilliant, not a plodder. Things had come too easily to him. But now, it seemed, he had made good. He had a splendid position in Toronto, wrote regularly to his father, was married, with a wonderful wife, children of his own, and did a lot of welfare work among today's youth.

Elissa said, 'Ever since I walked into Victoria's home in Haslemere and found you sitting there, drinking tea, I've just longed to see Glen Airlie again. It's almost as if it were meant to be. I met Victoria in the course of my work, naturally, because she was doing part-time for my firm, but apart from liking her for herself alone, I felt drawn to her because she came from Central Otago, even if we'd never even heard of each other. When she said her brother-in-law, Callum Doig, and Anna his wife, and her grand-parents were coming here and wanted to rent a house near them, I thought that was a godsend when I was thinking of taking off to see Mother—but for you to offer me a trip like this ... well, it must be my bonus year. Rupert, mad and all as it is, and so very costly to you, I'll do it, if you're quite sure you can afford it.'

He sprang up, eager as a boy. 'I'll cancel your flight to Canada and get you one to New Zealand. How about next week? I'm flying off then. It's all fixed up for Victoria to stand in for you, isn't it? I suddenly have a sense of urgency to restore Glen Airlie to its former glory. In the times when labour was so easy to get even in those remote areas, it was kept as it should be. If you can combine beautifying with making it more convenient, it'll mean a lot to me.'

Elissa's eyes narrowed. 'Rupert, there's something behind this. I'm going to be cheeky and ask outright ... are you thinking of marrying again?'

He burst out laughing. 'Oh, lass, you take twenty years off my age! No, there was only one woman, long ago, I'd have wanted for my second wife, but it wasn't to be.'

'Well, that's all right, because while a man might think a newly-decorated house might appeal to a woman, it would be only fair for her to have a say in the colours she wanted.'

'No, go ahead and decorate it as you would love to do it. Perhaps you've never had so free a hand before.'

'I certainly haven't, but I'll safeguard myself by saying I'll get all the preliminaries done, make sure certain fabrics are available there and not put anything irrevocable in the pipeline before you come home. I can see it all in my mind's eye, but I want you to outline a few preferences. Can we settle to that now? I'll write to tell Mother tonight, and perhaps you'd follow that up by seeing her in person? My Aunt Jean lives less than a hundred miles from Toronto, so how about you getting Douglas to drive you up to see her? She'd just love it. She hardly ever talked about New Zealand after we left there, except to tell me about my own father and their farm, but she had a soft spot for Doug and she's said once or twice she'd love to know if he made good or not. She was sure he would, and he certainly has.'

Before he could reply she said, 'On second thoughts I'll ring her instead of writing. Much more satisfactory. And I could tell her to expect you.'

Rupert said swiftly, 'No, don't do that. It'll be much cheaper if I ring her from Toronto. How about that? I'll get there before you get to New Zealand if we leave on the same day.'

Elissa had a strange feeling that this mattered to him— the timing. But why should it? Or did he fear that her mother wouldn't want her to go so far? Oh, she was being stupid. She must dismiss it from her mind. It was far too fanciful.

She said, 'But you'll be sure to go to see her, won't you? She was so fond of Douglas.'

Rupert didn't rush into speech this time. 'I'll see. Might just ring her, tell her, and leave it at that.'

Elissa knew a disappointment quite out of proportion to the proposal. Rupert continued: 'I'll send the Mac-Corquodales an air-letter. It gets even to the other side of the lake in five days. By the way, which way would you like to go in? By the new road? Or by launch as you used to go?'

She didn't need to consider that. Her mouth curved up at the corners in instant and delighted recollection. 'I'd like to go in by launch, to recapture the past. I'll never forget that first enchanted evening. The launch was delayed, remember, and we put in at sunset. Airlie House looked a dream, bathed in that sort of rose colour you see in films about deserts ... the little bay, and the dogs barking a welcome, and all the scents of Araby from the garden. I've never been able to understand Mother wanting to leave it.'

Rupert did not answer her. She continued on, more thoughtfully. 'Oh, that's stupid. What can children know of parents' feelings? I expect that, as she said, she couldn't bear to be away from her own folk a moment longer. Rupert, Mother always seemed so gay, so full of fun—had she ever spoken to you of unbearable homesickness? How blind and selfish children can be!'

He shook his head. 'Not selfish. Blind, perhaps. It's not just children who are blind, either. I was too. It's hard, naturally, for children to realise that their parents live a very different life from them, that they have needs children can't even begin to guess at. But *I* should have known— known and understood.'

For a moment he looked bleak, and a sort of pity swept her for Rupert who had lived without a wife for so many years, in mountain solitudes. He would have had needs too that they, Elspeth, Judy, herself had never imagined. Their happinesses needn't necessarily have been the happiness their elders would have desired. A longing to turn the clock back assailed her. But to go to Glen Airlie on a visit like this was the next best thing.

They left from Heathrow within an hour of each other, which was rather fun, one flying west, one south. It took a day and a half to reach New Zealand, another day to fly to the Deep South via Dunedin and Queenstown. Now, on a golden day of late winter that belied the snow on the high-tops, she was getting out of the Queenstown bus at Ludwig-town, in time to take the afternoon tourist launch across to Glen Airlie. Rupert had written the MacCorquodales to meet her at the launch office. Elissa had protested there was no need, but Rupert had insisted she be met.

But they weren't there. Neither were any tourists wait-ing, or any launch loading up supplies for the only-access-by-water homesteads where still no roads reached. The launch had broken down at Twin Hills Bay, the ticket office told her.

She said, 'Then I expect there's a message from the MacCorquodales for me. They were to meet me here. I gather they would be brought across from Glen Airlie on the return trip from Twin Hills, so I expect they phoned the launch people, and perhaps they're coming by road. I'm going to work at Airlie House.'

'There's no message. That's odd. Unless Logan thought he'd get here before you did. That must be it. Like to ring them?'

She couldn't raise them. They must be on their way. An hour and a half later Elissa was getting fidgety. She was tired of ringing the homestead. She said, 'It'll be one of those things. Probably stuck on the road, a puncture or engine trouble—probably engine. You wouldn't get many cars on the road, perhaps none. I'll hire a car and drive round there.'

He looked at her dubiously. 'It's some road, especially to someone English. The surface is ghastly, hewn out of solid rock in some places.'

She grinned, suddenly lighthearted. 'I'm not English. I've just got a veneer over my New Zealand accent. Can you tell me where I can get a rental car?' The MacCorquodales would be mighty glad when she turned up under her own steam. Right now poor Logan MacCorquodale might be hoofing it to the nearest house for aid, while Mrs Mac-Corquodale sat it out in the car. In a remote area like that, the *nearest* house didn't necessarily mean *near*.

She vaguely remembered the first twenty miles or so. In her day it had ended past the third homestead and unless some of these huge mountain holdings had been cut up, she doubted if there'd be any more dwellings till she got to Glen Airlie. The MacCorquodales must be between here and the homestead, poor things. They would be mighty glad to see her. Mr MacCorquodale would probably run her and his wife back, then take the hired car back to Ludwigtown to get a mechanic. That would save Elissa returning next day, with someone following her. Unless there was a launch tomorrow. She'd forgotten to ask.

The car bounced and jolted over the road ... if you could call it that. It would be years before it was tarsealed or widened, yet access like this must be a minor miracle for Glen Airlie.

Mile after mile stretched before her, swinging round sharp bends on the edge of the lake, occasionally a notice rearing up to say: 'Blind Corner' or 'Beware of wind gusts'. Well, at least there was no traffic to bother her and if she did meet a car she was on the inner side. She had to concentrate so much on negotiating the bends and driving in the ruts that the enchantment of being beside the lake of her dream-world just didn't exist. And where, oh, where were the MacCorquodales?

She *must* be nearing the Glen. Across the lake on an angle was Mahanga-Puke, Twin Hills, and surely that formation of rocks beyond the shoulder of the next hill must be Crenellation Bluff? It looked exactly like the cut-out edge of an old castle's ramparts ... but she'd never seen it from this side before.

She ground up a cutting in her lowest gear and the view before her brought her to a stop at the highest point. She drew in a deep breath of fulfilment as there before her lay the incredible beauty of Glen Airlie, something that had brought the first Airlie, Walter Ogilvie Airlie, to make his home and carve out a hazardous future on this remote inlet of the Lake of the Kingfisher. It was a miniature harbour, each headland clothed with native forest, but circling the curve of the shore were European trees, willows upright and weeping, Lombardy poplars, great oaks and chestnuts, rowan trees, and further in the well-remembered avenue of lime trees and the orchard, bare now of leaves, and scattered all through the garden, maples, pussy willows, liquidambars, ribbonwoods, great gums with multi-coloured bark, silver birches, beeches, spruce and larch.

Although the house might need refurbishing within it looked well-preserved without, gleaming in white paint, with black facings, and under the gable-ends were the diamond-paned windows the child Elissa had loved, still sparkling like the facets of cut diamonds. It was a long, low house, showing traces of many additions, and except for a quaint turret on the top of the far wing, single-storeyed. As far as architecture was concerned, it was odd, but endearingly odd.

One of the long-ago Airlies had built the turret for a beauty-loving wife who'd complained that when the trees grew they might shut out her view of the lake, so he'd given her one with windows set to all points of the compass ... her cup filled and running over, she'd said to him, the story went.

The front terrace had curved pillars, beautifully symmetrical, with balustraded rails joining them, and at each side of the top step was a Grecian urn which she could remember as cascading aubretia and gentians bluely in summer, with bright red geraniums topping them. Now, with winter still holding a grip on the land, there was only the greenery to promise colour come spring. But in the garden, sheltered from the cold sou'west by giant trees, were splashes of colour where pink and white and yellow daisies were massed, where Chinese bamboo showed russet leaves, and here and there a cineraria, escaping all frosts, glowed blue and purple.

Elissa got out of the car to look her fill, standing with the surprisingly warm sun glinting on her red-gold hair and the gentle zephyr off the lake lifting a strand of it away from her forehead, a touch that stirred memories and brought a surge of gladness to her heart ... just imagine, a month ago she wouldn't have dreamed what felicity awaited her.

Then something registered. The house had a deserted

air. It was unseasonably hot yet not a window was open. The double garage doors were wide and revealed emptiness. Only a Land-Rover stood in the stable-yard. She looked across to the cottage ... that garage was wide open and empty too.

Well, there must be some explanation. She'd missed them on the road. Perhaps they'd had to call in at one of the three homesteads nearer Ludwigtown, though if anything had delayed them there surely they'd have rung the launch office. Still, things could happen out here in the wop-wops. They'd turn up eventually, full of apologies, no doubt. Unless they felt she ought to have waited in Ludwigtown. She didn't like the idea of a hitch. She hoped the MacCorquodales wouldn't feel she was a jolly nuisance.

She stopped the car at the little jetty with its clutter of drums and ropes, saw a rowing-boat rocking gently at its moorings, and noticed something new from her time. Along the green sward of the lake-beach were picnic tables and forms, rough stone fireplaces, a couple of barbecues and litter-bins. There was even a notice close to these. It said, 'This is Glen Airlie Inlet and private property, but we are happy to share its beauty with you if you leave it as you find it. All litter to go in the bins, all ashes to be doused. May you leave here refreshed in body and spirit by the tranquility of the lake and the peace of the high mountains.'

She liked that. This must have come about because of the access road. Her spirits, slightly quenched because there was no one to meet her, began to rise. She drove up to the house, heard dogs barking. If anyone was at home, that would bring them out. It didn't. She knocked at the back door just in case, delighting in using the big brass knocker she so remembered, but no joy.

It seemed strange to find that door locked. In all the years she'd spent here she couldn't even remember a key. So when they had lost the perils of isolation, they'd also lost a little of their freedom from city precautions. She tried, without hope, a side door that opened off a stone-flagged closed-in verandah, but that too was fastened.

The verandah boasted metal garden chairs and a table.

She could always sit there and wait, but she wouldn't ...
this was a heavenly chance to revisit the beloved spots of
her childhood. She visited the dog-motels, kennels with
good runs attached, and saw with the greatest satisfaction
that they still kept to the endearing custom of having name-
plates on the fronts of them. Not that she'd know any of
them, the dogs she had known would have gone to some
canine Valhalla long ago. Here were Mungo, Ritchie, Bella
and ... oh, could it be? Bluey!

Had they just repeated a name? No, she remembered
Rupert hadn't cared for that, had said once that each dog
had a personality of its own and deserved a name of its
own. She grew excited ... this wasn't a young dog, it
could be her puppy. It had exactly the same markings, with
a little spot of brown set in the white patch on the bluish-
black face. She and the dog gazed at each other. He'd gone
quiet, although the others were still making a racket. She
said, 'Bluey?' and suddenly the dog went mad, yelping and
crying in near frenzy. Elissa felt tears in her eyes, kept saying his name over and over, longing to let him out, but not
daring to in case he got into mischief. She looked round,
saw the familiar green drum ... did it still hold dog
biscuits? It did. She scooped up a panful of the cubes and
scattered them through the netting for each of them. They
began munching and finally even Bluey settled down.

She spent a happy half-hour exploring the old orchard,
and was surprised to find the stables locked up too. The
horses, of course, were out in the paddocks, but it was odd.
However, the woolshed and implement shed weren't locked.
They must be afraid of fire; the stable would have hay in it.

By now she was wishing someone would come. She wandered along the jetty, gazed across at Twin Hills, wondered
if by chance the MacCorquodales had been picked up here
first and were stuck there, although the Campions at that
homestead had always had a launch of their own, and
surely would have brought them back. So had the Airlies,
long ago, but there was nothing but that rowing-boat now.
The launch could be away for a refit, of course.

She caught sight of the track that led from the jetty into

the cool greenness of the native bush that clothed the far headland. She and Judy and Elspeth Airlie had loved that path best of all, and had found names for every landmark, investing it with the excitement of adventure and eeriness. It led to all sorts of secret nooks and dells, and, best of all, to a series of little inlets where the forest grew down almost to the water's edge. There was no distance in any of it, and if they returned they'd see her car and know she'd not be far away. The depot would have told them she'd hired a car.

She remembered the well-locked-up house and decided she'd better lock the car. For one thing it wasn't hers, for another every bit of clothing she had with her was in it, her camera, her bag, her passport. She dropped the keys into the enormous patch-pocket of the jacket of her cream gabardine trouser suit.

It was delightful to have this grotto-like sylvan world all to oneself, to find that it still had that Eden-like quality despite that new road. She gave herself up to enchantment. The Secret Path wound and climbed and dipped. Ah, there was the side path leading up to the Crow's Nest, a jutting-out, leaning-over rock that overhung the Wai-o-Atarangi ... where in the deep pool scoured out before the tiny river fed into the lake, trout swam freely in the translucent green water. She climbed the track, gnarled roots intersecting it and giving toe-holds. Tree branches hung pendulously, brushing her hair, her shoulders.

She gained the Crow's Nest, leaned over, caught a movement; yes, there they were, brown trout swimming in all the grace of unafraid water-ballet movement. How unpolluted these waters were! She clambered down again, followed the main track. It skirted the lake shore and delight upon delight unfolded. The lake beaches were shingly, giving place at times to soft silty sand. She took her shoes off, stowed them beside a rock for a landmark, walked on.

Suddenly she froze. She could scarcely believe it. That was the scarcest of all New Zealand's water-birds, the white heron, the *kotuku*. The Maoris had given that name

to the young Queen on her first visit to these shores ...
the-pure-white-heron-of-a-single-flight. It stood as if carved
out of alabaster, on a rock partially submerged, and the lake
was so still, so blue, its reflection was a perfect twin, not
disturbed by the slightest ripple. If only she'd brought her
camera!

It was poised as if thinking deeply, but she knew it was
engrossed in watching for movement that meant food. Suddenly it lifted up its curving wings and flew to the far end
of the tiny curving bay, landing silently among driftwood
and weed at the water's edge. It remained supremely unaware of her presence and began wading away from her,
looking into the débris for succulent morsels. Elissa, a keen
bird-watcher in Surrey, began to stalk it.

The heron and Elissa rounded a miniature headland.
The bird waded round a huge tree-trunk that lay in its
path, bleached white by countless suns and rains. She
waited till it was well ahead, then put a foot up on to the
log and drew the other foot after it. The log rocked peril-
ously, she clutched at the air, cut all sorts of capers as it
rolled, then pitched clean into the lake at the far side with a
mighty splash.

The heron rose with an outraged squawk and soared
into the air. Elissa, after a moment of alarm, knew she was
lucky. The ground hollowed out the other side, but she
went in only to her waist. She floundered round till her feet
felt firmer footing than just ooze, then she scrambled out.

What a nuisance! Her lovely cream tailored trews were
not only drenched, they had ooze, bits of lakeweed clinging, and straw and leaves. She'd have to strip everything
off, for even her body-shirt was soaked for its lower six
inches. Well, she had plenty of changes in the car, but she
just hoped she could grab something and change before
the MacCorquodales arrived. She could flee into the woolshed if they hadn't. What a sketch she'd look if they were
there when she emerged from the bush!

Weren't wet clothes abominably uncomfortable to walk
in? Good job her feet had been bare, though. She scooped
up her shoes, put them on, took to the forest path again.

She shivered. The sun had been blotted out by an enormous cloud, and of course this path was cool even in high summer. And dark. She'd forgotten that. However, once the cloud had passed over and she emerged from the trees, she'd soon get warm.

But she didn't come out to a sunlit bay. The mountains were almost obscured by cloud now. She remembered how dramatically sudden storms could sweep down from the tops. She shivered again as a chill wind sprang up, sweeping across the immense expanse of water. It plastered her wet things to her.

She reached the car, put her hand into her wet pocket for the keys and met only emptiness. Elissa uttered a squawk of dismay. Oh, no, no! She knew instantly what had happened. They'd washed out into that hole in the lake, and sunk into the ooze, never to be found again. And it was a rental car! Oh, what *would* the MacCorquodales think of her?

They weren't back. The garages were still empty. Worse still! ... Better by far to feel a nit and be rescued from this predicament than to have to wait, for goodness knew how long, for them to come home. She was chilled to the bone now. She watched, fascinated, as thick fingers of rain from the far shore swept like malicious hands of demons across the surface. Oh, if only Airlie House wasn't locked up. She could have gone in, found some kind of clothing, made herself a hot drink. Anyway, they ought to have been at the depot, or at the least, have left a message. The full downpour reached her before she made the house, drenching her in seconds, so that now the upper part of her body was as soaked as the lower.

She took a short cut through the shrubbery, felt thorns catch at her, slipped on the wet track, fell flat on her face in the muddy surface. She scrambled up, went more cautiously. She almost fell on to the side verandah, and thankfully thrust the door shut against the force of the wind.

She had no compunction about wringing out her shoulder-length hair over the flagged floor. She slipped off her top and bra, almost splitting them with the vigour of her wringing, donned them again. It felt ghastly but was one degree better than streaming water. Off with her other things, then on again.

She gazed wrathfully at the contents of the verandah. Imagine sitting on cold metal chairs when you were soaking wet! If only there'd been clothes airing here . . . the lines were still up as in her time . . . or even a couple of cushions. There was nothing but an indescribable sheepskin mat that bore much evidence of the wiping of farm boots. When, oh, when would they come home?

Even if the couple in the cottage returned first, that would be something. If the rain stopped she'd explore there to see if by any chance a window had been left open. How heavenly it would be to be able to make oneself a cup of tea!

It was still winter, so darkness would close in early, which was a horrible thought. If only the stable had been open, she could have curled up on hay. She couldn't face the smells of the woolshed. She could hardly see the face of her watch now, the storm had darkened the sky so much. As she managed to focus, she realised with utter dismay that the last time she'd looked at it, it had been just that . . . the immersion in the lake had put paid to it.

But surely the MacCorquodales must arrive back soon? A horrible thought struck her. What if they'd had an accident . . . gone over the bank into the lake? They'd have been on the outer edge going in. She pulled herself up. Now stop it, Elissa Montgomery. Wild thoughts of breaking a window to get in occurred to her, but she couldn't bring herself to do it. It would cost the earth to get a glazier all this distance, and they could be cross enough with her as it was. So would the rental car firm, having to send two men round here, with keys, one to drive her car back.

The rain stopped and the resultant silence was even more eerie. She must investigate the cottage windows before it started again. She took off, sliding down the streaming path to it. She skidded right at the end, and landed on a rose-bush, scratching her face. She didn't think it had done the rose-bush much good either. She could only just see her way.

Not a window was even ajar. She stumbled on to an open porch and saw with thankfulness a row of nappies airing and a blanket. Tough on them, because it would need washing again, but she was past really worrying. If only farmhouses were like those of other days, when there was always a gauze-covered food safe outside. She was starving!

Her eye fell on a box against the wall, and she lifted the lid. Not apples, carrots, huge ones. They were newly dug, with a lot of earth still clinging. She grabbed half a dozen, took a nappy to carry them in and on second thoughts unpegged some more to dry herself with. She'd better leave some in case the poor mother had no others dry. The verandah up at the house was better than this.

She'd noticed a tap by the homestead steps, so thankfully washed the carrots and managed to regain her sanctuary by the time a huge flash of lightning lit the sky with evil green. Thunder followed, great claps reverberating round the peaks with frightening volume. The storm played for a full hour and she was almost thankful for the spectacular display, because at least it was something to watch now night had fallen. Better than huddling in that thick, almost tangible darkness straining one's eyes against it.

The carrots were hard and cold but at least filled up that aching void. By now she realised it was hardly likely the MacCorquodales would attempt a road like that, unlit, narrow, prone no doubt to slips in rain like this. They'd stay the night in Ludwigtown. Probably they had reached there after the depot closed and would have made up their minds that when no one had turned up to meet this girl from England, she would have made a sensible decision and gone to an hotel for the night. They'd never dream of anyone from England hiring a car and driving on that road.

If only that light in the ceiling could have been switched on, but like all such, it worked from the inside. A light would have given them warning that someone was here, if they did turn up.

In one of the vivid flashes she decided she must try to make herself as comfortable as possible. The chairs were too upright to doze in, so she dragged the table over, turned it on its side to shield her from the cutting draught that swept under the door, spread out the indescribable sheep-skin, put some nappies on top, and rolled herself in the blanket, thankful for even that much. All the same it was most inadequate against the seeping cold and her damp clothes, and she found herself muttering, 'A pillow, a pillow, my kingdom for a pillow!' Quite suddenly and blessedly she fell into exhausted sleep.

She knew nothing more till she was awakened by a terrific blow on her back, a muttered curse, and then a heavy body falling over her, held off to some extent by the edge of the table.

The muttering became, 'Hell and damnation ... what's this? And what in the name of——'

F'issa sat up, mazed with sleep, came into contact with a very hard head and said idiotically, 'It's all right, it's only me.'

What he said then wasn't half as mild....

CHAPTER TWO

ELISSA came horribly awake, felt afraid, but said sturdily, 'There's no need to swear. I'm Elissa-Montgomery-making-the-best-of-things. Are you Logan MacCorquodale?'

'I sure am, but what in hell have I walked into?' He was still sort of rocking and scrambling.

'It's the side of the table. To keep the draughts off me, of course. That's a very badly-fitting door.' She sounded accusing, which did nothing for him. In the darkness she was struggling to get up, but she'd wound the blanket round her like a cocoon. She clutched at the edge of the table to steady her and it fell back on her.

His voice held sheer exasperation. 'What *are* you trying to do *now*?'

She said, with an attempt at dignity, 'I'm trying to get up, but the blanket's swathed round me so tightly I can't, and besides I've got pins and needles in my legs, as anybody might, waiting all this time for you to come home.'

He made a grab at her, made contact, said, 'Now I've got you. Turn round on your knees and then try. Oh, if only I had a torch, but a chap can usually find his way into the house he's lived in for the last five years without stumbling over unidentified objects!'

Elissa was horrified to hear herself giggle and say: 'Like flying saucers.' Good grief, he'd think her an hysterical idiot! She pulled herself together, said, 'Ah, I'm up.' She freed herself from his grip, tried to take a step, teetered and fell against him again, with the edge of the table still between them.

He said, 'For the love of Mike stay still. I'll lean over this blasted table and try to get my key in the door so we can get a light on this dark subject.'

It was the weirdest feeling, clinging to a stranger, with a table edge digging into you and swathes of blankets holding your feet prisoner. His face came against hers as he stretched over. There were sounds of metal grating on metal, then the welcome one of the key going home and turning.

Then he said, 'This accursed door is sticking again. Look, can *you* give it a shove?' He added, too late, 'But not too much, mind.' That did it. Elissa's second shove was effective but overdone. They both hurtled through and sprawled over each other in the hallway. The man fell more heavily because he'd pitched over the table, and his howl of anguish meant he'd barked his shins on it.

He lay there for a winded moment, then scrambled off her and found the switch. What he saw bereft him of speech temporarily ... a sodden wreck of humanity with gingery elf-locks plastered about her and indescribable clothes, once cream, covered with moss and mud.

He said, 'Good God, even in a storm like this, how *could* you get in a state like that? You look as if you've been crawling in the lake-slime. And what brought you to *my* door, anyway? I've heard of people finding babies in baskets but—but this is ridiculous! You're not a Martian, are you?'

For some reason this made Elissa cross. It wasn't the time for levity. She said, glaring, 'Believe me, if I *was* a Martian, I'd have got back in my saucer and upped towards my own planet for dear life. You certainly do lock up when you go out, don't you? Not as much as a laundry door open. I could have perished from exposure!' She struggled over most inelegantly, and managed to get up.

He boggled, then burst out laughing. 'It's all my fault, is it? What a beautiful piece of feminine logic! Sorry about our remissness ... but vandals got in not long ago and it altered our style of living. We were very easy-osy before that. But tell me how you got here. Did you hitch-hike on the wrong road? Or get lost in the bush? People shouldn't tramp alone.'

'I'm not a hitch-hiker. I'm not a tramper. I tried to tell you at first—I'm Elissa Montgomery.'

He continued to boggle.

She said angrily, 'The interior decorator from Surrey. And all this *is* your fault. You were supposed to meet me.'

'Supposed to meet you? Why should I? And where? And why? What's an interior decorator to do with me?'

She stamped her foot. 'You and your wife were supposed to meet me at the launch depot. You seem remarkably slow in the uptake. I'm to do up Airlie House.'

'Do up Airlie House? Now I *know* you're bonkers. Look, you said Surrey, and you sound English. I think you've got your wires crossed badly. It can't be this house, and besides, I haven't got a wife.'

Now it was her turn to boggle. 'Haven't got a wife? But Uncle Rupert said——' she stopped, confused. 'Well, he said the MacCorquodales. And that Mrs MacCorquodale had said Airlie House deserved to be done up. But you *must* know this. Uncle Rupert wrote to you. He wrote in detail. He wrote in time. I'm from Haslemere in Surrey. Does that assist your memory any?' He still looked dazed, so she added, 'He was staying with Victoria Doig there.'

He looked a little more with it. 'Victoria Doig? Now we're getting somewhere. But *she*'s the interior decorator.'

'So that makes two of us,' she said sarcastically. 'It may surprise you, but there are thousands of interior decorators in Britain. Victoria is taking on my job while I'm away.'

He shook his head helplessly. 'You said a letter. I didn't get any letter about this. I did hear from Rupert—my boss —weeks ago. He said he'd met up with Victoria and Blair. My mother did say once this house ought to be restored to its former grandeur—Rupert's wife didn't have much idea— I'm sure Mother was thinking ahead for when I get married. But why send an English girl out here? He must be mad!'

Elissa said with dignity, 'I told him that too, but let's get the record straight. I'm not English, I'm a Kiwi myself. I only sound that way because my mother was English, and I've lived there the last ten years. Before that, for three years, I lived *here*. My mother was governess to Judith and Elspeth Airlie. I was born in South Canterbury where my father had a small farm. But by and by my mother, Meg

Montgomery, wearied for her own folk, and returned to her native land.'

She thought a peculiar expression crossed his face, but it was fleeting. 'Oh, I think I remember hearing something of this. Some woman who had her daughter here too, but left very suddenly.'

For a moment Elissa had a sense of unease, then she said lightly, 'That's Mother. A few weeks ago she decided over-night to go for a prolonged holiday to Canada, so she up and offed. The same from here ... oh, well, didn't Shakes-peare say somewhere "If it were done when 'tis done, then 'twere well it were done quickly"?'

He nodded, 'M'm ... *Macbeth*, I think. So she'd not be much surprised at you taking off quickly too?'

'Well, I don't know yet. Uncle Rupert—as I used to call him—thought she might veto the idea, so he said leave it to him. We left the same day, on different planes. He was off to stay with Douglas and said he'd tell her.'

'Is she near Douglas?'

'No, I meant by phone. I did ask him to go to see her later on—she's not more than a hundred miles away and she was very fond of Douglas, but he didn't seem to want to.'

This Logan MacCorquodale was a strange man. He said, 'H'm, I can understand that. What I can't under-stand is him sending *you* all this way. He could have got the woman who took Victoria's place to do it. Oh, well, if the old boy's got money to burn, that's over to him. He must have got carried away.'

She faltered, added, apologetically, 'He was so set on it —made it sound like a favour. I was free because I was packing to go to Canada for a surprise visit to Mother—I tried to dissuade him rather than to push it, so——'

The black brows lifted a little, he shrugged, 'So it's no business of mine. It sounds so unlike Rupert Airlie. I'd not be surprised to know he's carrying the damned letter round in his pocket still and will suddenly find it and cable me.' He pulled himself together, 'Look, I'm sorry there was this hitch—no one to meet you and that you couldn't get in. I say, where was I supposed to meet you? How *did* you get here?'

'You were supposed to meet me at the launch depot. I had a yen to come across the lake as we did thirteen years ago when I first saw Glen Airlie. So when they said the launch had broken down at Twin Hills and there was no message and I couldn't raise anyone here, I hired a car. Said I'd drive it round tomorrow and come across by launch.'

He said, 'You were pretty game to tackle a road like that on your own. But tell me, even if you did get soaked in the rain ... why on earth didn't you get your luggage out of the car and change? In fact, you'd have been warmer in the car. Sleeping in wet clothes could give you a frightful chill.'

The shaming colour ran up into her face. 'I couldn't get in to the car. I dropped the car keys in the lake and I'd locked it.'

He grinned, maddeningly. 'I get it. You walked on to the jetty, swinging them.'

'I didn't—I'm not such a dill. I *fell* in the lake. At Treasure Island Bay.'

'What on earth made you go right round there?'

'I was putting in the time exploring and saw a white heron. So I stalked it. I fell off the trunk of a tree—it rolled. There was quite a deep pool at the other side. I didn't know the keys were gone, or I'd have dived to try for them. Anyway, they'd have sunk deeply in the silt immediately.' She swayed.

He put out a steadying arm. 'I must be off my rocker firing questions at you like this. You're all in. Come on, the kitchen may still be warm. I stoked the range up before we left. We use such slow coal it ought to be still on. But the electric kettle will be quicker to get you a hot drink.'

The warmth hit them as they went in. How Elissa remembered the matchless comfort of this on winter mornings! He lifted the lid of the fire-box, said a satisfied 'Ah,' dropped in a piece of newspaper, put some dry kindling from the rack on top of it, and it lit from the red embers immediately when he pulled the dampers out.

Elissa's eyes lit on a batch of scones under a huge plastic cover. 'What a wonderful sight,' she said, and not asking permission, sank her teeth into one unbuttered. She said, 'I'm starving,' then shut up as she munched. With the last swallow she said with a sigh like a replete lion, 'Much, much better than cold carrots.'

'Cold carrots? What——'

'I dashed down to the cottage in a lull, hoping for an open window. That's where I got this,' she brushed a hand across the dried blood on her cheek. 'I fell in a rose-bush too. I found that blanket and some dirty carrots and the nappies. I left some for the mother in case she didn't have any more dry ones. They're going to be mighty late, aren't they? And with a baby!'

'Oh, the baby's not here yet, though perhaps it will be by now. I'll ring soon. Gwyneth had just made those scones when she got her first pain. She told us—Hew and me—that she'd be ages yet because firsts took a long time, but we weren't having any of that, cowards that we are. Hew took his car and I followed with mine in case he had to stay the night, as he has.' He cocked an eye at her. 'I'm afraid you're going to be unchaperoned. It can't be helped, but have no qualms, I'm no womaniser and anyway, I'm practically engaged to a Ludwigtown girl, Stacey Cressford.'

That was nice of him. Elissa said, 'I never gave that a thought. But what's happened to your mother? Is she away too? I hope she comes back soon. I didn't like taking this on without Rupert here, though he thinks he'll be back before I do anything really major. I can get sketches done, work out designs, and so on. I wouldn't care to decide everything on my own, and your mother will be the one to live with it, so——'

He pulled a face. 'My lady mother is an Australian and got an invitation to a school Centennial in Geelong. She refused to budge without Dad, so I packed them both off. Anyway, she's not here permanently. I'd say just go ahead.'

(Evidently Mrs MacCorquodale was just housekeeping

till such time as her son got married.)

'Gwyneth's sister was meant to come to stay when the baby was near, but it's beaten the gun.' He was pouring boiling water into a mug he'd tipped a Cup-a-Soup packet into; now he stirred it briskly and handed it to her, then cut some bread. Had ever anything tasted more heavenly? He filled a couple of coffee mugs, and said, 'When we've had this I'll run you a bath, then get you some things of my mother's and we'll have a proper meal. You're steaming right now. Don't flake out on me while you're in the bath, will you? And don't take too long, I'll be anxious.'

The bath was bliss. Elissa found a hairbrush and after towelling her hair dry managed to get it into some sort of order so that the ends curled up. She donned the clothes he'd put out for her. What a glamorous nightgown for a mother! It was in a gorgeous shade of apricot with a frilled yoke trimmed with forget-me-not embroidery and enormous pompons of turquoise brushed nylon to tie it at the throat. The dressing-gown, if you could call so flimsy a garment by that prosaic name, matched it. It was far too long. She tied it firmly with the girdle and hitched it up, and slipped her feet into pale blue sheepskin slippers. They felt the last word in luxuriousness. Two hours ago all Elissa had wanted was warmth and food; now, perversely, she wished for make-up. But she didn't like to prowl—she found some lavender talcum in the bathroom and patted some on her face to take off the boiled-lobster look.

She entered the kitchen a little shyly. A delicious smell of bacon and eggs met her. Her host turned round, egg-slice in hand, stared, said, 'Good lord, you looked about sixteen before. Now I really can believe you're a qualified decorator. Now you look——' He bit it off, said, 'You look mature.'

'I'm nearly twenty-five. When I'm at my boss's desk I look every minute of it, but when you've been falling in lakes, scratching your face on rose-thorns, sprawling in mud and dashing through thunderstorms, to say nothing of sleeping on a dirty sheepskin, it takes at least a decade off!'

He chuckled. 'Sure does. That's what made me so disbelieving, because I associate interior decorators with Victoria's sort of elegance ... to match the houses they do up. Not a cushion out of place, not a crumb on the carpet ... so the decorators usually come slick and smooth too. However, I daresay I'll get a surprise when you finally emerge in your own fine feathers. You're hardly likely to fall into lakes every day.'

The girl opposite said in a tone of deepest gloom, 'But I do. That's the trouble. I don't know what it is about water, it seems to have a fatal fascination for me. I even stepped clean into a toilet once when I was doing up a bathroom!'

He chuckled again. 'This relieves me. I thought Rupert must've gone clean mad sending out someone used to stately houses and converted windmills ... now I'm beginning to think he had something. Things are always happening here at the back of beyond, but perhaps *you'll* be able to take the rough with the smooth ... or do I mean the wet with the dry? I've just thought of something. I'll bet you're the youngster they talk about who went down the well to rescue a goat?'

'Just a baby goat.'

He nodded. 'And held it on your shoulders till help arrived, so it wouldn't sink into the ooze. Pleased to meet you, Miss Montgomery. But they called you Bunty. Is Elissa your professional name? Sounds like a made-up one. I've never heard it before.'

Her voice sounded indignant. 'Bunty was the made-up one ... that's always a nickname. Elissa, I'll have you know, is as Scots as Logan MacCorquodale. It's the Scots form of Elizabeth.'

'No, it isn't. Elspeth or Elsbeth is that.'

She pulled a face at him. 'They're both forms of Elizabeth, just as Isabel is in Spanish. You don't know much about Scots names for a Scot, do you?'

He challenged her, laughing. 'Well, how much do you know about the MacCorquodales? It's just that an Elissa hasn't crossed my path before.'

The blue-green eyes danced. 'Um ... let me see. You would wear the MacLeod tartan. And your motto would be: *Hold fast*. And as for Logan ... now, there's a romantic name for you. Two of your forebears were killed in Spain, taking the heart of Bruce to the Holy Land, so your Crest Badge is a pierced heart.'

She sat back, a smug expression on her face.

He said, dazed, 'What are you? A walking encyclopaedia or what?'

She burst out laughing. 'I'm being mean—couldn't resist it. It's sheer coincidence. We had a neighbour called Mac-Corquodale who was always talking about such things, and it so happened that my boss took me with him on a very fine job he did for some Logans at Glenelg. I worked out the drapes. Colonel Logan was interested in all clan histories, and we had great fun tracing my Montgomery connections. We were up there a month, you see.'

He said, 'I'm quite relieved. I felt I couldn't possibly keep up with such erudition and would feel very much a peasant the whole time you're here.'

Elissa felt as if a shadow passed over her mind. Oh, how ridiculous! A few hours here, some of them anything but enjoyable, and already she knew a surge of longing to stay.

He took some warm plates from the rack. 'I feel you need something more substantial than soup and coffee after an ordeal like that, and I'm starving myself.' He ladled out the bacon and eggs. 'By the way, I've put your outer things in the tub. I supposed you washed your smalls out in the bath? Well, put them on this newspaper on the rack, they'll be dry by morning. Mother's slacks will be far too long for you, as she's a beanpole like me, so if you like to come out for breakfast in what you've got on now ... I see you've managed to hitch them up ... I'll have a go at getting that car open. I've done it before. We've had tourists lose their keys. I'll let you have a lie-in—I'm up and out early. I've put you in my parents' bed.'

'Oh, what a pity. That means using double sheets, and a single was all that was necessary. Save washing when you're on your own.'

He hesitated, said, 'That room's the only one with a key. I thought you might sleep better that way.'

Their eyes met. Elissa thought irrelevantly that she'd imagined a man as dark-visaged as this one would have had dark eyes ... but he must have taken after his Highland ancestors. They were a vivid blue when his penthouse brows weren't drawn. 'Thank you, Logan MacCorquodale,' she said slowly, 'but I don't need to turn that key. Some things a girl just knows.'

He couldn't have known this had been Mother's room, but it gave her a sense of belonging, of returning. The little room off it, built in pioneer days for the current baby, had been hers. Tomorrow she'd renew acquaintances with that.

She noticed an electric cord leading under the sheets—oh, what bliss after the iciness of the verandah. She crawled in, only to experience a letdown. The sheets were quite cold. Then it dawned on her. This would have dual control, and Logan would have switched on one side only. She shuffled over and found it so hot and turned it off immediately, because she wasn't going to be able to stay awake long enough otherwise. Sleep claimed her.

She had a feeling that as it had been after one before they retired, Logan MacCorquodale mightn't have been up as early as he'd prophesied, but at six she came to the surface temporarily as he closed the outside door and she went forty fathoms deep again. Next time she stirred it was well after nine. Her conscience stirred too. She must pull her weight. He had problems of his own, no doubt, with his man not back. She was an additional one. He'd have to get some neighbour to come to stay with her ... or perhaps it would be all right if his man did when he returned. Otherwise there would be talk.

She girded the long apricot gown round her again, sped out to the kitchen. It looked as if Logan had just had a cup of tea and a biscuit, so he must mean to have breakfast with her later. The kettle was singing on the fire. She found a frying pan and oil. The bacon was evidently home-cured because it was in a huge piece. She hacked off some thick slices. She could do these now and put them in the oven, and just fry the eggs when he came in. She sliced toast, put the teapot on the hob to warm. It was fun, and made her feel not such a colossal nuisance.

A big ginger cat jumped in the window. Logan had left a saucer of milk on the hearth for it. It lapped, washed its whiskers, came and rubbed itself against Elissa's legs. She had a feeling as if time had stood still. There had been generations of ginger cats at Glen Airlie. It made it seem cosy and domesticated.

She heard an engine stop. Logan must have taken the Land-Rover. She dropped an egg into the oil, then two more—he looked like a two-egg man. She snapped the toaster lever down, and turned, smiling, to the open door, and there framed in it, with what seemed like several bodies behind her, was a tall exquisite-looking creature dressed in an elegant cream serge suit piped in brown, with a long dangling emerald scarf wound round her neck. This vision had stopped dead still from sheer surprise, brown eyes under dark brows wide with shock. The others cannoned into her and a rather stentorian voice further away demanded, 'What is it, Stacey? Do go on in.'

Oh, no, not *Stacey*. The girl Logan was nearly engaged to! All in that aghast moment Elissa realised she'd landed her kind host in one helluva mess!

The next instant she heard Logan's voice, raised in protest and, heaven help him, coming from the direction of the side passage that led to the bedrooms! 'Elissa ... where are you? I was going to give you breakfast in bed after a night like that!' And on the heels of his shout he pushed the other door open. It was like a scene from a farce, one of those corny *flagrante delicto* situations.

Elissa felt the hot colour rush up her neck and into her cheeks. She stood helplessly, one hand on the pan-handle, with Stacey at one doorway, Logan at the other.

Logan had stopped as if shot, said, 'Good lord!' and remained rooted to the spot. Elissa pushed the pan back, said with an appealing gesture towards the blonde girl, 'This isn't what it looks like, believe me ... it's ... it's not what you're thinking at all!'

There was pure scepticism in the look Stacey sent her, and who could blame her? Her voice was icy-calm, sharp-edged. 'No? But you can't possibly know *what* I'm thinking.'

Just then three children wormed their way round the rigid figure in the doorway and shouted, 'Uncle Logie, we've come to stay for a couple of months with you. Isn't it marvellous?'

Their uncle shut his eyes at this triple vision, as well he might, and the stentorian voice demanded again, 'What's going on? Stand aside, Stacey! Why are you behaving like this? Who else is here? Not your mother, Logan? Is she back?'

Stacey stepped aside, waved speechlessly, and in came a stoutish, grey-haired, beaky lady in a herringbone tweed costume, with a leather grip in her hand.

Logan MacCorquodale opened his eyes at the sound of her voice, looked as if he'd like to shut them again and said feebly, 'Aunt Claudia!'

Stacey Cressford's voice was cold, controlled, 'Logan, I'm waiting for an explanation,' then, as Elissa essayed speech, 'Hush ... not you. I want an explanation from Logan ... He's got to tell me who you are.'

Logan began, surprisingly, to grin. Elissa knew immediately it wasn't the right thing to do. He said, 'Oh, Stacey, stop acting like a mid-Victorian, all outraged prudery and virtue! It wasn't like that, you chump. This is the back of beyond where, if things happen, you make the best of them. Where, if waifs of the storm get washed up on your doorstep, you take them in, feed 'em, clothe 'em, and bed 'em down. Nothing else to do.'

He met, naturally, an uncomprehending stare. He continued.

'I actually did find her on my doorstep ... the one on the verandah. I literally fell over her. Nearly scared hell out of me. It does things to a man to fall over a table, and put his hand out and encounter a warm, breathing *something*. It was nearly midnight when I got back from Ludwigtown, and she looked like nothing on earth. She'd fallen in the lake, and got caught in the thunderstorm and curled up there.'

'Why hadn't she gone back to Ludwigtown? I see her car down there. The road wasn't impassable. It was only because Aunt Claudia wanted to see the Samsons that we spent the night there. The road wasn't cut with slips.'

He shrugged. 'I'd not have expected anyone to have negotiated the road in that storm who wasn't familiar with every bend, much less someone from England, but in any case she'd locked the car and the keys are in the pothole she fell into in Treasure Island Bay. Besides, she's here to stay —at Rupert's request. She's to do the entire place up. Apparently my lady mother's suggestion triggered this off, though I guess she'll find it hard to believe Rupert took her seriously enough to send out an interior decorator from England!'

Stacey's lip curled. 'That would make two of us. I don't believe it either. You'll have to do better than this, Logan. Even supposing this tarradiddle were true, the natural thing would have been to take her down to Gwyneth's cottage.'

Again he shrugged. 'Gwyneth's at the nursing-home— much too early. It got Hew and me worried, so I stayed with Hew till quite late. She hasn't had her baby even yet. I rang first thing. Hew stayed with her, naturally.'

'How very convenient! So you brought—this—back for company, I suppose. Glam company at that. I've heard red-heads are supposed to be ... exciting. And how were you to know Aunt Claudia and I would arrive with the family this morning? Sheer bad luck for you, Logan.'

Elissa saw the colour of rage run up from Logan's throat. She intervened quickly, striking her hands together in very real distress. 'Oh, please, *please!* Every word he says is true. Believe me, I didn't look at all glamorous when he fell over me last night ... he scared seven bells out of me and himself. I'd put the table on its side to keep the draught off me ... he must have barked his shins ... he could show you.'

Logan said hurriedly, 'There's no skin off, to my surprise.'

So that hadn't helped. Elissa rushed on, 'He swore like anything, but I didn't care. I was glad to hear a voice ... I was having a nightmare as it was and I thought it was a gorilla landing on me, or an elephant.'

At this, the three children who'd been staring goggle-eyed at these grown-ups having a real ding-dong fight, burst out laughing.

They were quelled immediately by the glance Stacey shot them. Stacey said to Elissa, 'Well, you hardly look now as if you're recently recovered from exposure.'

Oh, if only she'd put her rough-dried clothes on, instead of waiting for him to pick the lock of that door. She said sturdily, 'Only because he looked after me so well, had hot soup made in a jiffy, ran a bath for me.' Oh, dear, that wasn't so good.

When Logan managed to gain control of the conversation again he said coldly, 'Stacey, it seems incredible to me you don't believe me. You *know* me. You know me very well. I happen to be telling the truth. Adventures like this do happen, and people need to trust each other when they do.'

'They don't happen to me,' said Stacey Cressford, and Elissa thought that was probably right. This was an elegant girl, not a tomboy type who rushed round everywhere, not looking where she was going, and continually falling over things.

Her gaze shifted to Logan. The skin over the high cheek-bones had tightened, deep grooves were in his lean cheeks, he was pale again, and his lips were a thin line. He turned his head a little, said in a carefully controlled tone, 'Children, you'd better go in the playroom. Don't go outside, because the burns are full after that rain. We've got to sort this out. I know you don't understand it, but Stacey seems to think I've got myself another girl-friend. I haven't. So it will be all right soon. Scram!' They scrammed.

He turned back to Stacey. 'She arrived at the launch depot yesterday afternoon expecting to be met. She could get no answer from the homestead because Hew and I were on the road with Gwyneth. About the time we must have got to the nursing-home, she'd heard the launch was holed up at Twin Hills and decided to hire a car and just arrive. By the time she'd decided she couldn't stay in case we didn't come home, she'd fallen in the lake and couldn't get into the car. I'd like to haul you by the ear and show you her suit ... rub your nose in it if need be ... it's soaking in the tub.'

Stacey said, 'That might sound convincing, but it seems odd to me that she managed to get a ravishing négligé like that out of the car, and not something more suitable. That's doing it a bit brown.'

He uttered a scornful sound. 'That's my mama's. Her one weakness is frilly undies. Oh, I know that on the surface she's the tweed-and-tailored type, but not underneath, believe me.'

He actually grinned and it infuriated Stacey. 'This has been a revelation in more ways than one, Logan, in that I can almost admire your express reactions. As fast as I bowl you out you pick yourself up and produce an even more brazen excuse. The only thing is I don't believe any of it.' When he was too furious to reply, she added, 'And what's this about meeting her at the launch depot? So you *did* expect her?'

His lips thinned to a disappearing line. 'I didn't. She arrived unheralded and unsung. Not nice for anyone, that. Rupert said he'd write to Mother. He wouldn't know she was in Australia, of course. The only thing is the letter hasn't arrived. Oh, yes, look like that. Another lame excuse, you're thinking. Who cares what you think by this time? I can't give you anything but the truth. You too, Aunt Claudia ... you've not uttered a word yet, which is astounding in itself, and *you've* looked disbelieving too. First time in my life *you've* not believed me, and I don't like it. I expected you to fly to my defence like an old warhorse, same as always. So I can only assume you too believe the worst. What's the matter with you? Surely if you'd thought the same you'd have made mincemeat out of me!'

Aunt Claudia's voice was deep, almost mannish. She said, entirely without humour, 'I rather thought Stacey was coping with the mincing jolly well, and no wonder! You deserve it!'

It was too much for Elissa. She uttered a cry, said chokingly, 'How *can* you? He was so decent to me, so chivalrous. Look, Stacey, you're barking up the wrong tree in every single thing. What absolute rubbish to talk nonsense about redheads being exciting! I looked like something the cat had dragged in last night. And I'm not a redhead, I'm ginger, just plain ginger. And let me tell you, I've got a temper to match, and right now, as *I'm* accustomed to being believed too, it's red-hot. If you can think things like that about Logan MacCorquodale, you don't deserve to get him. Now look ... both you women are going to march down to that car and see for yourself the darned thing's locked up like a castle keep! Even my handbag's in it, and my make-up. Believe me, if this had been the sort of affair you two imagine, I'd have had all that in here with me instead of being trigged out in things of Mrs MacCorquodale's that trip me up every step, and having to use talc on my face after my bath to take away the boiled-lobster look. Come on!'

She stalked towards the passage that led past the bedrooms to the side door, which was a pity because the double bedroom door was open. Stacey halted, took one comprehensive look, said, 'How extraordinary. Most men would have put an unexpected guest into a single room.'

Elissa gave her a look of unutterable scorn and was about to retort when Stacey added, 'And ... I couldn't be mistaken, could I? That bed's been slept in by two people ... two pillows are dented in.'

Had Elissa but known it, the look she gave Stacey then was positively regal. 'I got in the wrong side. He'd switched the opposite control on, so I wriggled over, very thankfully. I can't prove it, so you can do what you damn well like about it, but I'll tell you *why* he put me in here. Most men wouldn't have had the chivalrous thought that a girl alone in a strange man's house might have had all sorts of feminine fears. They might have been frightened to go to sleep. Like you, I protested, said single sheets would be easier to wash, but he said it was the only door that locked.'

The silence that descended upon the two women then made Elissa think her tone, plus their knowledge of Logan, had convinced them. Elissa said, 'I didn't need to turn that key. I recognised him at once for a man of high standards, even if you, who should know him a thousand times better, don't seem to. You're going to get the sort of husband most women long for, and I just hope you've the sense to realise it before it's too late.'

The other girl didn't have as much confidence in her voice this time, when she said, as if trying to regain her fury, 'I certainly *won't* marry him if he gives me any more cause for doubts, ever.'

To Elissa's horror, Logan's voice came in, cool, hard. 'Oh, don't strain yourself, Stacey. I've no intention of asking you to marry me. I did, yes, but this last six weeks or so, ever since you brought up the idea that Rupert owed me something because his great-grandfather cheated mine out of a gold-claim all those years ago, and ought to make over some of the property to me, I've gone off the idea. That's nothing to do with this generation and nobody, at this stage, can prove or disprove it. I forbade you to mention it to Rupert when he comes back, you'll recall. And let me tell you this ... rumour can be very nasty, and if you spread any distorted version of this affair ... Elissa landing here last night ... I'll take legal steps to stop you.'

Stacey said, with relish, 'You're going to be in a real fix, now. You've got no housekeeper ... Aunt Claudia couldn't possibly manage house and correspondence lessons too ... that's why she brought me along. Says she's no intention of lifting as much as a hand to the housework. Said I'd better see if I could take this sort of life before I signed on with you. I can't imagine a high and mighty interior decorator from England as much as washing a dish. I'm going ... and you'll have to crawl to get me back ... but before I go, you'd better show me this locked car. This girl probably just put on an act about that, hoping I'd march off in high dudgeon without putting it to the test.'

Logan said savagely, 'Right!' and out they marched, down the fern-fringed drive, across the lawn above the blue-green lake, a lovely, lovely world spoiled only by discord and lack of faith. Elissa and Logan were in the lead. She waved at the stack of luggage on the back seat, and with a magnificent gesture, wrenched at that door ... the next moment she almost went sprawling as it opened with her!

Stacey's laugh wasn't good to hear, Logan's face wasn't good to see. Aunt Claudia made a sort of trumpeting sound, whether of triumph or dismay couldn't be told.

Stacey said, 'There's something very phoney about this. I think you made up a lot, both of you, as you went along, and overreached yourselves.'

Elissa said, but even to her own ears it sounded feeble, 'But I *did* try all the doors ... I went round them two or three times. You do, in a case like that, positively wrenching and rattling them. I needed that rug, believe me. See ... all the others are locked.' Suddenly, in the face of their disbelief and of Logan's chagrin, she was fighting tears.

She said forlornly, 'I'm sorry about this. I can't explain that. I've thrown a spanner in the works between two people who've only got their lines crossed. I'm sure when Stacey cools off, Logan, she'll realise there was nothing in it. Rupert's letter will turn up. I'll just clear off. Though what I'll tell Rupert, I don't know. I'm just a dill, falling into lakes and losing keys and making some hideous mistake like this.'

There was a drawl in Logan's voice that was meant to be provocative—to Stacey. 'Oh, no, you won't clear off, Elissa Montgomery. I'm landed with three kids and no housekeeper. If you're truly remorseful, you'll stay and pitch in. Even if Stacey did stay, in the mood she's in she'd hound the poor little devils day and night. On your way, Stacey, and don't come back, ever, to apologise!'

CHAPTER THREE

STACEY stood quite still for a long moment, which could have meant she was considering apologising. Then she said, 'That's something I couldn't imagine, Logan. Any crawling will be done by you, believe me. What a good job I brought my car too. Have a good time, all of you. I wish you joy ... imagine having three homesick children, Aunt Claudia, and an English greenhorn all cooped up together. Goodbye, I have better things to do.'

She wheeled round, took some unhurried steps towards an expensive car drawn up a few yards away, opened a door, took out some bags and dumped them on the shingle. At that moment the three children rushed helter-skelter towards them, evidently fed-up and curious.

Stacey reached in to the shelf above the back seat, caught hold of a battered teddy-bear by one drooping ear, and tossed it on to the pile of luggage with a disdainful air.

The smallest child, a little girl with shining blonde hair, darted forward just too late. The bear slid over the edge of a case and dropped with a splash into an exceedingly muddy puddle. Small Elizabeth scooped him up and yelled with spirit, 'Now look what you've done! You've made him even worse than what you said last night. I'm glad you're going!'

Was there to be no end to the insults? thought Elissa with despair. Then she looked down on the small offender, saw tears in the big blue eyes and a lip trembling, scooped her up with an instinctive gesture of comforting, said, 'It's all right, sweetie, teddy-bears wash. He'll be as good as ever when he dries.' The lip steadied.

Stacey turned her wheel, accelerated, dust spurted up, and puddles sprayed, and she was away. No one spoke till the car was out of sight.

Then the dark elfish-looking child, who was about ten or

43

eleven, stood on her head. Logan MacCorquodale said, 'What's that in aid of, may I ask, Isabel?' Then as she opened her mouth to reply he said hastily, 'No, don't tell me, I'd rather not know.'

It had looked like pure joy to Elissa. But whether because of coming to Glen Airlie, a child's paradise, or at Stacey's departure, she couldn't decide. She said quickly, 'Where do we go from here?'

Logan said, 'Well, first of all, the three children can start carrying their cases up to the house . . .'

Isabel looked up at him with her impish grin, but affectionately. 'Want to get rid of us, don't you?'

He smiled back, to Elissa's surprise, said, 'That's true. I'll get things sorted out with the others then. See you soon, love.'

He turned back to the two women. 'Elissa, we'll attend to your problems soon . . . look, put my jacket on over that flimsy garment. After last night's adventures, you'll be down with pneumonia. But while the kids are out of it, just tell me, my dear aunt, why they are here?'

'Because Roland and Sue are off to Cambridge.'

Logan's jaw dropped. 'You're having me on! Rol could never get Sue to leave them for as much as a weekend. People don't just go off to England at such short notice, leaving their children behind them.'

'Now let me get it out without interruption, because this girl should be back in the warm house. Rol had put in for this course of study, but only got into second place. Then the man who got it wasn't able to take it up for some family reason, and it was offered to Rol. He was to go off, get them a place to live . . . it's for two years . . . and send for them. But at the last moment Rol broke his arm. Fortunately it was the left, but Sue just had to go with him. He can't even dress himself. We couldn't let him miss an opportunity like that, so I proposed this.'

Logan swallowed, said, 'You *proposed* this? Aunt Claudia, I hope that in any family emergency I'll always pitch in, but you knew Mum and Dad were away, so why didn't you reach for a phone and ask was it convenient?'

'Because I knew that before I had time to pack their things, you'd have been dissuaded, even if you'd said yes in the first instance.'

His lips thinned out again. 'Dissuaded? By whom?'

She looked amazed. 'By Stacey, of course. She'd have said it was an imposition, that you'd be tied even more to the estate than you are now. You can't get out so much, with a family wished on you.'

He tried to digest that. 'But you brought *her* here. That would have tied *her* to the place too, and she already thinks I'm mad to stay here. Though I've told her I'm here for keeps.'

The mannish face gave nothing away. Her tone was entirely unrepentant. 'I know. But we don't want a repetition of Euan and Anne. I thought it would be good for her to know what it's really like living up here, with the responsibility of a family, with a road that's often cut by slips and a launch service at the mercy of mountain storms. I've never been here yet when some emergency hasn't occurred. I thought it was providential your parents were in Australia.'

Logan's face was a study. 'Providential? I could find another word, like catastrophic, hellishly catastrophic. Aunt Claudia, never before have I felt like ... like ...'

'Like boxing my ears?' she suggested, and when he didn't reply said complacently, 'That's one thing about being an aged great-aunt, people don't. Box your ears, I mean.'

He said, 'I was thinking more of boiling you in oil.'

Aunt Claudia burst out laughing. 'Good, you've got your sense of humour back.' Elissa thought she must be wilfully blind. She'd never seen anyone less likely to laugh.

She said hastily, 'Let's get my luggage out of the back seat so I can get into something decent, and cook some breakfast. I'm ravenous! I'll ring the garage after that and ask them to send a couple of men round if they can spare them, with a set of keys. They can book their time up to me. One can drive it back. It serves me right to go stalking white herons with hired car keys in my pocket.'

Logan's voice was milder, though firm. 'I'll pay the charges in lieu of some of your wages as a housekeeper. You'll have to wait till they come before you get your things out of the boot—that's much harder to pick than the doors. Those I could have managed.'

'But you didn't have to,' said Elissa miserably. 'One opened.'

Aunt Claudia gave way to a bellow of laughter. Tears rolled down her cheeks. 'It was the last straw! I'll never forget Stacey's face. Or yours, Logan. Or Elissa's.'

Fury rose in Elissa's throat. The humiliation of that moment was still with her. She saw Logan's mouth beginning to crumble. She said icily, 'I'm afraid I haven't got the sort of humour that seems to prevail in this family ... it's put me in an entirely false position and I don't like it. I won't run out on you, for the children's sakes, and Rupert Airlie's, but I fail to see anything funny in it. I'll work at my schemes for the redecorating in between washing dishes and scrubbing floors, and when Stacey sees me set off for the other side of the world again, she'll come to her senses.'

She grabbed two small bags and marched up the rise to the house, outrage in every inch of her.

She was quickly into warmer clothes and tipped out the board-like eggs and started again with the breakfast. The children decided they were hungry again too, but Aunt Claudia decreed they were to have toast only.

Logan looked across the table at Elissa, said, 'That door's faulty all right. It won't shut at all now. It's the mechanism on the inside. That's what I thought when it came open like that.'

Elissa said, 'Then *you* believed me? That I *had* tried all the doors over and over?'

'Of course. Nobody would leave any door untried in a storm like that, especially after being dunked in the lake. Car doors are quite commonly faulty. Stacey will realise that too, when she's cooled off.' He paused, said sharply, 'Rennie, what did you say?'

Rennie hesitated, but only for a minute. 'I said that'd

be a pity. I think she's better out of it.'

Aunt Claudia got up quickly. 'Well, least said soonest mended, and the fewer remarks like that one the better. Logie, when you're as old as I am, you'll never ask children what they say in asides. Now, you children know what rooms you usually have up here. I'll take the double one.'

They all trooped in and out of the house till almost everything was in. Isabel was like quicksilver and was likely to wear herself out. Elizabeth quietly sorted out her own things. Rennie had a list and seemed to have great enjoyment in ticking things off. 'Undoubtedly a future Government statistician,' said Logan out of the corner of his mouth to Elissa, as he stooped to bring out the last carton. Something fell out of it, and bowled down the slope. It was round and red. He managed to stop it with his foot, said, 'What on earth have you brought a dog-bowl for?'

'It's Benjamin's,' said Rennie. 'But we had to leave him at the Samsons'. He was sick twice on the way up and we didn't want it happening again. Aunt Claudia said Gordon Samson would bring him up in the back of a truck some time.'

Logan shut his eyes, said, 'Not *Benjamin*? Oh, *no*! I don't think I can stand it. Why on earth didn't Sue put him into kennels?'

'Costs far too much,' said Aunt Claudia. 'Besides, if they're going to be away for two years, it couldn't be done. You were the obvious one to take him. He might be useful. After all, Logan, he's half collie.'

'Useful!' he groaned. 'That crazy mixed-up animal! The only bit of collie in him is his pointed nose. The rest is Labrador and God knows what else. As far as sheep and cattle are concerned, he's a disaster.' He turned to Elissa, caught her disapproving look, said defensively, 'He's only three-quarter grown, but gigantic, and every inch is charged with dangerous energy. And to cap it all, he's accident-prone like you.' He groaned again. 'What have I done to deserve all this in one day?'

Elizabeth sidled up to him, slipped a small starfish hand in his, said, with confidence, 'But you always love having us, don't you, Uncle Logie?'

He looked down and the dark face softened, he bent down and swung her up. 'Of course I do, poppet. We'll all have such fun. And I have got a soft spot for silly old Ben. It's just that pet dogs on a property can be a problem, but if you promise not to mind that he has to be on a chain at night so he can never be blamed for worrying and killing sheep, I'll make him welcome too. Now let's get going. The first job should be the washing of Teddy. You can help Elissa with that, Bess.'

They washed the poor battered thing and hung him out in the glorious mountain air in a hammock of muslin suspended from the clothes-line. Elissa rightly guessed Elizabeth wouldn't like her boon companion suspended from it by a string round his neck.

Elissa had a feeling of great unreality as she helped them unpack, tidied the house, made beds, concocted the lunch. After it she went to find Claudia. She discovered the redoubtable soul putting her own things into the drawers of the dressing-table in the big room, said, 'Mrs Robertson, I'm going to take the little room off yours. It has another door leading in from the hall, so it won't inconvenience you at all.'

Claudia was surprised. 'It's very tiny. There are stacks of bigger rooms in the side-wing. There's a very nice one with glass doors that lead out on to a porch, very sunny.'

'No, thank you. I've found out that's where Mrs Mac-Corquodale sleeps. When Stacey comes back, as come back she certainly will, I want to have a room that leads off yours and is neatly sandwiched in between that and the girls' room. Puts a stop to her thinking any hanky-panky's going on.'

Claudia nodded. 'Sensible gal. Go to it!'

The room nearly overwhelmed Elissa with memories. There was the window-seat where she used to sit and dream, looking out on to the bush paths, where she had listened to bird-song early and late, a dearly-remembered view. Suddenly her eyes blurred with tears ... why, there was her triangular bookcase, the one Rupert had made for her, and it still held the books that had been left behind by mistake, by her mother, when she had packed, taken a launch across the lake, and called for her fourteen-year-old daughter at Cloudy Hill where she had boarded with old Trudi Klausner so she could attend Kotare High School at Ludwigtown.

She knelt down ... a couple of rows of Enid Blytons, her A. A. Milnes, the Anne of Green Gables books, and the Emily ones she had loved best of all; the old edition of Burns's poems Rupert had given her from his own treasures, two books on New Zealand birds, two on trees. Treasure-trove from a happy past. She sprang up, refreshed by this small delight; later she would revive the happiness of ownership when time permitted.

Suddenly she remembered she was cooking with a solid fuel stove. What if the fire had gone out? She flew out to the kitchen, took a poker, opened the fire-door, saw with relief a steady red glow in the grate. She'd like to keep it to an even heat all day, because it was a little tricky, cooking with this when you'd been used to just turning a switch. She filled the grate with some slow-burning coal.

It was quite a day. The Samsons, father and son, arrived with an excited Benjamin in the back of their truck. They all suspected it was more to get rid of him than to save Logan driving up for the animal. By this time Logan had heard from the rental garage that the car couldn't be picked up till the next day. The men eyed it curiously, made laughing comments on the perversity of door-locks, and Elissa felt they were summing her up at afternoon-tea time. It was quite evident Stacey had called there on her way back and had given them a decidedly biased account of finding some girl at Glen Airlie with Logan.

She carefully called him Mr MacCorquodale and noticed a twinkle in Claudia's eye. She was glad the old warhorse was there. She was certain the Samsons knew her well, and would know she wouldn't stand for anything irregular.

Aunt Claudia, as if reading her thoughts, said, 'I'm mighty glad Rupert sent Miss Montgomery here when he did, even if, due to his letter being delayed, the poor girl wasn't met. She'd no idea what the road was like, of course, or she'd have stopped in Ludwigtown for the night. She was expecting to be met by Mr and Mrs MacCorquodale, and had no idea Logan's father wasn't the manager. She'd never as much as heard of a son.'

Elissa nodded. 'He did say Logan, but I thought that was the husband of the housekeeper. I'm afraid he didn't put things as clearly as he might. I met him at Blair and Victoria Doig's place in Surrey. Do you happen to know them? They come from Roxburgh way.'

Gordon Samson grinned. 'I'll say! In fact I once had a mad crush on Victoria. She was Victoria Sherbourne then. Not that she ever looked at me. How are they?'

'Fine. Victoria's standing in for me while I'm away. I'm an interior decorator too, as I suppose you know by now. Not that I've ever been sent from one hemisphere to another before, but Rupert was all set on having all this re-decorated.'

Bob Samson boggled. 'The gay old dog! He must have got carried away by some of the stately homes of England. Not much wrong with the place, is there? Oh, I'd better watch my step. You're the professional, and can probably see a lot that needs doing.'

She laughed, 'As yet I've not had time to even look it over with what Rupert suggested in my mind's eye. I'm still recovering from the disasters that befell me ... I'm a bird-watcher and went for a walk when there was no one home, and stalked a white heron and fell in the lake and lost the keys. I was never so cold in my life. I curled up on the sheepskin on the verandah, with a blanket I found on the porch at the cottage, and turned the table on its side to keep out the draughts, and was scared out of my wits when Mr MacCorquodale fell over it in the dark.

'Nevertheless, the worst part of the nightmare was when he didn't know who I was. It sounded so crazy, an interior decorator all the way from England. When Rupert first asked me I thought perhaps he was thinking of marrying again—even that he'd met someone in England and wanted the place all prettied up. But he denied it.'

'Rupert?' This was Bob Samson, who was about Rupert's age. 'Not he! If he didn't marry again when the children were small, it's hardly likely now. He only once ever showed signs of looking someone's way long ago. But she was no good, I heard. When he found out about her he was completely disillusioned, and there's been no one since.'

At that moment all hell broke loose outside. The children had been happily playing in one of the home paddocks with Ben. Now they were screaming and shouting and Ben was giving vent to anguished squeals and yelps, which sounded slightly smothered. As one they left the kitchen table and rushed outside. Four figures were running madly round the paddock, seemingly chasing each other, three human, one canine, and the canine one had his head jammed in a paint-can. Ben was shaking his head madly from side to side, stopping now and then to thump it on the ground and claw at it, thereby wedging it still more firmly on.

They were through the gate in no time, tearing towards the commotion. Tears were pouring down the girls' faces; Rennie flung himself on Ben, pinning him down, but only for a few moments as the great dog shook his puny weight off. Fortunately he didn't see he was running straight at Logan, who pounced.

Isabel was shrieking, 'Be careful, that lid will cut his head off!'

She had cause for fear. It was an old one with a pushed-in lid stuck with old paint, so someone had cut round it with a tin-opener, leaving jagged edges. Ben had poked his head in, and the edges of the partly-cut lid had closed behind his ears. It took three of them to hold his thrashing hindquarters while Claudia issued advice. 'Hold him absolutely still. One of you flatten his neck a bit, and Logan will bend the lid over. He'll cut his fingers, but no matter. When you've got the edges bent over enough, Logan, exert force downwards and the other one will pull his head out very gently, holding his ears close to his head.'

Elissa's hands were smallest of the adults', so she slid her hands in, and flattened the writhing, jerking dog's ears down, and all of a sudden jumped and said, 'There's something else inside. A bird or a mouse ... no, of course I'm not frightened, it was just unexpected. Carry on, Logan.' She gritted her teeth as something ran over her fingers again and the big yellow dog heaved convulsively. Logan was speaking reassuringly to the animal as he worked at the tin, said, 'Now, Elissa, press his neck together, then pull his head out.'

Grunts, ouches, squeals, and suddenly Ben was free, one ear and Logan's finger dripping blood. Elissa peered into the tin, then tipped out a little white lizard. That explained why Ben had thrust his head in, in the first place. Ben shook his head, looked puzzled as gore flew in all directions, then lay down, like a couchant lion on a medallion.

'If I'm not sorry for myself,' said Logan, 'saddled with a mad animal like that. Isabel, Elizabeth, what are you still crying for?'

Isabel lifted a tear-drenched face. 'Because Ben's wounded. Look at his ear. Perhaps he'll die!'

'No such——' her uncle began, and had the kindness to cut off the next word. 'No such thing,' he hastily amended. 'Ears always bleed a lot, like lips. If you must cry, cry about me. I've gashed two fingers almost clean to the bone.'

'But *you* can tell us if you think you're dying,' said his callous niece. 'Ben can't. But never mind, Ben, I'll sit up all night with you.'

Elissa expected a scathing remark from the child's uncle, but he merely said, 'He can stay in the warm kitchen all night if that'll satisfy you. But you'll see, he'll have forgotten all about it in no time. Let's go back to the house. I meant to take some chops out of the deep freeze for our dinner.'

Elissa said, 'I did that. I put them in the cylinder cupboard to hasten the thawing.' He looked grateful.

Aunt Claudia, the three children, and Ben, by now dancing merrily all round them, walked ahead of them to the house. The other four followed, talking of the pranks dogs could get into. They paused by the great gum by the house-gate. 'But they have such wonderful memories,' said Elissa. 'I couldn't credit it when Bluey remembered me after ten years and more.'

The Samsons looked surprised. 'Remembered you? What——?'

Elissa said, laughing, 'Oh, I didn't realise you weren't fully in the picture. I lived here ten years ago. I don't remember you, but then the road wasn't through. It was a case of across the lake by launch. My mother was governess here for three years. I had a couple of years at Kotare High before she took me back to England. It was a wonderful surprise to meet the man I used to call Uncle Rupert one day at Victoria's.'

She looked up to see a peculiar expression on the older man's face. He said, 'Are you Meg Montgomery's daughter?'

She said, 'Why, yes,' smiling. 'Did you know her?'

He said slowly, 'Not to say know. I did meet her once, very briefly. It was more that I knew of her. We had a place at Arrowtown then, not here. Well, well!'

Elissa didn't know why his tone chilled her. Almost as if Meg Montgomery's daughter wasn't welcome here. She was glad when they left.

CHAPTER FOUR

The rest of the day simply flew. If it hadn't been for the sickening recollection of the word-battle with Stacey Cressford, Elissa would have quite enjoyed it. However, there was little doubt that when the two antagonists simmered down, they'd sort things out, though Logan had said some pretty unforgivable things, like not intending to ask her to marry him. Still, no doubt worse things had been said by other men and women, in the heat of the moment. Things that were forgiven and forgotten. Not that Stacey looked the forgiving sort.

If only it hadn't happened, if only her arrival could have been as idyllic in circumstances as in setting, from the moment of her arrival at the far side of the lake when she had been enraptured with its remembered beauty. How different it would have been had she been met by the middle-aged man she'd imagined, with a kindly wife, the one who'd proposed the redecoration of Airlie House. What a pity they'd taken off for Australia, leaving only their son. But even given that, if only Rupert's letter had arrived Logan would have expected her and probably arranged for some other woman to stay in the house till Rupert came home. What *could* have happened to that letter? Well, occasionally mail did go astray.

But if all this had gone according to plan, she could have looked on this as a long, paid holiday, recapturing the magic of childhood, revelling in the tasks she loved most, not stinted for money, allowing imagination and inspiration to have free rein, instead of which she was saddled with the care of a large house, cooking for five people whose tastes she knew not, and one of them was the formidable Claudia.

The children went off with Logan on some farm job; Claudia was busy in the schoolroom. Logan had put out potatoes, carrots, parsnips and a freshly-cut cabbage. Good, she'd do the carrots and parsnips together, mashing them when cooked. He'd also put out a jar of preserved apricots, and Central Otago apricots were out of this world. They'd need no cooking. Nice if she could do something to accompany them, something easy. Baked custard with coconut stirred into it? No, better not, some children disliked coconut.

What about a marshmallow sweet? Plenty of eggs and sugar here if she could find some gelatine. It was so quick. She did unearth the two dessertspoons of gelatine needed, but not a grain more. How lucky! She soaked them in half a cup of cold water and when dissolved, added another half cup of boiling water and set it aside to cool. She beat up two egg-whites, added a cup of sugar, beat it, added the cooled mixture and beat it again till it became marshmallowy, then folded in the yolks. What deep yellow yolks! No wonder, with the fowls on free range. It was so thick a mixture it piled up in pleasing whirls as she scraped it into a blue-and-white striped bowl. She experienced the glow of pleasure she knew when a decorating job had surpassed her expectations.

But what a time it took to peel this amount of potatoes! She would prefer grilling the chops to frying but wasn't sure about the fire-stove. In her preoccupation she'd let it get very low. Aunt Claudia arrived out.

'Do them in the electric oven,' she suggested.

Elissa said doubtfully, 'That one looks as complicated as a computer with all those dials and lights. We cooked with gas at home.'

The older woman said briskly, 'This is very new, but fortunately a friend of mine in Dunedin has one the same. You push in the grill button, that means only the top comes on, I suppose there's a grill-pan in the warming drawer . . . ah, yes.' She began arranging the chops. 'Put them as close to the top as possible, give them about eight minutes each side—we like our chops well done—and be sure to leave the oven door open.'

'Open?' Elissa was mystified.

'Yes, because if you don't, as soon as the heat reaches the number it's set at, it switches off. With the door open the elements stay red. Isn't it a trial finding your way round a new kitchen?'

Elissa's voice was warm with gratitude. Claudia chuckled. 'All women get uptight about new cooking arrangements, girl, even an old warhorse like me. Don't be afraid to ask me anything. I like you. You've got guts. Most girls would have walked out and left this household flat after what happened this morning. You didn't, and I liked the way you sailed into that high-and-mighty madam this morning. At first you were placatory, as befitting a stranger, and anxious to explain it away. But all of a sudden you fired up in defence of Logan. I liked that.'

Elissa smiled. 'Thank you, Mrs Robertson. I was horrified later to think I'd got so hot, only Logan did deserve better than he got. To suspect him of that—once it was explained—was unthinkable.' She stopped, looking puzzled. 'But—but it's just occurred to me. There was a time, during the fireworks, when you even added fuel to the blaze, when Logan thought you too didn't believe him. I thought he was even madder about that than Stacey's disbelief, oddly enough. You actually said he deserved to have Stacey make mincemeat of him. I don't get it.'

Claudia Robertson's face crumpled into laughter. 'I'm a wicked old woman. I was terrified she'd suddenly believe him, and if ever two people are entirely unsuited, it's those two.'

Claudia watched the expressions chase over the face before her. 'Go on, say it,' she urged. 'It's not good to bottle your feelings up.'

'Say what?'

'Say: "I couldn't agree with you more." Be true to yourself.'

Elissa burst out laughing. 'I did feel that! How odd. I thought I was feeling remorseful because my spending the night here had caused such a kerfuffle. I ought to feel that. Oh, we can't judge her on leaping to an unfortunate conclusion this morning, it's just not fair.'

'We aren't judging her on that. We're judging her on lack of faith in Logan when the explanation was given. And in any case, my judgment is based on unhappily watching this develop all year.'

'But—but you were the one who insisted she come here to look after the house while you taught the children. I know you couldn't be expected to cope with it all, but if you disliked her as much as that, then——'

'Fiddlesticks! I could have coped. I've governessed on some of the loneliest sheep-stations in Canterbury—right in the Alps, far more remote than this. I didn't marry till I was forty, so I had years of it and times without number when the station wives would go down to the coast to have their babies and be away six or eight weeks, I've managed house and children and shepherds. I just thought it was time for that daft Logan to see his lady-love under those same circumstances. It brings out the worst—or the best—in people.' She added, 'I'm glad Alicia and Nicol took off for Australia, they were just pussyfooting around, leaning over backwards not to interfere.'

Elissa looked thoughtful. 'Isn't it good when parents don't?'

'Yes, for sure it is, but if *I* do, it doesn't matter. I'm a little outside the situation and they can just think it's bossy old Aunt Claudia, a sort of eccentric. Every family has them, so they just put up with me.'

A little smile tipped up the corners of Elissa's mouth. 'I don't think that's true. I don't think Logan's sister would have left her darling children with you if she only puts up with you. She must trust you implicitly, as I would myself.'

Elissa was surprised to hear herself say that. Claudia must have that effect on people. It was the governess in her. You recognised authority and wisdom and good judgment. She was slightly fearsome, yet she made you feel secure. Sue would know that.

Claudia actually looked self-conscious, hurrumphed and turned away, saying briskly, 'Well now, I'll set the table while you grill those chops. The other vegetables are boiling, so I'll shred that cabbage for you.'

They all seemed to enjoy the meal, so for the first time Elissa began to relax. Her eyes kept straying to the west window in the corner where the sunset was gilding the panes and sending rosy lights flickering over the old rag mat in front of the stove. Claudia noticed it, said crisply, 'Now, we had a good dinner cooked for us. I'll wash up, Elizabeth and Isabel can dry, and Rennie can put the dishes away. Elissa ought to go out to see the sun set over the lake. It's really something. Out on to the terraces with her, Logan, we can have coffee later.'

Logan grinned. 'I always obey Aunt Claudia. It pays!'

Elissa looked up at him as they stepped out. 'Even when it goes against the grain?'

He cocked an eye at her, one of the penthouse brows up. 'Do you really think I didn't want to show a girl like you a sunset like this?'

She frowned, 'I don't care for obvious answers like that. I wasn't looking for a compliment. I was serious in wondering how much influence your great-aunt has in your family.'

His look wasn't so quizzical this time. 'I assure you it wasn't an expected gallantry. I thought I'd like to take you out to see the sunset long before Aunt Claudia proposed it.'

'Oh? Then why didn't you?'

He grinned. 'I was trying to think of some way to do it without the whole tribe following us. Aunt Claudia spiked their guns very neatly.'

She ignored that. 'But what about your aunt's influence on the family?'

He didn't set her back. He considered it. 'I don't really know. I can't recall, in late years anyway, ever being pushed into doing something I didn't want to do, but somehow her judgments are so wholesome, we find ourselves being influenced by them. It's not so much that she's dictatorial, rather that we're so certain of her affection towards us that we instinctively try to please her. Mother always says if it hadn't been for her Aunt Claudia she'd have married the wrong man. I'm damned glad she didn't, I can't imagine anyone but Dad as my father.' He laughed at his own absurdity. 'Elissa Montgomery, you aren't making the best of things. We were sent out to watch a sunset, it's changing every moment, and we're babbling about my aunt!'

They lifted their faces to the west and silence descended upon them. Through a cleft in the lower hills nearer them, across the lake, the Remarkables above Queenstown were flushed right along their jagged peaks with a coppery-rose more like American desert colour than New Zealand mountains. Close at hand, the waters of Moana-Kotare were stained baby pink and over the long shoulder of Ben Lomond that crouched above the unseen-from-here Lake Wakatipu was a changing kaleidoscope of colours, rayed up from still more distant mountains as the sun westered, great bars of hibiscus-red, japonica-coral, interspersed with deep violet and pale primrose and a clear, translucent jade.

Elissa said dreamily, 'Going down to waken that other world I love, the northern hemisphere and its people. Victoria will be waking to a new day, possibly travelling to a house in Midhurst that has stood there for four hundred years ... or to another near Porchester even older.'

'Porchester? Near Porchester Castle, where Henry the Fifth assembled his troops before Agincourt?'

Surprised, she turned to him. 'You mean you know it? Or just love history?'

'I love history, yes, but I've been there. It's one of my favourite spots. So has Aunt Claudia. I did three years in Britain, in England, Scotland, Wales, on various farms. I won a sort of award for eighteen months, but stayed on another year and a half. Aunt Claudia and Uncle Dennis had a trip at the time I was on a Surrey farm, near the coast. Dennis had come from Hampshire as a boy, so they spent a lot of time round there. I know Haslemere too. I remember it in spring, with the beeches in new leaf, arching over those lanes, and bluebells like pools reflecting the sky beneath them.'

'Oh, that could stop me feeling homesick ... to have two people here who know the places I love there.'

'Are you going to be homesick, Elissa? I thought that through the years you might have been a little nostalgic for here ... eager to see it again.'

'Oh, I was. I was disappointed Uncle Rupert wouldn't be here. He was my father-figure when I was young. But he's promised to be back before I leave. I thought the whole time I was flying here of visiting our old haunts ... that half-hour stalking the heron was so idyllic till I fell in ... only——'

'Only what?'

She laughed a little. 'It's so foolish to expect everything to be the same. How could it be? With Judy and Elspeth, my comrades of long ago, married and gone from here, and Mother not with me. *She* seemed never nostalgic for here. I couldn't understand it. She hardly spoke of it at all, only about South Canterbury, where she and my father farmed. I suppose this time here was a time of intense grief for her. So I bottled up my yearning ... for the lake and the mountains and the silences and the bird-calls. I hoped for the old enchantment to come flooding back, and it did too, momentarily, but I fell in the lake and the mud and I got——' she faltered.

'And you got embroiled in a horrible slanging match, something that seemed to destroy the peace you remembered at Glen Airlie? But not to worry—Stacey won't be back. It won't be all grind, you know, endless housework and cooking. When Gwyneth gets back she'll be able to lend you a hand to free you to get on with the decorating. Hers is only a small cottage and she's a terrific worker.'

Elissa opened her mouth to say she'd not resented the thought of that, but hated the fact that she'd been the cause of that scene, something that might not matter to *her* when she was gone from here, but had possibly changed the whole course of *his* life, but at that moment Rennie came dashing out on to the terrace. 'Uncle Logie, Hew's on the phone!'

Elissa followed him and they all unashamedly listened, heard him say, 'Great Scott ... twins! Good heavens, nobody so much as expected that, did they? Congratulations ... but how is Gwyneth? And the babies? Oh, good ... all well. She must be tired, though, it was a long labour, wasn't it? Oh ... the second one took its time? Hew, you mustn't come back for a few days. Aunt Claudia is here. If I want a hand I'll get hold of Gordon Samson or Olaf Haraldsen. Will Gwyneth's sister come over with her when she comes home, to give her a hand with the twins? Good. Give her my love and congratulations.'

The girls were bemused. 'One each,' said Elizabeth. 'One each to nurse. That means Isabel can't have first go in this because she's the eldest. What kind are they?'

'Boy and girl, and quite a good size for twins, and they were a bit early at that. I'd never have believed it. Well, things are certainly happening today ... oh, watch it, Aunt, Ben's on——'

He shot out his arms and tried to stop her falling over the dog and received half a pint of milk down the front of his tartan shirt. The three children collapsed into laughter, fully enjoying an accident they couldn't be blamed for, and Ben, delighted at this sudden appearance of manna from heaven, sat up and began lapping madly. It was no good, Elissa collapsed too, and the laugh they all enjoyed dispelled a lot of the tension of the day.

The sunset fires gave place to twilit purple and a stillness descended like a benediction to a too-eventful day. Claudia had proposed they stay in the big kitchen, rather than heat up the lounge, and that they would all have an early night.

Elissa had always loved the big deal table ... what a boon to have a table one could scrub, where children could spill paste if they must, drop crayons, build models and not worry about scratching. These big old homes were ideal for family life.

Claudia was busy sorting out lessons for the next day, Isabel cutting out paper dolls, Elizabeth drawing the cow that jumped over the moon, and Rennie was busy with some ploy of his own. Elissa, writing to her mother a guarded account of coming to Glen Airlie, leaned over to see and looked amazed.

Logan grinned at her. 'His father is a wizard at statistics, and Rennie takes after him. It's the breath of life to him—

filling in forms. His father supplies him.'

Rennie looked up, said, 'They're very interesting, Elissa. I've got forty different applications here, and there's at least one question on every paper you don't find on the rest.'

'Goodness,' said Elissa, 'but how did you work that out?'

Rennie beamed on her. She was really interested, not like some grown-ups who thought it a strange hobby for a boy and only took an interest if you collected stamps or cereal cards or something. 'It's basic, really. You do it by a process of ... of ... well, you 'liminate each question. I'll show you.'

Logan gave her a look which said: 'Now look what you've let yourself in for,' and returned hastily to his farm accounts. The little earnest voice went on, as eager as if he'd been explaining the intricacies of a steam engine. Unnoticed, small Elizabeth, from the corner of the table, purloined for herself half a dozen forms.

Finally Rennie said appreciatively, 'I suppose I'd better let you get on with your letter now.'

Elissa managed a sigh of regret. 'Yes, I expect so. Mothers expect letters regularly so they know what their children are up to.' Silence reigned again.

Suddenly Elizabeth's voice shattered it, and though often, as she knew so well, grown-ups had to have things repeated over and over before they'd answer, this time three adult heads jerked up, three pairs of eyes fixed themselves upon her. 'Uncle Logie,' she said, 'what *is* sex?'

Elissa heard Logan swallow even as she herself swallowed. What a moment to pick! It was all right, in theory, to explain these things to children as they asked, but this *was* a bit public. You always hoped they'd have the sense to ask when they had you on their own.

She had to admire the way Logan rose to the occasion. After that first flabbergasted moment he said crisply, 'Look, Bess, I'd like to get these figures finished first. How about if I explain it to you when I tell you and Isabel your bedtime stories?'

Isabel and Rennie seemed too intent on their occupations to join in. Elizabeth said, 'But I want to finish this now.' Elissa and Logan gazed blankly at her, but Claudia gave a short cough, said, 'You want to know what sex is? It means either man or woman, mother or father, boy or girl. But if you're filling in a form you put down either male or female.'

It was so simple. Just a question on a form! Elissa felt laughter well up in her and knew she couldn't control it. She rose, went out of the far door and scurried along the passage to be out of earshot, and was just crossing the threshold of the verandah where she'd spent such an uncomfortable night, when she realised Logan was on her heels.

She turned, he pushed her through, shut the door behind them and like Elissa gave way to great gusts of laughter. When their first spasms of merriment had spent themselves, they made for the window-ledge where the sliding windows had been pushed back all day, leant their elbows on it and let their laughs subside in little gasps and revivements.

'Kids!' said Logan feelingly. 'They're so simple, so direct, and we adults are so complex. And all in that one moment before good old Aunt solved it, I was trying madly to work out what I'd say to tie in with whatever Sue and Rol have told them. I know they're all for truth in such matters, but what a problem to know what progress has already been made, and how much they can take at a time. I mean, no one expects a kid in Primer One to cope with higher maths, and I expect it's the same with the facts of life. It should be a gradual awareness, otherwise you'd take a little of the magic off it, by being too clinical. Sue and Rol would do it beautifully, I'm sure.'

A new sensation washed over Elissa. She raised her eyes to his. 'So would you, I think, if you can express yourself like this to me, a stranger.'

He began to answer her, then checked. Perhaps he wanted her to enlarge on that, so she added. 'And even caught on the hop like that, I thought it quite inspired to tell Bess you would explain at story-time. You didn't make her feel she shouldn't have asked in front of everyone. You said, so naturally, that you wanted to finish your work. I liked that.'

Logan MacCorquodale said slowly, 'You're really doing things for my ego. As a bachelor I feel woefully inadequate for standing-in for parents like Sue and Rol. You're a great morale-booster. I suddenly feel I can cope.'

Elissa looked up at him curiously. 'You seem such a strong person, I just can't imagine you on speaking terms with doubts.'

He said again slowly, 'I used not to have so many, but lately I've been much less sure of myself. I feel I haven't as much get-up-and-go as I should have, that I'm inclined to let things run on as they've run on for years. Not enough ambition.'

She knew instinctively who had put those doubts into his mind: Stacey.

She said, equally slowly, 'I suppose ambition is all right, but it depends on what you're ambitious for. I prefer determination, I think. I like people to strive for what goal they have ... such as being good at their particular job, for couples to work equally hard for the finance necessary to educate their children suitably ... not to be able to give them everything they want. I don't like them to be ruthless about it or to feel the end justifies the means. My mother is a case in point. She was marvellous the way she supported us both till I could earn too. She was doing very well in a certain clerical job she was in. She could have gone to the top there.

'Then she suddenly realised the firm, a private one, was doing a big tax fiddle. What she was asked to do was simply to turn a blind eye. She wouldn't. She left, telling them why. She gave up a big salary well above the average one, and settled for a basic one with a firm whose integrity was beyond question. Her boss and a colleague told her she was a fool. I felt Mother didn't care that she herself had less, but she *did* care that some advantages she had planned for me couldn't then be attempted. She was very candid with me about it, and at the age I was, she risked my being resentful about it. But she said maybe it was meant to be and that I'd just have to work a bit harder myself, that although she couldn't expect me to appreciate it at that moment of frustration, it would be good for my character.'

She couldn't see his expression by now, it was too dark, but some real emotion deepened his voice, she thought. 'As it has been,' he said.

That compliment pleased Elissa. But she chuckled. 'Seems to be give-and-take. It's the night for boosting each other. How you can say such a thing about a witless female who goes round falling into lakes and losing car keys, I don't know.' She thought of something. 'How come we never heard of you, or your parents, when we were here? You seem like family to Rupert Airlie. Are you distant cousins or something?'

'I'd never met Rupert till I came back from Britain. Before I took a job on another farm, I came up here on a whim to see where my great-grandfather had prospected during the gold rush. No, my great-great. It led me up the Awawhio-whio. I was directed to Rupert and he went with me. By the time we'd spent ten days in each other's company in that Never-Never-Land, we were great buddies despite the disparity in our ages. So he offered me a job, later the managership, and he's so family-minded, he asked all my relations up here for holidays in turn.'

'You were great buddies, despite the fact his great-grandfather had cheated yours out of his claim?'

'Was *supposed* to have done so,' he corrected her. 'Stacey was working in the County Office for a time and unearthed some old records. I'm sure Rupert has never known a thing about it and I hope he never will. I must warn Aunt Claudia not to mention it. It would make for self-consciousness in our relationship, which I wouldn't have for anything. All unknowing, Rupert has put many advantages my way. Prices being so high these days, land, stock, the lot, I'd have no chance of buying in. Rupert allowed me to run some sheep of my own. That gave me a bit of capital, and he sold me some land too. It's a start. But as for expecting any recompense—even if there had been some chicanery in pioneer days—no, thanks.

'Rupert has been so good to Aunt Claudia since her Dennis died. Rupert enjoys her immensely, says that in her views on life she reminds him greatly of someone he loved and lost long ago.'

'Loved and lost ... his wife?'

'I don't think so. There's an old lady I often visit in Ludwigtown, old Trudi——'

He was interrupted. 'Trudi? She's still alive? Oh, how wonderful! I boarded with her when I was at high school. I loved her. Oh, sorry, Logan. You were saying——?'

'I once asked Trudi what Rupert's wife was like. She hesitated, then said in that way she has of putting things: "Me ... I should find that a hard question to answer. She ought to have been a person of whom one would say nothing but good. A model of rectitude, that one. But——" and she wrinkled up that little nutcracker face of hers and added, "She was a good housekeeper and gardener and cook, with everything neat and tidy and she was hospitable. Not a—springboard kind of woman."

'She saw my puzzled look and said: "She would never encourage any cow to jump over the moon. She would rather pen it up and make it content with hay. She would never sacrifice method for one crowded hour of glorious life. She did that with Rupert. She was always slapping him down, as you young ones of today would put it." Then she told me later, when his wife was gone, Rupert had met someone who saw his full potential and he responded to her encouragement, but she wouldn't marry him.'

'What a pity! I thought he was a darling. There was a special bond between us. I fretted for him dreadfully. He deserved the best.' She sighed. 'Wouldn't it be wonderful to have the power of rolling time back, and giving people who deserve it their hearts' desires?'

He laughed at her. 'I guess everyone feels like that at times. I should think God does too. He gave us our free wills, and must sorrow over the way we use them. We can often see the steps others should have taken, even when we're heading in the wrong direction ourselves. Occasionally a kind fate steps in and saves us from ourselves, suddenly erects warning signs.'

The silence that fell between them was suddenly too fraught with emotion for people so recently met. Elissa said lightly, 'Aren't we being profound? ... especially me, wanting to play providence. Time we went in, now we're over our giggles.'

He said, 'Oh, leave Aunt Claudia to cope. This has upset all your ideas. You came to do what you like best to do ... you ought to be going round with notebook and pencil and swatches of drapes and samples of wallpaper, planning how to turn this into a dream house, but instead you've been pressganged into housekeeping. I'm sorry about that. Once the children get settled down I'll try for a girl to help you. I'm terrified they'll get homesick. It may take Sue longer than she thinks to get a place in Cambridge even if she is a human dynamo. So, before you get immersed in humdrum things, take a few moments to absorb the beauty of this. Something you knew ten years syne.'

The Scots term slipped out most naturally. Elissa didn't think he knew he'd used it. A relic, no doubt, of that long-ago Scots miner. Some words were retained in families and handed on from generation to generation in their childhood conversings.

They looked over the shadowy void of lake waters to where the lights of Ludwigtown curved like a glittering scimitar round the edge of the boat harbour; looked beyond Glen Airlie to those other homesteads where, as yet, the new road did not reach and which were served by water only ... Mahanga-Puke which meant Twin Hills, the furthest away.

Lights from the homesteads run by their own power plants showed more dimly, but beyond Twin Hills were brooding darknesses, known only to the creatures of the night and the occasional deerstalker camped in one of the huts. As they watched and listened, they heard a faraway sound from the lagoon beyond Treasure Island Bay.

'The boom of a bittern,' Elissa said. 'Something I used to hear years ago, before dropping off to sleep. Last year I heard one for the first time since leaving here. It was in Norfolk, among the reeds. It's the male that booms. It must be within a mile of us to be so audible.'

'True, that lagoon is more than a mile away by the track, but that's coming straight across the water, which carries sound. Did you hear that? The morepork?' It was the native owl, out a-hunting. 'We must see you get some time off to recapture these things. I take it you're a bird-watcher?'

'Yes, but I'm here to do a job, two jobs now. I think you're worrying in case I can't cope, Logan MacCorquodale. Don't—I shan't run out on you. And now we'll go in.'

The girls had a request. 'It would be rather fun if *you* bathed us, Elissa. Then we could ask you questions while you did it.'

Their uncle said, 'For heaven's sake, you're big enough to bath yourselves.'

Isabel's long dark eyes disappeared into laughing slits. 'It's much quicker under supervision, Uncle dear. Mum says so ... and a lot less messy.'

'That sounds like sense to me,' said Elissa briskly, getting in before Logan could start throwing his weight about, because the children must be tired by now and she didn't want any tears to trigger off homesickness for their mother and father.

Rennie said, with a great air of concession, 'Well, I won't hold you up, I'll go right off to bed, and read.'

His uncle wasn't deceived. 'You will not. Just think of the sheets! You could scrape the mud and moss off your knees. You can make it a shower. That's separate.'

Elissa found bathtime unloosed tongues. Both girls talked flat out, putting her in the picture about the family. Some confidences she had to stem—not that they were easily diverted, especially over the events of the morning.

Isabel said, 'I expect she was jealous of you, Elissa. You're much prettier than she is.'

Elissa burst out laughing. 'I'm just a ginger-headed urchin always falling in pools and lakes and what-have-you.

Stacey is *very* beautiful, but nobody looks good, of course, when they're in a—when they are upset.'

'You mean when they're in a temper,' observed Isabel shrewdly.

'Well, people only get in tempers if they're upset,' Elissa said, 'so you didn't get a chance to see her at her best. She——'

Elizabeth poked a plastic duck along the bathwater. 'We've seen her lots and lots of times and we *never* like the look of her. Neither does Mum. I heard her say to Dad she only hoped Logie saw through her before it got too serious. She said——'

Elissa said quellingly, 'I don't want to hear any more. Your mother wouldn't know you were within hearing, because children don't always know when not to repeat things. So you mustn't tell what you overheard. Everyone can't like everyone else and your uncle may know her better than anyone. We mustn't hurt his feelings.'

Isabel muttered, 'He wasn't worrying about hurting her feelings this morning, the things he said.' She added, with relish, 'I'd say, if anyone asked me, that he *has* seen through her. I'll write to tell Mum that tomorrow.'

'Nobody *has* asked you, Isabel, and you mustn't tell your mother things like that. It would make her worry about you and she shouldn't have to worry about anything just now. She'll be scurrying round Cambridge looking for a lovely cottage for you to live in. There are some beautiful houses round there. What fun you're going to have! There are lots of zoos in England, lovely outdoor ones with gorgeous animals and birds. You'll be going to London often too, I suppose. Fast trains get you there in no time, and you'll be able to take a boat up the Thames. Would you like to hear about some of the places you'll see ... when you're all tucked up in bed? If we hurry, we might have time before Uncle Logan comes to tell you your stories.'

While Logan was busy Elissa helped Claudia tidy up and they had cups of coffee ready when Logan came out. He looked at Elissa, said, 'Well, Isabel may have used a spot of blackmail in saying it was less messy to have you bath them than let them loose on their own, but you're splashed from top to toe.'

Elissa laughed. 'That was when Bess asked me could I touch my bottom with my heels. I said. "How on earth do you do that?" and she leapt out of the bath like a frog, a little pink frog, and sprayed me. Then she jumped up and down, kicking her legs backwards. I declined to try it.'

Claudia picked up a book, Logan settled with last night's paper, Elissa went off to her room and came back with an armful of books that she dumped on the kitchen table. Claudia looked at them, said, 'Don't bother sorting out the children's books tonight. Give yourself a break.'

'They aren't theirs. They're mine from long ago. I was so glad to see them still here. I hated the fact that Mother left these behind. I'd not realised how attached I was to my early books till I saw them again. I want to see if I can find a lovely nursery rhyme book I had. It had happy endings. Someone had written much less gruey finales. The three blind mice only had their eyes shut, and the farmer's wife just pretended to cut their tails off. Bo-Peep's sheep were found, Little Boy Blue didn't get scolded for sleeping while the cows got into the corn. I told Victoria that if by any chance it was still here, I'd send it to her for her step-children. I——' she broke off, because Claudia was absolutely staring at her.

Claudia said, '*Your* books? *Still here?* What on earth do you mean?'

Elissa boggled. 'Weren't you round today when we were talking about this—when the Samsons were here? That my mother was governess here, ten years ago. I was at high school in Ludwigtown by then. She just suddenly yearned for England and the scenes of her girlhood and took off.'

Claudia had a strange look on her face. It was reminiscent of the expression on Bob Samson's. She said sharply, 'Are you—oh, surely not *that* w——' she bit something off, substituted, 'Are you that governess's daughter?'

Elissa knew perfectly well that Claudia had been going to say: 'Surely not *that* woman's daughter?' There had been a hint of that in Bob Samson's voice too. But why, why?

As if they hadn't—quite—approved of Mother. But who *wouldn't* approve of Mother?

She said quietly, 'I suppose so. Meg Montgomery's daughter. That's why Rupert asked me to do this job. I met him again at Victoria's place. Oh, here's the book—how wonderful!' But she didn't feel wonderful. She felt uneasy. How much had she ever known of her mother's true reasons for leaving here?

CHAPTER FIVE

UNEASINESS was still with her after she'd had her bath, unpacked her clothes, brushed her bright hair. She got into bed, picked up her paperback, determined to read to dispel such stupid ideas. It was pure imagination. Till this moment she'd never thought of her mother as being anything but immensely popular when she was here.

Even in Ludwigtown she'd seemed part of the community, joining in the church activities whenever it was possible to get across and back by boat, helping with the catering for the rodeos, being a member of the horticultural society, entertaining various groups over here on special occasions, something Uncle Rupert had loved. She'd pitched in to help the housekeeper, at the times when seasonal activity created so much more work for Donsie, freed the men to work on the farm by putting in long hours in the garden she loved.

Nevertheless, there must have been something. But it was almost as if they'd known something shady about Mother. How too absurd! Oh dear, this book wasn't keeping her mind off it. She needed her sleep, too, after last night's fiasco and this morning's stramashings. If she didn't sleep, she'd not be fit to cope with tomorrow's strange routine, feeding a household of six. She might get crotchety with the children, perhaps feel the strain of doing things under Claudia's eagle eye, Claudia of the Julius Caesar look. She mightn't always be as lenient as tonight. Elissa snapped off the light.

Immediately the magic of childhood flooded back. There was no need to draw the curtains here, so the moon, riding high and palely over Mount Serenity, struck in through the faintly stirring curtains and pooled silver on the snowy-white lambskin in front of the window-seat as it had done all those years ago. Mother had covered the window-seat with a fleece too, and it had been a wonderful place for thinking the long, long thoughts of youth.

Elissa climbed out of bed, slipped across to the seat, pulled back the filmy white curtains, saw the loved contours of mountains and foothills, dark against the starry sky. There were the silver-netted barriers of the tennis court, the spread of the drying-green, that had a herbaceous border before the flowers gave place to currant bushes, rows of vegetables, and, at the far end, an orchard sheltered against the hard fronts of the region by a row of pussy willows backed by pines.

Off to the right, the long wing of the annexe ran out where the schoolroom was, the spare bedrooms, Logan's room. He still had his light on, he must be reading too. Compassion touched her. After an exhausting night and day he might have been expected to drop off the moment his head hit the pillow, but perhaps disturbing regrets were keeping him awake, recollections of hot words bandied back and forth, treadmilling in his brain.

It wasn't much of a life, emotionally, for a single man up here. He must be in his thirties. He would have looked forward to the day when he would share this home with a wife. Uncle Rupert probably wanted that too. Housekeepers would always be hard to get in this remoteness even if they were served now by a road of sorts, but most women liked positions handy to their family and friends. He had said they were almost engaged, so that meant his future plans had included a wife. Still, it might yet work out, only both contestants would have to eat humble pie.

At that moment Logan's window went dark and Elissa's silvery world suddenly seemed cold, yet her moments of communion with the loved scenes of yesterday had soothed her. She slipped into the softness of her bed and went out like a light.

She woke to a sense of having overslept, thought the early sun wouldn't reach this room as much as this, so now she was sure. She tore along to the bathroom, becoming guiltily aware of voices in the kitchen, the chink of cutlery and china. She had the sketchiest of washes, hastily donned trews of the deep blue Montgomery tartan, pulled a bulky-knit jersey that matched its dark green squares over them, thrust her feet into blue sheepskin slippers and tore for the kitchen.

Isabel looked up from setting the table, 'Oh, Elissa, we were going to bring you breakfast in bed. Uncle Logie said to let you have your sleep out.'

'Well, he's got enough on his plate, with his man still away, without having a lie-abed on his hands. I ought to have set my alarm.'

Logan, stirring porridge, turned to smile at her. 'Oh, not to worry. We'll work you hard enough from now on. After all, you not only had a rough time on arrival, but you'd travelled across the world before that. It might have been different had we been lambing—I'd have had everyone up at the crack of dawn then, but we don't start till mid-September. Aunt Claudia just wants tea and toast, so I said I'd send it in to her.'

'Aunt Claudia has changed her mind,' said a crisp voice from behind Elissa, 'and as you sound ready to serve out, I'll have my bath after breakfast.' She had on a tweed dressing-gown in a very masculine style tied around her. 'This mountain air is having an effect on me. I'll have everything that's going, please.'

'Right, Aunt. Elissa, make the tea, will you? Kids, I believe you prefer chocolate for breakfast. Spoon some out and pour some water on. I switched on the heaters in the schoolroom, Aunt, when I got up.'

It all seemed extraordinarily normal, even if a week ago Elissa had been in London, the hub of the universe. Yet hadn't someone said that each person carries the hub of the universe within them? At this moment, the centre of her world was here, with children who needed her to look after their well-being; with Claudia who must be freed from domestic duties to governess them, and with Logan Mac-Corquodale. After that, what? A return to the other side of the world, leaving this place again? The place she'd always loved best on earth. Suddenly she felt bleak.

She looked up to find Logan's eyes fastened on her. He

said, 'What's the matter? You suddenly looked appalled. Had you just realised what you've landed yourself into? That an exciting flip across the world to pretty up an old homestead has, out of sheer ill-luck, turned into a tough grind. Would you rather I tried for a housekeeper from Ludwigtown so you can do what you were engaged to do, then quit?'

Elissa felt as if someone had just jerked a prize out of her reach. She said coldly, 'What makes you think you can read my thoughts? Are you omnipotent or something? I'm looking forward to *everything* this entails. It means I can stay longer. Not all women hate domestic chores. I wasn't brought up to be a lily of the field, I knew Glen Airlie long before you even saw it. I know exactly how much work it entails. My mother wasn't the sort of governess to do nothing but teaching. She used to lend a hand during lambing and tailing, and with the cooking if the shearing gangs lost their cook suddenly. That happened at least twice, I remember. And believe me, I had to help with the farm chores and the household chores always. I'm here to do whatever needs doing, not just titivate the place!'

There was a quite a tense silence. Logan's expression was grim. Before he could speak she added, 'And don't go on thinking of me as an outsider. I'm a New Zealander, same as you, exiled as a child from all I loved most. My father was born and bred in South Canterbury. This is my sort of existence. You needn't think I'll pine for the city life.'

'Easy to say in the first flush of joy at seeing familiar places. But who's to know how you'll feel in a month's time? Reaction may have set in then, and you'll be homesick for Britain. I wouldn't blame you. I loved Britain.'

He cut off as there was a loud wail from small Elizabeth, sitting up to the table, with a napkin tucked under her chin. They stopped levelling looks at each other and swung round to her. The blue eyes were full of tears, the lip trembling. 'You're fighting! And yesterday when there was a fight, Stacey went away. I don't want Elissa to go away. She's like Mum.'

They both felt appalled, guilty. Elissa said quickly, 'Oh,

Elizabeth, we're just being stupid. Your uncle didn't mean it—and I was an idiot to get cross with him. Wild horses wouldn't get me away from here one moment sooner than I need to go. I'm glad I'm staying longer than just for the decorating. I'll be here long after your mother has come for you. Now, let's have breakfast—I'm starving!'

Elizabeth dashed the tears away with her hands and fell on the porridge ravenously. There was one thing about having children at a meal, tension dissipated in their flow of chatter.

Aunt Claudia got the children into the schoolroom quickly after the meal, not without demur. Isabel said: 'What? As early as this? We wouldn't even be leaving home by now!'

Aunt Claudia said with authority. 'I'm running your schoolroom hours exactly as I've always run them for other high-country children. You'll like it, I promise you. You start earlier, you finish earlier, and that means you get hours more sunshine outside. The sun goes down behind the mountains earlier here, not like living on the coast. Rennie, your teeth, and no skimping—I make inspections! Girls, your beds. No skimping there either. I'll supervise you. Rennie, make yours when you've finished, then the girls can have the bathroom. Playtime at nine-thirty, lunch at twelve, if that suits Elissa.'

'It does. Thank you, Mrs Robertson. Just tell me first if you prefer midday dinner or a night one, Mr MacCorquodale?'

'Night. I like to relax after the big meal. We usually have soup, and either eggs in some form, or sausages or cold meat after, for lunch.'

She nodded, 'Same routine for meals and the classroom that I remember. Those were my mother's rigid hours.'

He began clearing the table with her. 'And she really stuck to them?'

She looked at him sharply. 'Do I detect a note of surprise? Yes. Even if Mother had to pitch in with chores when there were emergencies, we were given essays and such-like to write. In her own way, she was as great a disciplinarian as I imagine your aunt to be. We never got away with anything.'

He didn't deny he'd been surprised. 'I'd certainly not thought of her as like Aunt Claudia.'

Elissa's russet brows drew down. 'She didn't look like her. Mother is essentially feminine—dark and petite, not a ginger-headed tomboy like me. Not accident-prone either. But in the schoolroom she was almost a martinet.'

'In the schoolroom, yes, all teachers have to be.'

'They ought to be. Not all are, unfortunately. But what did you mean? Not thinking of her as like your aunt? You only dimly remembered one of the governesses here had a daughter.'

She had a feeling he sought carefully for words. Finally, 'Oh, you know how it is. You start thinking back, and you gain a slight impression. Oh, well, I daresay the isolation up here was suddenly too much for her. It's never easy to live in an only-access-by-water sheep station. Too few leisure-time distractions.'

Again Elissa was assailed by unease. She said directly, 'Mr MacCorquodale, you sound as if you're making excuses for my mother. She upped and offed, yes, but she was, after all, alone in New Zealand but for me. My mother isn't the sort of person who needs excuses made for her. So what?'

He put his pile of plates on the bench. 'So of course she isn't. You know her best, and if you'll excuse me I'll be off. I've a lot of work to catch up on.'

Elissa, thoroughly incensed by now, said tartly, 'I wasn't expecting you to dry the dishes. I'd much rather do it on my own. *You* were the one who tarried. There's nothing here I can't manage.'

'Fine,' and she hated the amusement in his voice, but he turned at the door, said mildly, 'And the children won't expect us to be so formal. Drop Mr MacCorquodale and make it Logan. It's too damn silly for words.'

Her anger carried her through doing the dishes, making her own bed, and sweeping the kitchen floor. Anyway, it was just as well to work at speed. No need then for him to magnanimously offer aid. She remembered Donsie had always made a batch of either scones or pikelets each morning. Pikelets, which she'd learned to call drop-scones in England, would be quicker. She hunted out the girdle, heated and greased it, and soon had bubbling batter in circles cooking on it. She put a clean tea-towel on a cake-cooler and flipped each one on it in turn. She'd butter and jam some just before the play-break. Meanwhile she'd inspect the pantry, the deep-freeze, the store-room. A cook must know what she had to work with, and to re-order, because even if they had an access road now, many water miles or petrol mileage lay between here and Ludwigtown. She wondered if you could still have as much stuff sent across by launch. She took a pad and notebook with her.

She resolved as she worked that she wouldn't get too involved with the station manager. No good could come of that. She must be impersonal, running the household with efficiency as one on the pay-roll, but never assuming any sort of apparent attachment to the post, even if she'd had to pretend to that to reassure Elizabeth this morning. Pretend? She pushed that thought away.

Promptly at nine-thirty the schoolroom door opened and the children spilled out. She handed them their pikelets and an apple each, told them to go out into the near-spring sunshine, and asked Rennie to ring the bell so Logan, busy in the woolshed, would hear.

Aunt Claudia's eyes lit up at the sight of the fresh baking, and she sat down. 'They settled remarkably well. Even after all these years, I can be surprised at the way children love routine. Oh, like us they enjoy the occasional break from it, but most of the time they weary more of freedom than routine. Elissa, aren't you going to sit down yourself?'

'No, I'm taking mine in my hand too, and going to wander down to the jetty. I want sun and fresh air.' She saw Aunt Claudia's mouth twitch and knew she was not deceived, that she realised Elissa didn't want too much of Logan's company. He came in as Elissa went out. He checked, glanced at the mug of coffee in her hand, but said nothing.

The children were now busy with the bat and ball and didn't notice her. She was glad of this. She needed solitude. She wandered on to the jetty, drank thirstily, sat down on the seat. The lake lay before her in all its kingfisher colours, iridescent green and blue, flashing facets of light in the sun. Over there, quite discernible, lay the homes of Ludwig-town where many of her childhood friends would still live.

Round the edge of the lake where she had ventured so disastrously her first afternoon were all the secret haunts of that magic time. Had she been wise to come? Was she going to wish, when she'd said goodbye to it again, that she had never walked into Victoria Doig's home, to find Rupert Airlie there? Was it going to completely unsettle her, set up longings to remain ... which was quite beyond possi-bility?

When Logan's sister returned for her children, Claudia would probably stay on long enough for Elissa to complete her plans as far as possible. Rupert would arrive, she might gain two or three weeks after that, then she would be gone. Logan's parents would probably stay till he married Stacey, as no doubt he would, when they made it up. They ex-pected him to do just that ... hadn't Claudia said they were bending over backwards to try to like the girl? She won-dered how Rupert liked Stacey. It was to be hoped he liked her, otherwise he'd feel unwanted in his own home. It was a tricky situation. Suddenly Elissa didn't like the way her thoughts were heading. She was building up a prejudice against a girl she'd seen, so far, only in a temper. She was probably quite charming when she wasn't upset by finding a girl in her near-fiancé's house, in odd circumstances. She heard a cough, and turned. Logan!

He said, 'What's the matter, sulking? I wouldn't have picked you for the sulky sort. More the kind to flare up, then subside.'

'And you were right. That was only a silly spat and we ought to be ashamed of ourselves, quarrelling in front of the children. But though I'm never sulky, I am, in some ways, a loner. Only children often are. They're used to living in their own little dream world. I wanted to get—I wanted to be by myself for a few moments to savour the beauty of this.'

'You were going to say you wanted to get away from me.' She didn't see his lips twitch, so replied coldly, 'I find it most irritating to have you think you can read my thoughts, predict my words. But perhaps I did, subconsciously, think just that.'

'Why? I thought we shared this beauty last night in a very companionable way.'

'We did, but this morning you sneered at me, thought I was nostalgic for Britain, then when I said I wasn't, you curled your lip and prophesied I'd be sick of it in a month, as if I was a new broom sweeping clean. I resent being made to feel a stranger here. Why, all those years ago, when I had to go to live with Trudi for high school, I couldn't get back quickly enough each weekend on the launch. There was no other way then, but I never thought of it as a prison, rather as a paradise.'

'So it is, for children, but limited in its appeal to a girl of your age, I imagine, used to being within reach of Covent Garden, the Festival Hall, all the West End theatres. We've had no end of New Zealand girls up here during the vacations, to earn money by helping Mrs Prince, our house-keeper. About ninety per cent of them thought they couldn't have stuck it all year round. Even beauty, with no distractions, can be deuced monotonous.'

'Do you find it so?' This with a challenging look.

'No. But then it's my kind of life.'

'Well, you ought to know. You've lived with yourself thirty-odd years, I'd say. I've had nearly twenty-five of living with myself, so allow me to know my own mind too. Don't be afraid I'll want to settle here, Logan MacCorquodale. I can see what you're after. When Stacey comes here again I'll make it quite plain to her I'm here today, gone to-morrow. I can understand how you feel. If I stay on, it could make Stacey wonder again—hold up a reconciliation. Don't feel sore. You're at outs with the one you love and I'm responsible, even if inadvertently.'

His eyes held anger. '*You* had a go at *me* for imagining I could read your thoughts. Don't presume to read mine!' He turned on his heel and strode off.

For some reason Elissa felt this had cleared the air. Back to her chores she went. During the time Logan's mother had been away, Gwyneth, naturally, would have had time for little more than cooking the meals and skimming over the rest of the work. The whole place needed a thorough vacuuming, but she contented herself for today with doing just the big lounge and the hall. The kitchen required a good scrubbing, not just a push-over with a sponge-mop, and it looked good when she'd finished. She rubbed over the black top of the blue enamel range with a damped newspaper, knowing she could black-lead it some night when they'd let the fire out, and went outside in search of something for the empty vase standing on a small side-table.

She couldn't hope to find much at this time of year. Perhaps just a few ornamental leaves would have to do, so she fared forth into the dense shrubbery, and was enchanted to find a japonica already rosetted with coral blossoms on its dark twigs. She could remember her mother planting that. It gave her a curious feeling, and every time her eyes rested on the vase, it was as if her mother was in the kitchen.

Plain meals, Logan had said, probably feeling she couldn't cope with more. No harm in going the extra mile, and showing him interior decorators could supply other interior needs too! But she mustn't fly too high, there wasn't time. Her eye fell on a bowl of bananas. Why not add bacon-and-banana rolls to the scrambled eggs he'd suggested? Children always liked novelty dishes. She'd grill them right away, keep them hot in the oven. She had an anxious moment looking for toothpicks, but finally found them, snipped off rind, stretched strips of bacon over a table-knife, rolled them round two-inch pieces of banana, stuck the picks through, and put them under the grill.

She'd always taken pride in a well-set table, and the utility stainless steel cutlery was an attractive set, quite new. She loved the floral chintzy patterned china in cake-plates and butter-dishes remembered from her childhood, and a squat set of salt and pepper containers, done in the form of Friar Tucks in tomato-red pottery, were some she'd given her mother one Christmas. One more thing Mother had forgotten in her haste. It *had* been odd.

Why had there been such haste? It wasn't as if she'd applied for a post in England and had to take it up by a certain time. Why hadn't her mother waited till Elissa came home for the weekend, and told her then they would be leaving soon? In fact, it would have been far better had she let her daughter finish out her school year, so near.

Other things came crowding into Elissa's mind, things not thought of for years. How she'd commented on the fact that her mother wasn't writing to Rupert and Donsie. How her mother had come down with finality on the suggestion that Elissa herself should write, even to old Trudi. She'd wanted to cut herself off from everything. It had been so out of character.

Elissa stirred her egg mixture, looked at the clock—dead on noon. She went to the bell-post and rang the bell.

She was glad Logan didn't raise his brows at her oval platter of bacon rolls and say, 'I thought I said no frills.' Instead it was: 'Much better than bachelor cooking. I can begin to look forward to meals again. I wasn't fancying the time Gwyneth would be away. A roast or a casserole and enormous pans of soup and my variety is finished. That makes for monotony.'

Aunt Claudia said shrewdly, 'Elissa, I suppose you are studying the *Home Beautiful* type of magazines all the time, and attractive meals and well-set tables are all part of the decor. Good show!'

Gratified, Elissa smiled, 'But I won't make a fetish of it. When lambing starts and I have to lend a hand outside, it'll be a case of very plain meals.'

Logan looked startled. 'Lend a hand with the lambing? What——'

She looked at him squarely. 'I was fourteen plus when I left here. And I'd been going round the sheep for years prior to that. I always helped at lambing and tailing. I daresay Gwyneth helps, normally?'

'Yes, she does, but——'

'But me no buts. Uncle Rupert put no time fix on this job. I'm to have as much ready for him as possible. I'll be writing him, and will tell him I may take a little longer than we first thought. He would expect me to pitch in.'

She couldn't tell whether Logan was glad or sorry. Perhaps he felt he was being put in his place for doubting her, but was aware he might, in time, be glad of her help. The meal finished the children ran out to play. Aunt Claudia began to clear the table.

Logan said, 'I'll help with this, Aunt. You buzz off and have a few moments with your feet up. Can't let you wear yourself out.'

Elissa felt it was more that he wanted to speak to her alone. It put her on the defensive. 'All right, Logan, I spoke out of turn. Sorry about that. I keep slipping back into the atmosphere I knew ten years ago, when it was taken for granted everyone pulled their weight outside when needed. I realise you don't like the idea of me staying on here too long. That you just need me till your sister comes for the children, and I get my ideas under way for the house, then depart for the other side of the world so that your world can return to normal. I know you're worrying about the injustice of the situation, but Uncle Rupert's letter is bound to turn up sooner or later. When you give it to Stacey to read, she'll know I was just a calamity on your doorstep.

'It was very tough on her seeing what she saw, and she was humiliated in front of the children and Aunt Claudia. Some take a bit longer to say sorry, that's all. I'll guarantee that right now she's missing you horribly. If Rupert delays at all in Canada, it might be wiser for me to just set things in train, pending his approval, with the firms I'll contact.'

She got it all out and looked up to surprise a strange look in the intent dark-blue eyes. 'Did you work all this out between my surprise at your offer to help with the lambing, and now?'

'Yes. Why not? You can suddenly realise you've made a mistake and know exactly what you should do to retrieve it.'

'So you think you can play God, manipulate Stacey and myself and depart smugly home again?'

A flake of angry red appeared in Elissa's cheeks. She lifted her chin, said, 'I hadn't thought there was any smugness about it. Just an honest desire to put things right.'

'You're a fine one to accuse me of trying to read thoughts! You're at it again. You assume I want a reconciliation with Stacey despite the fact I said to her face that her insistence on using that incident of chicanery long ago to feather my nest here had put paid to any idea of my asking her to marry me.'

'You said that in temper. You didn't mean it. You were just lashing out because she'd doubted you.'

'Will you stop it? What strong ideas you have about how I feel! You don't know a damned thing about me. You've nothing to base that on.'

'But I have.' Her eyes were more green than blue right then. 'That very first night you said you were practically engaged to a girl, Stacey Cressford. So it *was* just the quarrel made you say that to her.'

She was most surprised to see that austere expression soften completely. 'Oh, Elissa Montgomery, I was saying that to you to still any fears you might be experiencing, at spending the night on the shores of a lonely lake with a man about whom you knew nothing.'

She felt warmth in her cheeks. Her eyes fell. Logan took her elbows, said, 'Girl, look up at me and be frank. Was that not so?'

Elissa looked up, grinned. 'It was so.'

He gave her a little shake. 'Then stop feeling stupidly guilty about it. It gets on my nerves. You were entirely blameless. And while I forgive Stacey her first startled conclusion, she ought to have accepted my explanation.'

The phone rang. Logan answered, said, 'Right, I'll hang on.' He put his hand over the mouthpiece, said, 'It's from England—my sister. We'll be connected in a moment. She may want a word with the children; would you wait in case I want you to get them?'

She nodded. She liked the way Logan spoke to his sister, sheer affection in every sentence. Presently Logan said, 'Oh, we're managing fine. Manna from heaven fell into our laps.

You remember Victoria Doig—now in Haslemere? Well, Rupert was visiting her when another interior decorator friend turned up and believe it or not, this girl's mother— now in Canada—was once governess here. Had the child with her. The girl was just taking off on a three months' visit to her mother, but Rupert persuaded her to come here first to redecorate Airlie House. Yes, honestly.

'No, you dope, not with the idea of his retiring and me marrying Stacey. That's all off. Sheer infatuation, that was. No, he just took it into his head. Well, she fitted back into the life here immediately and is keeping house while Aunt looks after the schoolroom. So you have no worries, Sis. Go about your house-hunting with a free mind, not dogged by any urgency. Glad to know they've given you quarters. Pity they aren't suitable for children, but it gives you time to get your breath. Get something suitable for you, with room for a study for Roland, and near schools for the children.'

He asked after Roland's arm, their trip, and suddenly Elissa caught his arm, and gestured to something she'd scrawled on a pad: 'May I speak to her briefly?' He said, 'Elissa, the girl I told you of wants to speak to you. Here you are, Sue.'

Elissa said, 'I won't take much time, but in case it might help you, and save you money, if I can possibly work out my ideas for the house, while keeping the house going, by the time you can get into a house there, perhaps I could be free to accompany the children to England. No, it wouldn't spoil my trip at all. They're darlings, and I'd enjoy the company. Now, it's just an idea for you to talk over with your husband. I'll hand this back to your brother now.'

Logan's eyes met hers as she did so. He went to speak, changed his mind, picked up the conversation where he'd left it off. Sue evidently thought it might unsettle the children if she spoke to them. She'd written them letters which they'd get in a day or two. She thought it wiser not to mention that she'd rung. He hung up.

They looked at each other uncertainly, then Elissa said, 'I think you wanted to say something, but had to continue with the phone conversation, because it was costing so much.'

He considered it, then grinned, 'No. I did want to, but I'm having second thoughts. I'm not rushing into rash speech again. You'd impute all sorts of motives to me if I did.' He added, 'Sue thought I shouldn't say she'd rung. What do you think?'

'I think she's right. Children that age have no idea how much it costs to ring from the other side of the world, and they're settling very well. Children live in the present. You find that out if you try to comfort them, in times of sadness, with promise of a happier future. So we have to make today happy for them and let tomorrow grow out of today.'

How different that dark Highland face was when the blue eyes smiled and the brows didn't overhang. 'I like that, Elissa. It's the sort of philosophy one expects from a mother rather than a girl, though.'

'I learned that from my own mother. Nobody could understand children more. She's got child psychologists knocked into a cocked hat. She ought to have had half a dozen children—life cheated her out of that when my father died so young. But her years of teaching made up for it, I think. She was only a few years older than I am now when she was widowed. She's gone it alone ever since. Not many women would have come to a lonely place like this, to give her daughter the chance of living with other children, of feeling a member of a family. At times she must have felt tragically lonely.'

He nodded, sombrely. 'And the devil of loneliness drives hard. Makes people act foolishly sometimes.'

He spoke as if thinking of something in particular, she thought. Was he thinking he was foolish ever to have fallen for Stacey, but had felt the need of a wife here? She went back to the sink. 'I'll finish these. You must want to get back outside. You're working short-handed as it is.'

'Thanks. Hew will want to be away over in Ludwigtown a fair bit the next couple of weeks—he's coming back tomorrow, by the way—so I'm going to ask a chap at the other end of the access road if he can give me some time. He's just back. He's a bit footloose, but a good worker. Better warn you not to lose your heart to him. He's broken more hearts than anyone I've ever known—Olaf Haraldsen.'

'I'm not susceptible,' said Elissa, suddenly feeling more lighthearted for no reason at all, 'but I like his name, Olaf.'

'Good. It's my second name. As you know, the MacCorquodales are offshoots of the MacLeods, who were descended from Leod, son of Olave the Black. The name has persisted.'

'And it suits you. You have true Highland colouring—black hair, blue eyes.'

He cocked an eye at her. 'And while we're on the personal touch, I must tell you you were wrong in one thing you said to Stacey.'

Oh dear, her name cropped up all the time! He couldn't leave it alone, despite his protestations of being finished with her.

'Yes?' she said tautly.

'You're standing right in that shaft of sunlight. You aren't just plain ginger, Miss Montgomery. You're pure copper . . . and very, very glamorous, just as Stacey said.'

'She didn't say glamorous. She said exciting.'

He laughed outright. 'Well, I can *see* the glamour, but how exciting you can be I've yet to find out. Perhaps I will now we've called off the sparring.'

'I doubt it. The only excitement you'll get from me will be due to having an accident-prone female on the property.' Then, while he tried to phone Olaf Haraldsen, she wiped the bench and disappeared into the store-room.

CHAPTER SIX

OLAF the heart-breaker couldn't come for a couple of days, but that night a beaming Hew came in, for the evening meal. Gwyneth and the babies were doing well, her sister was coming over for the first few weeks of coping with two babies and he was raring to get to work.

Elissa slipped into a routine totally different from her round of visits as a consultant in Surrey and Hampshire, with an ease that surprised her once she got used to the quantities she needed to gauge for the cooking. Enchantment had her in its grip and a dozen times a day she would look up from the most prosaic of chores to see over her shoulder, or through the windows that rarely had a curtain drawn, the blue-green of Moana-Kotare, sometimes heightened by the opalescent flash of kingfisher wings as the bird took swift flight downwards to filch some tiny morsel from the homestead brook. She knew in her heart of hearts that this was her true home, though she could not stay.

Olaf was certainly handsome, with a pulse-stirring vitality. Not in the least like Olave the Black, but golden-fair, with broad shoulders, ruddy skin, eyes as blue as the sea, and an attractively insolent way with him.

He very much approved the latest addition to the Glen Airlie household and wasn't slow to say so. He slept out in one of the *whares* used for seasonal workers but ate at Airlie House. He was good fun, and under his huge, lusty enjoyment of life, some of the earlier tensions between Logan and Elissa disappeared.

This afternoon Logan left Hew and Olaf on the hill and came back to the house alone. He went to the schoolroom first, had a word with his aunt, came along to the kitchen, and saw Elissa put a huge casserole of lamb chops into the oven complete with vegetables and with sliced potatoes on top for a lid.

'Good,' he said. 'That sort of thing looks after itself.

You've been a Trojan the way you've stuck to the house all this while. How about a jaunt, seeing you won't take a day off? I had the glasses on the hill with me, looking for deer, and I brought them down on Treasure Island Bay. Your lone heron is there, picking its way along the shore, feeding. Your last stalking of him was so disastrous, I thought I'd let you know.'

She flushed with pleasure. 'Oh, thank you. I'll just get my binoculars.'

'Oh, we can use these.'

'We?'

'Yes, I'm coming with you. No protests. I'm not there to stop you falling in—I like bird-watching too. I've told Aunt Claudia where we'll be.'

Elissa had on blue jeans and a fine white sweater with a blue yoke, but pulled on an emerald green jacket that tied round the waist, because sometimes the wind off the vast expanse of water was chilly and though it was spring in the Antipodes now, September was always a treacherous month.

They padded along the Secret Path, well-named, snaking in amongst great trees, mainly taking the easiest way, but leading up and down too. In the mossy crevices of the small leafed native beeches and *kahikateas* sprang myriads of small ferns and creepers, giving that moist tanginess inseparable from the New Zealand bush. Light filtered through, giving it an underwater look, a grotto-quality. Tiny birds rustled as they foraged in the bark for the insects they loved. The slightest zephyr was stirring the tree-tops far above their heads, but in here it was as still as if the forest held its breath, broken only by the cracking of twigs under their feet.

Fallen giants barred the green mossy track at times, so they had to climb over them; others thrust gnarled branches and roots grotesquely, in hoops and arches, so they bent down and went under them. It was an intimate, darling world of its own like a Walt Disney fantasy, and its signature tune was the silver music of miniature waterfalls, dropping from rock to rock and level to level as they had done for so many years that the brain reeled from trying to imagine what eons of time this had known.

It was close in here. Logan took Elissa's arm. She wasn't aware of the way he marked the eagerness in her, the delight that was in her parted lips, her lowered voice. Forests like this had an effect on sensitive people, such as she, as if they walked through dimly-lit aisles in some great cathedral, while a mass was in progress.

Suddenly she was shaken by another awareness ... that she didn't want to emerge from this closeness. She missed her step, swung towards a thorny patch, was caught, held. Absurdly she felt as if her heart missed a beat, and she hoped he didn't notice her heightened colour. He steadied her very carefully, went to say something, but laughed instead. She wondered why.

The path took its steep turn up to the Crow's Nest. They fell silent again and with gentle tread mounted it and peered over at the trout ballet, then looked further. Logan put a protective arm about her shoulders, bent his dark head, whispered, 'There it is. Beyond that ridge of shingle.'

Once again it was standing in the rim of flotsam at the edge, as motionless as if carved in alabaster, intent on watching with its trained eye for the slightest movement. Its beak darted forward and downward, it swallowed, moved on a few feet, grace inherent in all its movements, the lift of its feet, the arch of its pure white neck. Logan handed her the glasses. She focused them, caught her breath in with the magic of it all. To be, seemingly, so close to one of the most magnificent birds of the world, was to step back into Eden, where there was no fear of man. She looked her fill, gave them back for him to look. The bird walked on, repeating its performance over and over. They came down to the shore, shed their footwear, walked along the silty ridges, around blanched tree trunks, the bird well ahead, and because they didn't even whisper, it remained unaware of their presence. Time ceased to matter.

The little zephyr had dropped. The sun, high in the north this Southern Hemisphere afternoon, beat down on their backs. They eased off their jackets, dropped them on a rock against their return, went on, sometimes wading across small inlets, or through the countless streams that trickled down the hills where the water was colder because it came from the snows.

They crested a miniature headland, and because the *kotuku* had walked right round it, feeding, came upon it at very close quarters, standing immobile on a rock just a couple of feet from the edge. What did it dream of, staring out across the kingfisher-blue waters towards the west? Did it dream of its mate? Of Okarito where in the giant *kowhai* trees across the Great Divide, every heron would return presently to build a nest? Logan's arm held Elissa rigid within its half-circle.

Then, as if it sensed their presence, the bird lifted its flawless wings and with what looked like effortless movement, took off across the lake towards the mountains in the west.

Logan said, 'How idyllic! We were fortunate to have it in view so long.'

Elissa nodded. 'Thank you for coming to get me, because while you will have season after season, just as the heron has, this may well be *my* heron-of-the-single-flight.'

Again he started to say something, stopped. They sat down on one of the bleached logs, dabbling their feet in the shallow water. 'How warm it is,' said Logan. 'Not often like this. It must be the false spring.' He produced an apple from each trouser pocket. They munched away, sat on, loth to stir.

He answered her, then, as if she'd just spoken. 'Yes, I am glad you saw that today. You won't feel so cheated then if you've had that to remember. As you might feel cheated if you——'

'If I what?' She looked up at him as he paused.

'If you get through what you were sent for, fairly soon, and Sue takes you up on that rash offer you made her.'

He was looking at her most intently, but she didn't know. She was keeping her face turned towards the lake, away from him, because dismay had clutched her. What if Sue found a house very quickly? What if Rupert's son begged him to stay longer, and he wrote to say just put things in train, and return?

Return? It struck at her with a pain she'd not thought possible. She realised Logan was watching her, said, 'I'm thirsty.' She looked towards the lake.

He said, 'Mountain streams are better,' and put out his hand for her to take. He took her to the edge of the bush where, shaded by mountain beeches, a narrow torrent tumbled over a mini-cliff. 'No sheep on the hills above here, they're still bush-clad, and the fertilisers from the top-dressing planes don't reach this far. This water is as pure as if the world has just begun. As if this was the first Tuesday of all time.'

They both laughed at the idea of a day named that in the first week of creation. He said, 'There are only my hands to serve as a cup for you,' and put them together, holding them out to her, brimming over. Elissa drank deeply as he filled and refilled them three times. While she wiped her lips with her handkerchief he did the same for himself, drinking three times as if in ritual. Again a new feeling assailed Elissa. Like breaking bread to cement a friendship?

Friendship? She turned hastily from the traitor thought, said, 'I expect we'd better move on, I've a pudding to make.'

'How prosaic,' he teased, 'after a venture into fantasy-land!'

They talked of farm matters on the way back and Elissa was glad of this. She felt her emotions were swamping her reason. They entered the twilight of the dense bush again, close together of necessity. Just before the bush ended was, on one side, a tiny glade. They stopped and looked at the carpet of moss, white-speckled with tiny alpine flowers.

'I found a fawn here once,' said Logan. 'I think its mother must have been shot. I built an enclosure for it in the garden at Airlie House. When it was old enough I took it to the deer park at Queenstown. We missed it.'

Her eyes were dreamy, trying to visualise it. 'Oh, how truly idyllic ... I can just see a little spotted fawn against that emerald moss ... a moment that might never come again.'

She turned, to find him very close. He said, 'Not that

particular moment, perhaps, but this too could be idyllic, don't you think? For two people, Miss Elissa-Montgomery-making-the-best-of-things? What about this for magic?'

His arms came about her, bringing her against him. She couldn't have struggled against those whipcord muscles, even did she want to. Elissa was tall, but he still had to bend his head to reach her lips. She put out a slightly protesting hand, why, she didn't know. He caught it, held it against him, said, his mouth very close to hers, 'Don't spoil it, Elissa ... it's meant to be an idyll. Something to remember.' His lips reached hers.

It was all a first kiss should be, seeking, but not too demanding, tender but with a stirring feeling of leashed emotion behind it. She moved a little in his arms, but he didn't let her go. When he was satisfied he lifted his head a fraction, smiled down on her, and said, 'Thank you. You certainly made the best of that. Oh, dear! That doesn't sound as I meant it to sound. I meant—thanks for putting so much into it. Oh, aren't words clumsy?'

The smile lingered round his well-cut mouth, his eyes seemed to be searching hers. She smiled back, at ease, content. Surprisingly so. She said, laughter in her eyes, 'You do yourself an injustice, Logan. I think you are very articulate. All along I've liked your choice of words, the way you express yourself.'

The blue eyes danced. 'My dear girl, you sound exactly like Aunt Claudia! Quite pedantic. That could be an anticlimax. One doesn't go round kissing one's great-aunt—at least, not like that.'

Their shared laughter rang out. He brushed his lips lightly over hers again, released her, and they walked towards the last few yards of forest path, away from the glade, hand in hand, and in that moment heard the familiar hooter of the mail-launch.

Logan stopped dead. 'We had mail yesterday. Why an extra call? Though it doesn't necessarily mean there's anything wrong. Come on, Elissa. I don't suppose the lads are down from the hill yet, and Aunt Claudia may not want to let the kids go.'

But the lads were down. They were nearer the jetty than

Elissa and Logan were, and by the time the two of them, hand in hand, running, emerged from the dark cloak of the bush, two or three figures had disembarked and one of them was unmistakable. Stacey Cressford!

Stacey in less formal garb than before, yet still so elegant. Brown slacks immaculately creased, a buff jacket swinging open over a cream top, with a brown, polka-dotted cravat type of scarf knotted loosely about her throat, for all the world like a riding-stock. Her pale flaxen hair was tied back with a brown ribbon, beautifully shaped eyebrows arched themselves above her lovely brown eyes at the sight of two people running hand in hand from the dark tunnel of forest trees. As they might well arch!

Elissa's copper hair was swinging freely, shoulder-length, she had a streak of moss on her cheek where she'd brushed a wisp back; her jeans were water-splashed and silty at the cuffs; drinking from Logan's cupped hands had ruined her make-up (a good thing, she thought later, or his mouth might have borne traces of her lipstick) and the sudden transition from a solitary idyll to company had made her feel guilty.

She tugged her hand free, glanced swiftly up at Logan. She had thought to see him faintly embarrassed too. What she did see was even less welcome. Logan looked delighted, as glad as anything. So what he'd said, over and over about his feelings for Stacey was nothing but a mask to cover his real feelings!

Elissa felt exactly like a snuffed candle. Hew and Olaf were greeting Stacey; Hew's face was expressionless, Olaf's most appreciative ... as well it might be. The two men swung round, saw where Stacey was looking, and looked amazed to see their boss and Elissa running from the trees.

Hew said, 'What's up? Some trouble in there? Don't tell me the goat's got away again? You'd never get her out of there.'

Logan grinned, 'Oh, it wasn't a case of alarms, only excursions. We've been bird-stalking.'

Hew boggled. Olaf gave a great bellow of laughter, said, 'I couldn't think of a better term for it, myself, and a very nice bird too!' His audacious glance roved over every inch of Elissa.

Elissa saw Stacey stiffen, tighten her lips, and felt her own colour rise. Logan didn't look one bit set back, he too glanced appreciatively at Elissa. 'Well, you've got something there boy—but it happened to be a white heron.'

Elissa flicked the binoculars round his neck a little feebly and said, 'His glasses are so much better than mine. I've never had such a close-up. I ought to have taken my camera, but when he tore down off the hill to say the white heron was round there, I didn't waste any time.'

Hew said, 'And to think we went on straining fences while you were having a picnic! I'll be most suspicious next time you say you're off to your office, boss!' He too wore a huge grin now.

Elissa could have smacked them all. The launch pilot was taking a great interest in all this. He brought up the Airlie House mailbag. 'I know it's not your day, but we had a short run, and my brother at the Post Office said there was a special for you today, very much charred and damaged. Seemingly it was in a mailbag fire at Heathrow. Took a frightful time to get it all sorted out. They've done their best with it and apologise for the delay. Rod thought you might appreciate having it a day ahead of the usual delivery. Stacey decided to come along. I met her just after I got it and asked her if she'd like the run. Said if she liked to stay the night I'd pick her up again tomorrow, unless she wants to stay longer.'

'Sure,' said Logan. 'All right with me, either way, as long as it's right by my housekeeper. How about it, Elissa?'

She felt a spurt of annoyance. He oughtn't to have brought her into it. There were four more people in the launch. She managed an easy tone, said, 'Of course. It will be just lovely. Have you time to spare, Rod, to come up for a cup of tea, and your passengers too, of course? If they can spare the time?'

A warm Canadian voice said, 'I surely have. I do hope everyone else has. Are you tied to a time-table, Mr Ewart?'

'It's my last trip, so that's fine. I'll get you back to your hotel in plenty of time for dinner. This used to be a regular thing years ago, bringing tourists here, but at the end Mrs Prince was finding it a bit much. Folks, this is a bonus, one of the oldest and most beautiful homesteads on the lake.'

Elissa wondered the children weren't out by now. Hew said Aunt Claudia had driven them off to visit the Mendelsons down lake. She felt they needed some different companionship at times and Ingrid Mendelson had rung up to invite them. They were staying for an early tea. Elissa felt relieved. She didn't feel like facing candid comments from the children about Stacey's unexpected return.

Logan picked up Stacey's overnight bag, said, 'Well, I guess that burnt letter explains why Elissa arrived unheralded and unsung. Glad the mystery's cleared up.' He turned to Rod Ewart and gave an edited account of Elissa's arrival at the lake. He omitted all reference to Stacey's arrival next day, merely mentioning Aunt Claudia and the children, and added lightly, 'So the poor girl got the job of keeping house, instead of getting on with the redecorating.'

Rod said, 'Your guardian angel was certainly on the job! The Campions at Twin Hills are advertising for help and haven't had as much as an answer. You got one dropped on your doorstep—literally.'

Out of the corner of her eye, Elissa saw Stacey beginning to relax. If Logan could be so open about it, then it must have been exactly as he said. The letter, of course, would prove completely that Logan hadn't brought a girl in from Ludwigtown in Hew's absence. All this vindication ought to have made Elissa feel good, but she didn't. She felt lower than low and hated herself for the knowledge.

The presence of the tourists smoothed things over. Blithely unaware of any undercurrents, they chattered away, interested in all they saw. To anyone seeing Airlie House for the first time it looked like a dream come true. The last few days of sunshine had caused the daffodil buds to swell, and the snowdrops made white and green fans all over the garden. The forsythia had a few golden stars on the twigs and the japonicas were in full bloom now, making rose and coral banks of colour among the myriad greens of the shrubbery. Violets scented the air and everywhere polyanthus made jewel-bright clusters of colour in the flowerbeds.

Melissa Cooke, the tourist's daughter, turned to her brother and said, 'Perry, you must find yourself a farm like this in Canada ... across a lake ... the trees would be different mainly, but so much is the same ... we could create a setting like this. I'd come and keep house for you.'

Perry laughed, 'And how would I winkle you out of it when I met my dream-girl and married her?'

'I'd marry your partner or your hired man and you could build me a log cabin. Imagine how pleased Grandpa would be. He missed the woods so much.'

Mrs Cooke looked delighted. 'It's an idea. Oh, how glad I am we came here instead of going to the Far East for our trip. This is so ... what's the word I want? ... so idyllic.'

Logan's eyes and Elissa's met and held for a moment. She disentangled her gaze quickly. No, not any more. She dared not forget the gladness in his face when he beheld Stacey on the jetty. In that forest glade, for some foolish seconds, she had felt she was on the brink of a new and wonderful future. Here. What fools women were!

She sped into the kitchen to prepare tea: cut shortbread and nutty fingers, piled scones with raspberry jam and whipped cream, made tea and coffee. She looked up to find Stacey beside her. Elissa knew a spasm of nervousness. But Stacey smiled, a smile that changed her whole face, even dimples appeared. 'I owe you an apology. Logan has just handed me Rupert's letter. The gist of it is there. I wonder if you can understand how I felt when I walked in with Aunt Claudia to find a girl very much in charming undress, in the house of the man I love?'

Elissa put the last scone on the plate, said, 'Believe me, I do realise what it looked like. I felt terribly mortified and embarrassed myself and of course I lost my temper in return. I was flummoxed to find myself involved in even the slightest hint of scandal, and appalled to think it might break up an engagement. Logan told me, when he gave me the room with the key, that he was almost engaged. As for that car-lock, when the men came for the car, they admitted it was the most temperamental lock they'd ever had. I couldn't tell them just what trouble it had got me into, but I said very tartly I didn't think hired cars ought to be lent out in that condition, that it meant less than safety. Does all this help to get things into their right perspective now, Stacey?'

Even as she said it the words stabbed at her. Right for what? Right for Stacey and Logan, of course. Anything that had happened in that forest glade had been in false perspective, born of a mood, a setting, a shared interest, the solitude.

Stacey said, 'Yes, it does put it into the right perspective now.' She hesitated, said, 'I'm not very used to losing my temper and having to apologise, so it doesn't come easy.'

Elissa grinned. 'Well, I've had great experience in that line. Ginger-tops like me fizz up, then subside, so not to worry.'

Logan opened the door, looked relieved to see them apparently co-operating, and said, 'Can I give you girls a hand?' Elissa decided to go the second mile, so after she said, 'Well, you could scatter some small tables round the lounge, for the cups, and we'll bring the trays,' she added, 'Logan, do persuade Stacey to make a longer visit.'

She thought, without looking directly at him, that he stiffened, but Stacey said, 'I'd like to, very much. It would help us to get back on our usual footing again.' Logan went off to get the tables.

Elissa asked Stacey to pour, to underline that she now looked on her as the hostess. It was very pleasant, outwardly. They exchanged details about their lives, not only with the Canadians, but with the other tourist, a Miss Renaldson from the North Island. She'd always earned her living in cities, but had retired to a bush-surrounded bay on the very fringe of Auckland and was a constant traveller within the shores of New Zealand.

'My mother always said New Zealand was a whole world in miniature in the variety of its resorts, so as I haven't the money for world trips, I'm going to explore every inch of it.'

Elissa said, 'My father farmed in South Canterbury, so Mother knew that pastoral country well, with the backdrop of the Alps, and then, of course, the Lake Country down here, but she never had a chance to sample the thermal area of the Central North Island, or the semi-tropical delights north of Auckland. I've only read of them myself. It seems a pity she saw so little of the country, and somehow has never had a yen to come back. I can't understand it.'

She caught a look she didn't understand either, on Logan's face. Was she getting imaginative? Logan, Bob Samson, Aunt Claudia ... they all seemed to have some reserve about her mother. Oh, stop it, there just couldn't be anything known to Mother's detriment.

She was determined on one thing. She wasn't going to remain the spanner in the works as far as Stacey and Logan were concerned. That look on Logan's face had been too revealing. He'd been all uptight at the time Stacey had wanted to make capital about Rupert's ancestor having built a fine homestead out of Logan's ancestor's goldmine. But perhaps Stacey had just been solicitous for the welfare of the man she loved. She had used that phrase of him.

One part of Elissa's mind busily sorted this out, the other responded automatically to the conversation. Finally the pilot and his passengers took their leave. It was a beautiful sight, the white and scarlet launch cutting a creaming swathe of waters from the blue-green lake, and curving round beyond the headland towards Ludwigtown.

Hew and Olaf went off on the tractor for the late afternoon feeding-out, Logan departed to feed the hens, the dogs, and to break up the mutton he'd killed and hung the day before, ready for the freezer, leaving the two girls to wash up.

Stacey was most amiable, donned an overall, making even that look modish, said she'd do this while Elissa made the pudding. She'd stewed and sieved some dried apricots earlier, so now she rubbed butter and sugar into flour for a crumble topping, put it in the oven to brown, began to peel potatoes and pumpkin.

Logan stuck his head in the door. 'Elissa, would you take that bucket of scraps out to the goat, please? It'd save me a bit of time.'

Elissa went up a hill path to where Perdita was tethered. As she got out of sight of the house, Logan joined her. 'I wanted a word with you. If I get Stacey out of the house would you give the Mendelsons a ring and ask Aunt Claudia to tell the children Stacey has turned up and I want no candid remarks from them to upset things. She's full of sweet remorse and apologies and I want no more rifts in the lute. It's better this way.'

Elissa's throat went dry. How casual could men get? One overture from Stacey and it seemed as if the sweetness of the kiss they had shared in the forest was completely blotted out from his mind.

She managed: 'I'll do that, Logan. It's much nicer than feeling one was the cause of so much discord—however unwittingly.'

He nodded. 'This could cancel out any talk. The Samsons will soon get to know Stacey is here. As far as we're concerned, it can just fade out. No hard feelings that way.'

She nodded too. 'No hard feelings. Very sensible.'

'Good girl, I knew I could rely on you to play it along.' He disappeared downhill.

Elissa put Perdita's bucket down and stared into space, trying to get a grip on herself. Fade out? Could he possibly have guessed at her suddenly aroused feelings? At her thoughts, her hopes? What had he said, then apologised for putting it so crudely? 'You certainly made the best of that.' Now, humiliation washing over her, Elissa wished she'd not responded so naturally. With him it had been the whim of the moment, an unguarded one. He'd been missing Stacey ... and here was another girl at hand. Rage superseded the humiliation as it rose within her and for two pins she'd have kicked that bucket. Perdita gave a pathetic bleat ... she'd seen that bucket of goodies coming and now it was parked on the hillside, far from her reach. She bleated again.

Elissa picked up the bucket, trudged on uphill. But all

joy was gone from the day.

What Claudia said on the phone, blunt as ever, did her good. But Elissa had to water it down, to make it seem as if she thought it for the best ... as indeed she might, if that was what Logan desired.

Aunt Claudia said then, 'Faugh! The lad must be out of his mind. I thought he knew he'd had a lucky escape. And I thought he knew by now that having you cast up on his doorstep was a great stroke of luck for him. I didn't want it to start up all over again. Dammit, I've written to his mother and father to say for goodness' sake don't come home yet, that I wanted you there as long as possible. I said if Elissa stays, Logan might get that hoity-toity madam out of his hair for good. This one is the Glen Airlie calibre.'

In her agitation Elissa used the name she always thought of the old warhorse by, 'Aunt Claudia, do be careful! One of the children might hear you, or Mrs Mendelson. And besides, I'd be humiliated if anyone tried to matchmake on my behalf. If you'd seen the gladness on Logan's face when he saw her on the jetty, you'd know she was the one for him. What did you say?'

'I said bosh! And bosh again! And don't be stupid, girl, I've more sense than to talk like this if anyone was in earshot. I can see them all out on the lawn, playing French cricket, Ingrid and Oscar too. It's a setback, yes, but it won't last. Stacey won't stay sweet for ever. We'll think of something.'

Elissa panicked. 'Oh, no, no, we mustn't interfere.'

A chuckle was the only answer to that. 'Don't worry, child, I won't involve or embarrass you. And I'll drill the children. Not in the way you would, perhaps, but apart from the fact they don't like her, they have to learn not to be outspoken or make anyone feel unwelcome. Mind you, don't expect any warmth from them, but open hostility I will not allow. Goodbye till later.'

Elissa stood staring at the wall. The uppermost thought in her mind was that Logan's world had appeared to right itself when he saw Stacey in all her elegance silhouetted against the kingfisher-blue lake.

CHAPTER SEVEN

AUNT CLAUDIA had evidently drilled Isabel, Rennie and Bess well, for their behaviour on meeting Stacey was impeccable. However, it was a good thing it was near their bedtime, for it was hard to believe such angelic conduct could last. Elissa took herself to task for also thinking Stacey's conduct towards them was rather unnatural. Was she being uncharitable in supposing that Stacey wasn't really fond of children? The fact that Hew and Olaf stayed on after the youngsters' bedtime, watching television, helped the atmosphere. When the men went off, Elissa said, 'I'll make up your bed now, Stacey, or would you prefer to do it yourself? I suppose you've often stayed here?'

Logan answered, 'No, she hasn't. Her visits have all been by the day. But would you mind doing it, Elissa? I want to take Stacey off for a walk. We've things to talk out, naturally. Perhaps you'd take the one the far side of Aunt Claudia's, Stacey. Elissa's is the one between hers and the children's.'

He was underlining that fact for Stacey. Elissa managed to smile and said, 'Because that was mine when I was a child, and I love it.'

Logan brought out a camel-hair coat of his mother's for Stacey, held it out for her, turned her round, pulled its hood over her shining blonde head. 'It's clear and starry but cold. Goodnight, Aunt. Goodnight, Elissa.'

He might just as well have spelled it out: 'Don't wait up'.

A heavy silence descended upon the two women left. Then Aunt Claudia said vehemently, 'Well, men are fools, that's for sure.'

For very pride's sake Elissa strove to sound placatory.

'I don't think we must really judge her on the strength of a few bad-tempered moments in what was, on the face

102

of it, a trying situation.'

'Don't be absurd. I told you I brought her up here to look after the house and children so that Logan could see her in her true colours. She'd never stand up to the rigours of the life here. I'd made one mistake, though. I thought lambing was a lot nearer than it was. I'm glad—in a way—that you've asked her to stay on a few days. I hope they come thick and fast ... I wonder how that veneer will stand up to bleating, sick lambs, stubborn to feed and with dirty tails, taking precedence over everything. It's not exactly gracious living then! She'd be fine as a business executive's wife, queening it over social gatherings. But during lambing Logan will be dog-tired and not up to ambling in the moonlight then. I'll help you put the sheets on her bed, and I'll pray hard that stupid nephew of mine sees her in her true colours before long! Come on.'

Suddenly Elissa giggled. Aunt Claudia stared, gave a sort of trumpeting hoot and joined in. 'I know, girl, I know. You needn't tell me. It's not exactly a Christian sort of prayer. All right, I'll modify it. I've always said the good Lord must have a mighty sense of humour to cope with all His creatures. I'll cool off and ask Him to give Logan a bit more gumption and save him from the consequences of his own folly, without getting too personal and detailed about it.'

Elissa felt her continuing laughter had done her good. She put her arm about the older woman, said, 'Oh, Claudia Robertson, I do love you. I think your Dennis must have been a very fortunate man.'

For an instant the aquiline face was changed, even transformed. A look of pure tenderness swept across it. '*He* thought so ... which proves my point, of course, that men are gullible. Come on, girl, let's kill the fatted calf. The best sheets and nothing less. Lead on!'

Elissa got sheets with lilac sprays dotted over them, plain lavender pillowcases to match, and they went off to the best spare room in the big old house. The other rooms were very ordinary, reminiscent of the days when a large pioneer family had romped through, eleven of them, plus domestics. This, under Logan's mother's artistic hand, had been completely transformed, but with the best of both worlds, the old and the new.

The twin beds were sturdy ones that had come out from Scotland in the eighteen-sixties, with the spool ends that had come back into fashion again, but the mattresses were modern ones and the last word in comfort. The deep-piled carpet was a medley of greens, merging into each other like the greens of the New Zealand bush, and at the windows fuchsia-purple drapes framed misty white Terylene curtains that were almost always pulled back to reveal much the same view that Elissa saw from her room.

Elissa said, switching on the light between the two beds, 'What perfect taste Mrs MacCorquodale has! Very few people would think of making this lampshade a splash of red against the purple. It's so charming I'll incorporate it in some future work in England.'

Claudia took a quick look at her, said, 'You're sure you're going back, then?'

Elissa said sturdily with no trace of emotion, 'Of course. That's where my home is. Unless, for any reason, Mother decides to stay in Canada near Aunt Jean, in which case I'd join her. This is just a job. Uncle Rupert sent me out here for that.'

'Did he indeed? He's a wily fellow at times. I thought it might just have been an excuse to get you here.'

'Eh? You mean to housekeep? Oh, I hardly think——'

'I didn't mean quite that. Rather more of an—let it go. I'm speaking out of turn.'

Elissa couldn't fathom it. 'But the MacCorquodales will be coming back, anyway. Even if they go when Logan marries. So——'

'When I told his parents not to hurry back, Alicia wrote to say she and Nicol might just go on to England after this trip, not bother coming back here first. They have another son in England. Alicia thinks he needs her more than Logan does. He had a marriage break-up and has never settled since. He was high-country farming too, but a place even more remote than this. No road, not even lake transport. You had to ford a river to get there. She was a Bristol girl who just couldn't take the life, and no wonder. Plenty of New Zealand girls couldn't either. Poor bairn, I was sorry for her, impatient sometimes, but more often sorry. And I was used to that sort of life. I've an idea that Alicia thinks that by now she might persuade Euan that a compromise would do. It wouldn't have worked once, but since he's been working on farms in Britain, so much easier of access, he's realised what a catastrophic change it was for Anne. After all, he could farm on the Taieri, within an hour's reach of Dunedin City. Anyway, to return to my muttons, I've an idea Rupert had more in his mind than just interior decorating.'

Elissa paused in the act of shaking a fat pillow into its case. She looked very thoughtful. 'You could be right. When I see what Alicia MacCorquodale has done to this room, there was no need to send me. But as for what he had in mind——'

Claudia hid a smile, said, 'She used these colours because either side of the windows is a Victor Hugo fuchsia— you know, that one with the frilly purple petticoats and an overdress that shows the red beneath it.'

Elissa clasped her hands together. 'Oh, I know it. Not by that name, but you have a knack with words. I can see it in bloom, even if as yet it has only a leaf or two.'

Claudia actually blushed. 'Oh, you've kissed the Blarney Stone. As Dennis had. He used to make me feel so different from—from how I look.'

Elissa's eyes lit up. 'That's the way it ought to be. My mother said something like that once—that my father used to make her feel lovely and desirable, even in a sack apron, washing the clothes in an old farmhouse laundry. They were just getting a start and putting everything into stocking this rundown place, so she wouldn't allow him to improve the house too soon, felt it was better to sacrifice the present for the years ahead when life would be easier. But she didn't have that dream future. Dad worked too hard even so, and she lost him.'

Claudia said, 'It must be even harder to lose your mate when you're young. I've always been glad Dennis and I had the later, richer years together, except that it meant we had no family. I had a great sense of fulfilment in my marriage. But a woman in her thirties, just a girl! She must have found the days—and nights—very lonely, when she was used to sharing all the hours there are.'

Elissa dropped her pillow, put her arms about Claudia, said, 'Oh, I *do* love you.' She kissed the leathery cheek. 'You're like my mother ... steel-true, blade-straight.'

She thought a peculiar look crossed Claudia's face, but perhaps it was just a little embarrassment at such a display of emotion. Claudia hurrumphed, picked up the pillow, punched it into shape, put it in place, drew up the green bedspread under the fold-back of the sheet, said, 'Was Rupert going to call on your mother in Canada? He'd have found it interesting after all these years. We mellow as we grow older.'

Once more the disappointment Elissa had known in Surrey touched her briefly. 'No. I asked him to. It isn't really far, and my mother always had a soft spot for Douglas. She'd have no idea he was so near. But Rupert said he'd just ring her to tell her he'd persuaded me to do this job for him. It's nice that Doug's turned out so well. Did you know him?'

'Not in those days. But you know how hospitable Rupert is. When Logan got settled in here, he had all of us up here in turn, sometimes as a crowd. How Dennis loved it here! Rupert talked a lot to him about Doug. Dennis was a schoolmaster and understood adolescent problems very well, and I think he took a lot of the remorse away from Rupert. Rupert felt he must have mishandled Douglas—but it's not always that. Varsity life made a big impact on the boy, coming from isolation like this—he'd gone to high school in Ludwigtown, which is very different—and he got into bad company. But fundamentally, the lad was good. Some things he drew the line at, I believe.

'However he made good, first in Australia—he left here to get away from the crowd he was in with, I believe—then in Canada. Came back with his wife and family, and we met him then. Rupert and the girls—it was before they

were married—were so delighted to have them. He's
turned out a very fine man. Does a lot of work to assist
youth clubs. He's exceptionally good with even some of the
hardened cases. He said once that he always thinks that but
for the grace of God and someone who stood by him, he
might have known what it was to have a record too. He's in
his right sphere, no doubt of that. That's why Rupert
wouldn't press him to return to carry on here. Rupert
raised money to give Doug his share—some of it from the
land Logie bought, and apart from some that Doug in-
vested over there, for his family, he put it into providing
more recreational facilities for the youth he's interested in.'

'I must write to tell Mother. Unless Rupert's told her
when he phoned. She would be bound to ask after Doug.'

Elissa checked that the drawers of the dressing-table
were empty, said, 'I'll put some flowers in here tomorrow
morning. Oh, I've an idea. I've some violets in mine. They'll
go well with the fuchsia drapes. Well, that's done.'

Tonight she decided to draw her curtains. Stacey and
Logan might just come round by the hill path, and it
looked right down into her room. She went across, not yet
switching on the prosaic electric light, because once more
the silvery peace of that moonlit, starlit sky, spelt calmness
to her. She felt close to her mother, kneeling on the sheepskin seat she had upholstered for her little daughter, and
because she'd been talking of her to Aunt Claudia. Besides,
who could look on the classical slopes of Mount Serenity
and not feel it was well named?

Suddenly she felt chilly. It would be good to snuggle
down now on that electric blanket, read, forget her
moments of elation and disappointment. More than that,
disillusion.

She reached up her hands to draw the curtains, and with
cruel precision, two figures rounded the corner of the house.
Stacey, she thought, put out a hand and stopped Logan.
He looked down on her, seemed to wait for her to ask
something. Elissa, of course, couldn't hear as much as a
murmur. But she saw the shadowy outline of his head nod,

then Stacey reached up, drew his head down and kissed him.

Elissa swiftly and silently drew her curtains, undressed in the dark, switched off her blanket, snuggled down, found herself saying, 'Please God, sleep and a forgetting?'

She woke with a sense of heaviness. For the first time at Airlie House she found herself reluctant to rise. She made herself sit up, pushed her tangled coppery tresses back, shook her head a little as if to clear it of all unwelcome thoughts, sighed, then with sudden resolve, sprang out of bed, wrapped her short towelling dressing-gown about her and tore for the shower-room.

She collided with Logan, returning from it, just in pyjama trousers, his black hair gleaming sleekly from the water. He steadied her, laughed, said, 'Hey, why the hurry?'

She had a hand on his chest and pushed herself back with it. She sounded breathless, more by his nearness than her pace, and said crossly, 'I should think you'd know the answer—this household just grows and grows, and I do like to get a good start with the breakfast.'

His hand clutched her wrist. 'I see ... not as hospitable this morning, are we?'

She said coldly, 'It's your house, Logan, so naturally I had to appear welcoming yesterday, but——'

'But not to worry, Coppertop. I'll see the fair Stacey pulls her weight. She's not one of the dumb blondes, you know, ornamental but useless. Who knows? She may prove so good, in spite of Aunt's doubts, that you'll be able to get on with your real job here.'

'You mean so I can finish it and get back to my own place? That would suit me beautifully. I could take the children, then *all* your millstones would be gone.'

His grip tightened, he peered into her face and laughed. 'Did you and Aunt Claudia have something wildly in-digestible for supper last night? I think your liver's out of order.'

She couldn't help it. 'Then it must be *gall* you're suffer-ing from!'

She could have gnashed her teeth when he laughed. 'And don't dare, Elissa Montgomery, call my nieces and nephew millstones. Or yourself. You've been a godsend to me.'

She said coldly, 'You've used me, yes. But not any more. Turn over as much as you can to Stacey. *You* can tell her, not me. And I'll get on with my sketching and measuring up. And if Sue should ring with any good news, you can say I'll be able to bring the children over quite soon. I'll write to Rupert and say if he can't put a date, I'll make one myself.'

He said, 'Have a heart! Imagine me being left in a place this size ... a lumbering great white elephant ... without a housekeeper, Gwyneth coming home with twins, which means she can't be counted upon, and lambing starting in two days?'

'Well, for goodness' sake, the lambing'll be nearly over by the time I'd be able to leave, and if Stacey and Aunt Claudia can't manage without any children or lessons to be taught, they ought to be able to!'

'Elissa, what's got into you? Can you imagine Aunt Claudia and Stacey running a house together? For some reason, *you* can wrap my redoubtable aunt round your little finger, so for my peace of mind, you'd just better stay on.'

'What makes you think your peace of mind matters to me? I never heard of anything more selfish! All I want is to finish my job and get back. I thought I could recapture the magic of my childhood, but I find I can't. It's not surroundings that matter, it's people. I miss my mother too much to stay too long. I want that holiday in Canada with her. And for goodness' sake let me go, you madman, the children will be up soon and whatever would they——'

It was too late. Isabel and Bess erupted into the passage, stopped dead as they saw them, looked at each other and giggled. Logan let Elissa go and strode off. Elissa said sharply, 'Back for your slippers. We'll be nursing sick lambs next week ... we don't want you two down with colds.'

She thought she'd handled that quite well, but her self-delusion was exploded when, at breakfast, Isabel said,

'Elissa, you know that towelling dressing-gown you were wearing this morning when Uncle Logie was kissing you? Well our mum's got——'

Elissa swallowed, choked on a crumb, then said furiously, '*Kissing* me? We were doing nothing of the kind! What on earth made you think that?'

Isabel rushed on, waving a hand as one interrupted with an irrelevant detail, 'Well, he was holding you, so I thought he probably just *had* ... well, Mum's got one the same except that hers has got big blue buttons on.'

'Has it?' asked Elissa weakly. 'It's the same but for that? I got that at Marks and Spencer's, a big shop in Guildford.'

'Oh, Dad brought it back from Australia for Mum. Uncle Logie, why *were* you holding her?'

He was quite bland, and quick. 'Because I wanted the shower first.'

Elissa felt an inward sigh of relief.

Small Bess wiped her lips on her napkin, said in her dear little matter-of-fact voice, 'But your hair was wet.'

He looked quite unrepentant. 'Was it? Then it must have been something else. Elissa, what made me grab you?'

She was only too aware of Claudia's amusement and Stacey's riveted attention. She said clearly, 'Sheer bad temper, I think. And he said that about the shower because he didn't like admitting to you children that we were fighting. I'd told him he was bossy and pushed past him to end the argument, but you know what *men* are. It's just a myth that *women* like the last word.' She turned to Stacey. 'He said I could drop the housekeeping while you were here and get on with the job Rupert was paying me for. Then if Sue gets a house, I can push off by plane with the children. It looks as if I'd better do just that, Stacey. I guess you know your way round here fairly well, but if you do want any help, just sing out. I'll get my notes and swatches and my sketch-book and go right ahead.' She marched off.

It didn't make her feel any better to hear Logan say, 'As temperamental as they come. Maybe you had something there, Stacey, when you said redheads were exciting. But I could do without that sort of excitement early in the morning. How about it? Will you take over?'

Elissa made her bed, flinging the sheets over with wasteful energy, dusting furniture, tidying, till her feelings abated a little. Then she picked up the notes she'd taken from Rupert in England, and went running up to the little turret room at the end of the passage beyond Logan's room.

This had been a playroom when Elissa had shared it with Judith and Elspeth, and was the one that the second Airlie bride here, Charlotte, had begged from her Hamish. The west window faced down-lake to Twin Hills between the two promontories that formed Airlie Bay. The north one looked across to Ludwigtown through a gap in the trees on that headland, to give a perfect view of it, nestled on the lake shore. The south one framed Mount Serenity, and the east one gave a view of the access road, the only scene that differed from that of yesteryear, when only a bridle path had led along the lake towards the other homesteads.

Here they had spent all their rainy days, played with their dolls, painted, crayoned, squabbled. Here Rupert and her mother had adjudicated, sometimes spanked, often played with them.

This was the only room Rupert had had definite ideas about. He wanted it turned into a room that a woman might take for a sitting-room of her own, where she could spin, if she so fancied that, weave, sew, or just sit and read.

The bookshelves were dusty and shabby. They were to be painted off-white. There would be gold-and-green chintz curtains and window-seats, the colour of the daffodils under the orchard trees, and between the sets of windows were to be bird portraits. The one that framed the lake was to have a kingfisher. That had caught Elissa's fancy and she had shown Rupert a framed print she had of a kingfisher, one of Ted Chicken's. That would pick up the blue-green of the lake beyond it. One would be of a New Zealand native pigeon, the *kereru*, with its beautiful white breast, and its coppery green iridescent plumage. One would be a *tui* with its beak deep in *kowhai* flowers, and last, the symmetry and grace of the *kotuku*, the pure white heron, a print Rupert had treasured for years. Now it brought to Elissa a pang for that idyllic afternoon at Treasure Island Bay with Logan.

She wondered if Logan's mother had suggested just this to Rupert. Surely some woman had put it into his mind. Or was it something his grandfather had told him, old Hamish Airlie? Had Charlotte sat up here weaving, looking over the lake she loved?

Despite her heavy heart, the artist in Elissa began to stir. She thought a carpet in a shade between duck-egg and teal, and if she could procure that white and gold beading in New Zealand she would have it attached to the window-sills to pick up the white and gold of the bird portrait frames. The small bow-fronted cabinet in the lounge was to come up here. It had Queen Anne legs, and latticed glass. It should hold dainty china, perhaps that small rosebud design, or the violet one, equally old-fashioned. The door could have a floral design white china knob to match the contents.

An elegant gate-legged table could stand there, a small shelf here, with a kettle on a spirit lamp. That kerosene lamp from downstairs with the brass base and the painted shade could be brought up for the odd times when lake storms could bring down the power lines. There ought to be an armless knitting-chair, beautifully curved, beside the fire, and a whatnot in that corner for some tiny ornaments.

She thought a couple of balloon-back chairs for sitting up to the tea table, and those two Edwardian lady's and gentleman's chairs in the lumber room covered with some sort of muted brocade, with blue and green and metallic gold merging into each other. Perhaps a rosewood writing-desk. Oh, no, Rupert had mentioned the davenport in his bedroom for that.

She laid her swatches out, found a chintz that would be ideal, and knew, as she'd enquired before leaving, that these were obtainable at certain firms in New Zealand. She would order them, by telephone, almost immediately.

She heard steps on the uncarpeted stairs that led up here: Stacey's. Stacey entered with more confidence and less of the apologetic humility that had sat upon her so quaintly the day before. That walk and talk last night must have restored her equanimity, to say nothing of the recent scene at the table, when Elissa and Logan had been at such cross-purposes.

'Why start on this room, Elissa? It seems so unimportant. Or have you some particular reason?' She laughed. 'Or did you just want to get as far away from Logan as possible? Don't worry. Look at all that passed between him and me that morning after you'd landed on him, and now ...' she spread her hands out, 'it's as if it had never been.'

Elissa managed a grin. 'No, that wasn't my reason. His moods needn't worry me; I shan't have to live with them. Rupert asked me to do this first. I've an idea he wants it restored to much what it was like in his grandmother's time, for whom it was built. A woman's very own retreat. I liked the idea.' She indicated her sketches, done in England to show Rupert, the patterns, the prints of the birds carefully slotted into a protective folder. 'I think it was partly Mrs MacCorquodale's idea too. Like Logan, she must love birds.'

There was a faint asperity in Stacey's voice. 'It's odd—for him to do it on her say-so, I mean. Because from now on I don't suppose she'll be up here for more than the odd holiday. That's very charming, admittedly, but some would prefer a modern décor, tweedy, in divan materials, or a sort of Mexican motif, made for relaxation, but not cluttered.'

Her meaning was obvious. She could see herself as mistress here. But would Rupert Airlie, born and bred in the tradition of Colonial pioneer style, ever allow a manager's wife to set her seal on his house? She could imagine him building a new house for a manager, but not to surrender the atmosphere of this.

She made herself say evenly, 'I can only carry out Rupert's wishes. He'll have many years here yet. Other décors can come about when he's gone.'

'But the money that it will cost ... for a mere whim.'

Elissa said, a little tartly, 'Rupert's worked hard enough and suffered enough too, to be able to indulge a whim like this, and after all, it was nothing to do with me what a customer ordered.'

Stacey, turning to go, said, 'How true. Nothing whatever to do with you.'

Had she stressed that last word? Did it really mean: 'But it could be everything to do with *me*?'

But if Rupert wanted it like this, he was going to have it. Stacey Cressford couldn't, yet, do a thing about it.

Stacey turned out some delicious scones for morning tea and wasn't above asking Elissa what she'd had in mind for lunch. 'Oh, you'll find three bacon-and-egg pies on the pantry shelf behind gauze, thawing out, and I thought of opening a big jar of Mrs MacCorquodale's preserved tomatoes to go with them. There's a leg of hogget mutton for tonight, beside them, on an ashet.'

Logan said smugly, 'My lady mother would never dream how well I've got things organised. I must send her a cable to say I've dual help in the house now and to go on having the time of her life. That the lambing will be nothing this year with five women in the house counting Isabel and Elizabeth, to help feed motherless lambs and to help in the fostering shed persuading bereaved mothers they have a duty towards the orphans. Olaf, I hope you can stay on till lambing's right through.'

Olaf smiled, his sea-blue eyes looking across the table at Elissa. 'Wild horses wouldn't drag me away, old boy. I could hardly leave you in possession of all the field.' He included Stacey in his glance. 'I've never struck it so good before. There's the Kotare High School Ball in aid of the new library coming up, how about——'

Stacey said quickly, 'Logan's taking me. We planned it long ago, didn't we?'

'And ratified it last night,' said Logan. 'Elissa——'

Olaf interrupted, 'Then if I'm lucky, Elissa will partner me.'

'If I'm still here,' she said slowly. 'It could be I'll be away with the children by then. Unless Rupert insists I wait here.'

'You'll be here all right, Elissa,' said Aunt Claudia.

'We're going to need all the help we can get. Gwyneth will be out of it. I'm sure it would ease her mind to know that Logie has extra help. Because although the weather's so ideal at the moment, I've never known a lambing yet without storms sweeping up from the South Pole.'

Logan looked amazed. 'I've always thought of you as a super optimist, Aunt. Always thinking we just might have conditions ideal for bringing lambs into the world. You've let me down!'

Stacey rang to ask her mother to put some more clothes on the launch for her, and stayed on, managing the house quite creditably, though when Logan had cooled off, he asked Elissa to give her a hand in the mornings and do her planning and designing in the afternoons.

But Aunt Claudia's Cassandra-like croaking proved only too true, and on the Monday the first of the lambs were born in a flurry of sleet and a bitter wind that blew from the tops of the mountains and penetrated every inlet on the lake.

Elissa resented it strongly on behalf of struggling ewes and just-born lambs, thinking of the past sunshine of the false spring, and the green pastures that now were rapidly turning into quagmires. They rescued all they could from the harsh elements, out all day in gumboots and balaclavas, turning with slithery little creatures in their hands to try to find something less than a puddle to lay them in. Hillside paddocks weren't as bad, as the water streamed off them, lakewards, and even the rocks, cropping out, provided some sort of shelter. They'd kept a lot of hedges here, and though they seemed inadequate against the searching wind, they were better than nothing.

Their faces stung from the icy particles of snow in the rain, muscles aching as they struggled on, bent against the force of it, searching, finding, helping the births, rescuing ewes and lambs.

Stacey looked harassed to death as the kitchen floor became slithery with water and worse, as they brought in sodden bundles dripping from being immersed in tubs of hot water, and putting them on sacks, rubbed them vigorously and lengthily. Those that responded were put into clothes baskets, with old blankets and rubber hot-water bottles, then, as they revived, they were fed with warm milk made up from dried milk, and egg and glucose, and relegated to the various verandahs in cartons with old fleeces in them. Elissa was tired of filling bottles, or lamb revivers, of trying to decide which lamb to attend to next, and she was moved when she saw how the children worked.

Isabel's little face grew pinched with pity and tears rained down at every casualty; Bess worked away stolidly, but Elissa heard a gulp or two and hoped she wasn't bottling it up too much, and Rennie put his occasional sniff down to a bit of a cold he'd picked up. He seemed to find a comfort in working out the percentage of casualties. As fast as the kitchen ones were sent out to the verandahs, new victims of the storm arrived in.

At night they listened desperately to forecast after forecast, hoping the sou'westerly air stream would blow itself out, but fresh reinforcements of icy winds seemed to be driven up from the South Pole itself. The whole country, even right up to the North Island, was lashed by gales, and it was going to be a most disastrous season for farmers and for the economy as a whole.

On the third night the wind dropped dramatically, but the men didn't look much happier. There was a leaden look over sky and lake, menacing, brooding, and the level of the water had submerged the roots and lower branches of the willows that, till this had blown up, were bursting into glad leaf. Even from the turret they could see Twin Hills no longer, and soon Treasure Island was blotted out. They all knew what this meant.

'Indian summer in August,' groaned Olaf, 'winter in September.'

The men worked furiously, bringing the sheep down as far as possible and as many as possible, hunting them out of gullies where snow would pile up. Many, from the higher ground, were making their own way down, some instinct warning them. But it was too vast a property to cover with the dogs in the short time vouchsafed to them. By the time night fell and the weary men came in, snow was already falling, beautiful, powdery, treacherous, death-dealing snow.

There was a great stamping-off of snow from heavy boots once the dogs had been fed and housed, wind-cheaters were shaken on the back porch and the snow swept out over the steps, and they thawed out their frozen faces with warm water. They were philosophical, as befitted high-country farmers, who took the weather as it came, glad beyond measure when they did get a bonus lambing season, when the sun shone, and the skies were blue, and lambs fluffy dry atoms of sheer mischief ... but this was the bad to be taken with the good.

The children had been allowed out the last hour to build snowmen. Elissa had brought up a huge stack of nappies from the cottage to be dried in their electric drier, because the bigger reserve they had, the better, in case the snow brought down power lines. The twins were adorable, and thriving, and the young sister Gwyneth had brought back with her had done part-time nursing, but Logan said to Elissa as she held out a warm towel for him to dry his hands on, 'I'd sooner the power lines went out than the telephone ones, with two small new lives to be cared for. This is the sort of thing that drives married men to farms closer to civilisation.'

Elissa nodded, 'But at least if Bronwen or Gwilym take anything, it's not like a woman being alone, and afraid. I know Claudia, with her experience of stations more remote than this, would be a tower of strength.'

The dark Highland face above her softened a little. 'And so would you, Elissa-making-the-best-of-things. You'd battle through.' He reached out a finger, just beginning to thaw, and flicked her warm cheek with it. 'You've certainly pulled your weight during the last few days.'

Warmth flooded her at his touch, making her despise herself. 'So has Stacey,' she said.

The blue eyes mocked her, 'Giving the devil her due, are you, bonnie lass? Yet I think it goes against the grain. Am I right?'

'Trying to be omniscient again? I'm speaking as I find

her, making, as you sometimes taunt me, the best of things.'

He caught her arm as she turned away. 'Good grief, girl, it was never meant as a taunt. I think you do make the best of things, even see the best in people. That you always have done. Your loyalties do you credit.'

What could he mean? What loyalties?

On the television news at six-thirty they saw truckloads of pathetic little woolly corpses being carted away in the pastoral counties of the North Island where rain had fallen non-stop for a disastrous length of time, only the very early ones having escaped. Would it be like this for them too? Outside it fell thicker and thicker and thicker, with an evil noiselessness. By nine they were without power. They had their last snack by the light of kerosene lamps, left torches at the children's bedsides, candles by their own, banked up the range with wet slack, to last the night, and went to bed full of foreboding.

CHAPTER EIGHT

WHAT a tragedy that so beautiful a morning world was spelling death to so many little lives! Elissa drew back the curtains. The virgin snow, a mockingly bright sun, the glistening particles, each one, she knew, a kaleidoscopic creation in itself, in shape if not in colour, the dark stretch of water against the purer whiteness of the fall, the blackness of twigs and branches in etched relief, the music of little torrents rushing down to join the lake waters was a lovely, lovely, cruel world.

But this was just a comprehensive glance. Every moment was precious. Nobody showered, everybody hustled, breakfast was eaten at speed, with nobody checked for table manners, the dishes just stacked. Stacey had begun to wash them, but Logan said, 'I say ... first things first. Into gumboots and anorak, Stacey, and out with the rest of us.'

She turned an astonished face. 'Me? I don't know a thing about lambing. I thought I'd keep the house warm, cook the meals, make the beds.'

'Not in an emergency like this. Even your dainty feet will help tread out a track to the sunnier faces. For that matter, even the dogs' feet do. We're damned lucky it *is* sunny, not still snowing or blowing. And as for beds ... if need be we can turn into them as we got out of them.'

Stacey was evidently still not sure enough of Logan to demur. The children were delighted to skip lessons, though Aunt Claudia, true to type, assured them they'd make up for most of the time, later. Out on the slopes Logan said, 'I want the sheep looked for first near Danger Creek, where the banks overhang so much. If this sun lasts and we get a quick thaw I want them away from where they've taken shelter under the banks or they'll be swept into the lake, waterlogged and helpless.' He said to Stacey, 'You'll see little air-vents in the snow where their breath is coming

119

through. But you children must work away from the stream, on to the slopes. I don't want you near the edge. With snow this thick, you could disappear into a drift and go clear into the water. Hew and I and Olaf will take the edges. We'll take the old sleds up, cover them with sacks, and bring back any weak lambs to the sheds.'

Fun at first, the novelty soon wore off. The children stopped throwing snowballs, trudged on, dragging their feet out of the clogging snow with a sort of automatic precision that did them credit. They soon recognised little patches where the snow was thinner. They tramped paths to them, clearing tufts of grass and tussock, urged cast sheep to their feet, and along to these patches where soon the sun would thaw the thinner crust.

There were many casualties, but it was encouraging soon to see rescued ewes and lambs standing on the cleared spaces, shivering but recovering. But their hearts were heavy at the thought of the further away numbers who couldn't be succoured.

Memories of similar scenes flooded back on Elissa. She was taking animals from Logan and pushing them along towards those sunnier faces. She said, 'Is there still that scoured-out place across the creek, with a huge overhang, like a shallow cave? I remember once when a score or so took shelter there. With a bit of feed taken to them, they stayed in good shape, but we had to free the snow from the entrance. Mind you, they weren't lambing. That fall came much earlier.'

Logan nodded. 'Glad you reminded me. How about coming across the log bridge with me and seeing how they are? Bound to be some there. Stacey and Aunt will see to the children.'

Olaf and Hew nodded approval. Elissa and Logan made their way up the bank, breaking away crusted overhangs as they went, to show the men better where the sheep were. Crossing the bridge, which was simply three trunks of trees lashed together with fencing wire, was very tricky. Logan said, 'Don't look down, and take my hand. I'll kick off some snow as I go. Put your feet in my footprints and take it easy.'

He went over his knees in a drift at the other side and because he still had her hand, Elissa pitched over him and sprawled across him. They heard laughter from the other side. He laughed up at her. 'You make a habit of this, don't you? I forgot it was so hollowed out here.'

They scrambled up, plunged on, testing each step with their sticks, and came to the scour. Elissa thrust forward, eager to see, but Logan caught her. 'Steady! Wrong thing. I know that lots of roots reinforce the overhang, but we don't know what weight of snow is on top. We'll go up the side, here, where the rocks are showing through, and get a minor avalanche going if we can. That'll get rid of some of the weight.'

They came up, cautiously. Logan brushed some snow off some fallen branches, explained what he wanted to do. It was like an enormous birch broom. They slid it into the mass of snow on the lip of the overhang and pushed hard. A passage appeared, snow banking up against the twigs, drew back their ramming-rod, pushed again, and an enormous amount of snow went right over the edge. What they'd cleared looked very firm ground, but Logan held Elissa back. 'We go *down* to investigate, lass.'

Down again, they found that though it had added to the deep snow in front, it had created a huge gap through which they could see a dozen or more ewes standing patiently and perfectly all right. They could safely leave these here and return with feed later. Now they'd free the ones on this edge of the creek.

They worked away, pausing now and then for a breather. In once such pause Logan said, 'Not a bad test this ... snow at lambing-time.'

'Test? For whom?'

'For any girl. If she can take this, she can take anything.'

Stacey? But somehow she didn't think so. Though undoubtedly Stacey was trying to prove herself. Good for her.

Elissa said, 'Are you thinking of your brother? That if he'd been able to give his English bride a foretaste, she mightn't have embarked on a marriage she couldn't take? I hope you don't mind, but Aunt Claudia told me.'

'No, we've learned to live with it. Euan's a grand fellow,

made for family life. Mother got very thin at the time it
was breaking up. But she loved Anne too, and saw how she
felt. So did I, because I'd had that time in Britain, knew
how she must miss the little villages, the community life,
the spires on every skyline, the sense of the whole country
being a garden. Where Euan was she looked out on bare
shingle-fans, and great towering mountains ... it was on
the grand scale, but not beautiful like this. Grim, challenging country. Oh, it wasn't fair to her. He was adamant that
she must take his kind of life. I'm not sure he was right.
But after she left him and went back to Hampshire, he
missed her so much that he just took off. Said he wasn't
going to see her, but wanted to see what she'd been used to.
I think he's bound to see her, and may be big enough to
compromise, now. It will hurt him to give up his mountains, but it shouldn't be all on one side. Oh, there are
three more air-vents here.' They bent again.

This time the picture wasn't so good. Two ewes were all
right. The third had given birth to twin lambs and had
died. Elissa steeled herself. Farmers had to be sensible,
and Logan had his knife in his belt. The lambs were pretty
far gone. It was hardly worth saving only to lose them
later after much work, probably. That bridge had been
hard enough to negotiate unburdened. The dark Highland
face turned, and she couldn't read the expression. He recognised the hint of pain and acceptance on hers. 'I'll take
them back,' he said. 'They've got a slender chance.'

She clutched his arm. 'We've packed the snow on the
bridge hard with our first crossing, Logan. It will be more
slippery than ever. You couldn't do it, carrying these.'

He grinned, and, to her amazement, began to unzip his
wind-cheater. He had wound round him under it, a short
length of plaid. 'I worked on a mountain farm in Scotland
and I found this invaluable. I'm a bit self-conscious about
using it in front of some New Zealand shepherds, but Hew
and Olaf have seen me in it before.' He rewound it, bringing
it under one arm and fashioning a sort of loop in front of
him.

Then he picked up the almost lifeless creatures and

tucked them into it. 'I'll make it across like this.' He surprised an emotion that quivered over her face and said, 'What is it?'

She looked a little embarrassed, then, 'It's—it's almost Biblical. How that would appeal to my mother! She likes the fundamental things.'

'You get homesick for her, don't you?'

'Yes. Not that she's possessive—indeed the opposite. She's afraid we might become too close, too dependent upon each other, so there are no apron-strings. But it will be wonderful to be back with her before too long.'

He seemed to hesitate. 'Would she come for a visit to you while you're doing the redecorating? It takes such a short time by air from Canada.'

'It would be heavenly for me, but for some reason, I think she wouldn't. She may not want to waken memories.'

Logan held out a hand. 'Let's get these two down to some warmth.'

She said, 'You mustn't help me over this time. Too awkward.'

'But we want no accidents with the road impassable and only the lake for transport, so I'll come back for you.'

He edged over slowly, put his burden down, edged back. A pace from that side and he held out his hands. 'Hold fast,' he said. Elissa could feel the warmth of his hand through her mittens. Hold fast ... the motto of the MacCorquodales. She knew it was what she wanted most in life, to hold fast, always, to him. But it wasn't to be. It was quite evident what was in his mind. He was going to work Stacey hard. She was going to see life at Glen Airlie under the worst possible conditions. Maybe he had more gumption than Aunt Claudia gave him credit for. They might have had an ardent reconciliation under the stars that night, but he didn't deem that enough. He was trying her out. For one unworthy moment everything in Elissa wished for Stacey to fail him, that she couldn't face the prospect of the best years of her life being spent in this isolation.

She said, 'Logan, do give Stacey a bit of a break. If

you're going down with the sleds of lambs, take her with you.'

He gave her a strange look. 'I'm the boss here. *You're* coming with me. So are the children. If Aunt Claudia can carry on, so can Stacey.'

Elissa said, 'Yes, but though I've been away from it ten years, this is Stacey's first taste of it, so it's not fair——'

'She's not as soft as she looks. She's whipcord tough because of all her riding. Running a riding-school is more elegant than this, of course, and carries more status, but she came back full of resolve ... so you're the one to be with me.'

They'd been ploughing on through the snow as they talked. Logan made no apologies to Claudia and Stacey, but told Hew and Olaf to pour some hot soup from the flasks for the women and themselves while he and Elissa took the lambs down. 'I want the children for feeding them, so come on.'

Down at the house they tubbed the lambs quickly, put old towels and sacks on the laundry floor, rubbed them vigorously, the children doing an excellent job, though Elissa saw Isabel shedding tears over the two that were beyond saving, and Bess's lip trembled as her uncle took them outside. 'Think how many we've saved,' urged Rennie, rubbing away.

Before they'd gone out they'd filled every available hot-water bottle, and covered them up with old pieces of blanket to keep warm. The heat from the kitchen stove was marvellous. The ones from the day before were out on the back verandah, barricaded in with a few hurdles, all bleating madly. There was no time yet to feed them, while there was a chance of reviving these inert bodies. Finally, their turn came, and they subsided drowsily again.

Elissa dished out hot ladlefuls of thick broth, dropped broken bread into it. They all supped gratefully. She and Stacey had cooked a huge casserole of sausages the night before, for their lunch, so Elissa popped it back to warm up now, and put Stacey's scones on the rack, flung china and cutlery on the bare table, because there'd be no time for frills today, just to eat and return to the snow-raking.

The day would soon close in, and so much depended upon how much stock they could save. Out they went again, toiling up the hill with the sleds this time piled with boxes of sheepnuts. Now there was no crisp crust on the powdery snow, it was thawing fast. It lightened their spirits, though they were all glad when the lunch-break came. Oddly, Aunt Claudia looked ten years younger. Olaf said so, admiringly.

She flushed, pleased. 'I feel it too, though come night I'll be stiff enough to creak, I know. But it takes me back to my younger days in the Mackenzie Country. That exhilarating feeling of pitting your strength against the elements and making it less than complete disaster.'

Stacey said, 'I still think, if one had a choice, that men could find easier places to farm. Makes you wonder.'

Claudia was surprisingly gentle with her. 'Indeed, yes. That always amazed me, in the Mackenzie, but it seemed as if the mountains got into a man's blood so the plains were not for him. It's always been like that. New Zealand pioneer history was still within living memory when I was young. The old folk were the sons and daughters of those who first came to these shores. They had shared their parents' struggles. I was always lost in wonder, love, and praise that, faced with tough conditions even near the coast in a new, raw country, there were some who took on tougher challenges still, crossed unbridged rivers, driving their stock before them, going further and further west, right to the Alps. It's something their women had to accept. But there again, there were some men who, for their wives' sakes, came back to civilisation. But what it cost them only other mountain men would know.'

The children were all eagerness to be out again. Elissa said to Stacey, 'Would you like to see to the dinner, and come out again later?' The men had gone.

Stacey shook her head. 'No, I'm sure Logan thinks I'll turn it in. I'll show him I can take it.' She looked at Elissa, said, 'Aren't you lucky? *You'll* soon return to that gentle Surrey countryside. Oh, yes, I know it too. I had a trip over there. I'd like nothing better than a riding-school there ...

access to all that music and theatre within an hour ... the Continent on your doorstep. But failing that, if only Logan would play it the way I want him to, get some money, rightfully his, out of this estate, we could take a farm and riding-school in much less rigorous surroundings. Just outside Auckland for instance, and have the best of both worlds.'

Elissa had to reply, for Logan's sake. 'Perhaps it's like Claudia says, the high-country gets into a man's blood. Central Otago is noted for that, dramatic, challenging terrain.'

'Easy to say when you don't have to face years of it. Marriage is supposed to be a partnership these days. Some sort of compromise ought to be made.'

Elissa supposed she must be old-fashioned ... she still felt in her bones that it was right for women to follow their men. Or was she being quite honest? Was it more that she loved Logan so much she couldn't imagine him elsewhere? This country tied in with the grandeur and harshness of the Highlands of his ancestors. If you fell in love with a high-country man, would you love him as much if you tamed and gentled him?

But she must careful here. She said lightly, 'Stacey, I'm sure you and Logan will work it out, given time. Well, if we're going up the hill again, we'll refill these flasks. We may get further up now it's thawing.'

What a blessing they'd freed the sheep under those banks, because now the stream was roaring down as clump after clump of snow softened and fell into it. It was a cheering sight to see tussock heads appearing, even though they still had to work hard in the gullies that intersected these hill-sides, where shade kept the drifts deep. Late snowfalls like this were disastrous enough, but they seldom lay for long.

The best sight of all was the snow melting from the higher slopes where as yet they'd not reached. When, late, Logan and Hew decreed that the women had worked long enough, they demurred, at least Claudia and Elissa did, but the men were adamant. 'It will do us good to know you've got another feeding over, and apart from what we bring down then, to revive, we can relax. Don't forget to put the transistor on to get the forecast and reports.'

It was only when they reached the house that they realised how bone-weary they were. They sank down on kitchen
chairs and groaned, disregarding the ceaseless bleating that
greeted their coming. Aunt Claudia said, 'I know they're
fair clemmed, but so are we. We'll revive ourselves first. Oh,
my back!'

'The best thing in this house,' said Elissa fervently, 'is
that stove, glowing fiercely ... instant bath water, instant
tea, instant soup.'

'You may sing a different song,' said Stacey, 'the first
time you have to clean the flues. I once stayed at a place
that had one. Soot everywhere!'

Elissa giggled. 'And I'm so accident-prone, goodness
knows what would happen, but all I can think of at the
moment is that if this house was all-electric, where would
we be?'

The children, revived, tore off to see how the twins were,
cautioned to kick off their gumboots on the cottage verandah and not to dare waken them if they were asleep.

Elissa said to Stacey on the quiet, 'Let's get Claudia
lighting the lamps and doing the vegies. Though she's such
a goer, it's tough at her age. If you like to make up some
more mixture, I'll clean up a bit. I think I'd better bring
some clean sacks. These are indescribable by now.'

Stacey said on a deep sigh, 'It's not what I'd call gracious
living. Not even civilised.'

Elissa dared not sound critical; she just said, 'There's
only one thing to be grateful for ... with the road closed we
can't get unexpected visitors. I imagine farmers on the
Taieri just dread city visitors dropping in at times like this.
But if only they'd stop bleating! A big noise at one end and
no sense of responsibility at the other—that's lambs! What
a hypocrite I am, when with each almost lifeless body
brought in, I'd give anything for any sign of movement.
These could go on the back verandah now, to make room
for what the men bring in, and the ones out there, on the
side one. But if so, I'll cover that stone floor, and put something against that door. I know from bitter experience what

a draught sweeps under it.'

Soon, with darkness falling, the house became irradiated with the mellow glow of lamplight. The big pull-down one, suspended from the ceiling, left for such emergencies, was a boon. 'Safer too, for the children,' said Claudia thankfully, 'especially present-day children. In the old days, on my most remote high-country runs, they were so used to lamps, and if any high jinks went on, it was well away from any table with a lamp. They were careful with candles too. Our children can stay up later tonight. I won't risk them reading in bed.'

Stacey groaned. Elissa said, 'I feel like that too, but they'll be so tired after all that work, they'll probably fall asleep out here. Unless they perk up madly once they get more food into them. I can never understand why repletion makes adults drowsy, and children bounce back.'

The men looked fagged to death when they came in, but cheered to find only one lamb occupying the kitchen, the rest, more perky, on the verandahs. Logan's eyes lit up when he saw what Elissa had arranged at the right-hand recess by the range. She'd brought down from the turret an old iron fire-guard and a large play-pen, long disused, and wedged them against the wall, and lined the space cosily.

Finally, when the lambs were in the corner, and the men had scrubbed up and changed, rest from the labours of the day descended upon them.

They got the news, though with extremely poor reception, and though the snow wasn't expected to last long, it had blanketed the entire province to the coast, some roads were impassable, motorists advised to stay off them even with chains and—fearsome thought—a severe frost was predicted.

The men groaned. That could mean an even more hazardous day tomorrow. They'd hoped to take the Land-Rover up some of the hill tracks. Ploughing through snow-drifts on foot was bad enough, but ice on the coating left was horrifying.

Elissa, going to her room for something, heard Logan getting into outdoor clothes again. She expressed surprise.

He said, 'I know you fed the fowls and locked them up, but if this frost is as bad as predicted, I want to take one more precaution. I've got two of those frost lamps you can use in a garage to stop the water freezing in the radiator. Our cars are all drained, of course, so I'm going to hang these in the fowlhouses. Once when I was getting experience in the Mackenzie, the hens froze to their perches. I won't be long.'

'Could I come, to hold the torch, or would I be a nuisance?'

The dark face softened. 'If you'd like to come.'

Something in his eyes made her add quickly, 'Oh, just because if you slipped out there and broke a limb, we'd be in a worse plight than ever.'

He chuckled. 'Not solicitude for my welfare, just for the collective convenience of everybody?'

She said lightly, 'How, after such a day, your brain isn't too tired to produce expressions like that, I don't know. You're as bad as Rennie. Even when we were busy feeding those dratted lambs tonight he kept firing questions at me ... did I know how many people lived in Greater London? How many facets there were in a single snowflake? ... How many taste-buds a snail had on its tongue?'

She zipped herself into what she called her Edmund Hillary jacket, pulled the fur-lined hood up, tied it, stepped out with him into the snow. He put an arm around her to stop her slipping. The icy air froze their breath, stiffened their lips. The whole world seemed hushed, and dimmed, for in Ludwigtown only a few makeshift lights were glowing across the miles of water. Their side of the lake showed only faint glimmers at the three homesteads. 'For which I'm callously thankful,' said Logan. 'If ours had been the only place out, they couldn't have reached the break, with the road out with snow, but if it affects all Ludwigtown, it's a major one and will have to be repaired smartly. Watch here, Elissa, this already looks icy.'

The hens squawked protestingly, but not for long, they were too sleepy. They had deep litter on their floor, but it was cold enough. 'These lamps seem so small, but it's enough to keep the frost at bay.' Logan stood on a box to reach the hooks, with Elissa steadying it. Even so, as he got down, it went from under him. He crashed against her, but did not fall because she caught him. His cheek, slightly rough, brushed against hers. She steadied him, then his arms came about her. She put up a hand, said, 'No, Logan, no. It's not wise.'

Surprise sharpened his tone. 'What do you mean, not wise?'

She floundered, tried for words, but didn't find any. He gave her a shake. 'Come on, you can't utter like that and go back on it. Why isn't it wise?'

She couldn't say it was because, unlike him seemingly, she couldn't take it merely for the pleasure of the moment. Or that she just couldn't forget the look of gladness on his face when he saw Stacey had come back to him.

She got another shake. 'Give me one good reason why I shouldn't kiss you?'

'Does there have to be a reason for kissing?'

'No. I wasn't trying to find a reason for kissing. I'm not so cold-blooded. Kisses just happen. I'm trying to find a reason—*your* reason—for *not* allowing me to kiss you. After all, I'm damned sure you enjoyed it the other day.'

She felt her temper rise. 'You high-and-mighty male! Logan, you may as well know I'm not normally the casual-kissing type, but perhaps even I can be—at times—in the mood for kissing. The other day was idyllic, the heron-stalking, the sun and the lake and the two of us alone in a forest glade. But that was all. This isn't my world. I belong now to the Northern Hemisphere. I came out to do a job for a man I loved as a child. But I've a mother back home, and I love her dearly. I'm going back to my own world of Surrey woods and villages. I don't want to get my emotions all mixed up. I'm enjoying all this, but it's just a flash in the pan as far as I'm concerned. Oh, perhaps I'm making too much of it, but let's play it cool. And, don't you think, honestly, that this has brought out the best in Stacey? I put a rift in the lute once before. I don't want anything on my conscience when I go back to England. You wanted

Stacey to apologise, didn't you?'

Logan seemed very taut, as if he'd like to lash out at her but he said between his teeth, 'I did. I very much wanted that.'

'Then don't foul it up again, if she grizzles about the remoteness of this. It *is* remote, it *is* tough. It does have many drawbacks, even to women who like country life apart from that. You've got one compensation, with Stacey's love of horses, she doesn't want to live in the city, only near one. I feel you and Stacey could reach a very happy compromise. It's quite good advice.'

'Thank you very much,' he said. 'Thank you very, very much. Well, that makes things all cut and dried. We know exactly where we stand. Right . . . out, so I can put the hasp on the door. I'll be in shortly.'

He didn't care tuppence, Elissa realised, if she did slip on the path this time. She went carefully, unwilling to cause any mishap to complicate things further. The night seemed dreary now. Coming out, despite the intense cold, it had been a world of magic . . . a white moon riding high over dark waters, forest trees sprinkled with gleaming snow, a sky of midnight blue spangled with stars . . . the ice-cold touch of the air against lips and cheeks, then the warmth of his arms, his nearness . . . oh, it could have been so different had Stacey not come back. But she had, and he'd been glad, and that night had taken her along the Secret Path. Had he kissed Stacey too, in the solitude of that forest glade?

Aunt Claudia was reading to the children, a breathless tale of smugglers, wild rescues on a savage Cornish coast, of villains outwitted, family fortunes restored. Elissa was glad of the lamplight, it wasn't so revealing.

Logan came in, sat down in one of the shabby old wing chairs. Aunt Claudia finished the story. In a trice Bess was across to Logan, putting an appealing small hand on his arm. 'Uncle Logie, are you too tired to let me sit on your knee?'

She must be missing her father, poor lamb. 'Of course not, poppet,' Logan said, lifting her up. 'Snuggle down . . . after all, cuddle a girl a day is my motto . . . though I don't always bring it off.' His voice was derisive.

'What girls?' demanded Isabel.

'You, Bess, Aunt Claudia, Stacey, etcetera, etcetera. The women of the household, who else?'

Isabel came to sit on the arm of his chair, then slid down on to his lap too. 'Tell us about our gold-mining ancestor, please?'

He'd been adventurous, that long-ago Torquil Mac-Corquodale, first a Forty-niner on the Californian gold-fields, winning and losing a fortune, thence to Bendigo in the eighteen-fifties and then to Central Otago after gold was discovered there in 1861. Up the Awa-whio-whio at the far end of the lake, he had struck it rich again, but, thinking it had petered out, had packed his swag again and made his way to the West Coast diggings.

By now, however, he had learned his lesson and built up a prosperous supply business, entered local politics and became quite a figure on the Coast, known for his bigheartedness and generosity towards anyone in want.

Stacey said, not quite looking at Logan, 'That was because he'd known what it was to be reduced to the breadline himself, cheated out of his wealth by his best friend.'

Rennie said quickly, 'His best friend cheated him? Did the police catch up on him? Did he have to repay? What was his name?'

Logan tried to drown out the reply but failed. Stacey's voice rang clearly. 'His name was Walter Ogilvie Airlie, Rupert Airlie's great-grandfather, who prospered on his ill-gotten gains.'

The three children looked shocked. Excited, but dismayed to think they knew the great-grandson of someone criminally dishonest.

Logan's voice was harsh. 'Don't take that for gospel, kids. It's just a rumour. I don't think it adds at all. From all accounts Walter Airlie was a steady, honest man. My own ancestor, and yours, was a ne'er-do-well, a fly-by-night character, hard-drinking, gambling, not a stable type. Stable doesn't mean horsey, it means dependable. Torquil, as a young man, with no ties, won and lost his gold. There is a story that in the first place, when he landed here, Walter Airlie took him in when he was starving. People on the diggings really did starve. Prices were sky-high, because everything came in on pack-horses or on foot. If you hadn't gold, you hadn't the price of a pannikin of flour for your damper. So Walter and his wife took Torquil in.'

Stacey said, 'It's not to say Walter's motives were entirely disinterested. It would still be cheating if Walter bought Torquil's claim to give him enough to live on and get to the West Coast, as seems likely, then stuck to the claim when it turned out a minor bonanza.'

'It's very doubtful that Walter made anything out of it. It's all rumour, revived because of the spate of centennial celebrations in the last fifteen years or so, that made people delve into old records.'

'But there must have been something. Those papers I found.'

'Only relating to the money Walter paid Torquil. There's one thing that to me proves as nearly as can be proved that there was no double-dealing. Torquil was born 1833, went to California as a mere youth, but didn't marry till he was forty-two, in 1875, many years after he'd departed from Central Otago, but he named his first son Walter Airlie MacCorquodale. That was long after the working yielded more gold. You don't name your son after a man who's defrauded you. Besides which, it's all water under the bridge now. I wouldn't care if there was skulduggery. It's nothing to do with us.'

'*I* don't believe Uncle Rupert's ancestor cheated our ancestor,' said Isabel sturdily. 'But it makes a lovely story, doesn't it, Uncle Logie? When I grow up I'll write a proper ending for it. About me and Bess. And I might put Rennie in it if he doesn't try to boss me into giving him all the credit.' She sat up, fixed her brother firmly with her dark sparkling eyes. 'Bess and me'll find some—er—proof that Torquil's friend didn't cheat him. I'll jot that down. I'm going to be a writer when I grow up and Bess will do the illustrations.' She looked doubtfully at Rennie. 'What can he do?'

His uncle said hastily, 'Rennie'll do all your checking for you, dates, quantities of gold, etcetera. You have to have dates and figures absolutely correct when you're writing an historical novel. It'll be a good effort by the whole family.'

Thanks to Isabel, the discussion had ended on a lighter note. He added, 'Now, mugs of milk, biscuits, and teeth-cleaning. Bess is just about dropping off.'

Elissa looked at the three of them, Rennie with his proud dark head, beautifully shaped, leaning against his uncle's chair; Isabel, quicksilver, impulsive and lovable, with an exquisite profile; small Bess, her incredibly dark brows and lashes lying on roses and cream cheeks, the light shining tenderly on her pale gold hair with the darker streaks in it, and she experienced a moment common to most adults with loved children, of wanting to hold time still, of not wanting them to grow up.

She bent to lift the sleepy Bess, who opened vivid blue eyes and said, 'Elissa, if you take us to Mummy and Daddy in England, will you be living near us?'

'Not in the same town, love. I'll be living about the same distance from London, in the opposite direction, but that's just an hour by train each way, lovely fast trains that run often, so we'll see quite a lot of each other.'

Over the shining head her eyes met Logan's.

'That's good,' said Bess drowsily. 'Uncle Logie, I don't want any supper, I just want to go to bed.'

'I want lots of supper,' declared Isabel. 'I'm starving! It's all that hard work today. Elissa, will we be able to come to see you? I love trains. Wouldn't it be fun to go through London and out the other side?'

'Yes. We'll have a lot of fun together. Your mummy and daddy can come for a weekend. It's a lovely ride.'

'Do you know how many trains go in and out of London every hour? Or is it every day?' demanded Rennie. 'I'll just check.'

'Not now, you won't,' said his uncle. 'I used to employ these delaying tactics myself when I was a boy, so you can't teach me anything. Cookies and milk, then the bathroom. Working men go to bed early. I want your help to-morrow again.'

Rennie looked saucy as he finally went out of the door, and said over his shoulder, 'Are *you* going to bed early, Uncle, or are you staying up with the women of your household?'

His uncle pulled a face. 'I'm going early. I feel out-numbered. I shouldn't have let Olaf go with Hew, but he's going to sleep down there. It's too cold on a night like this in the quarters. Oh, listen! The chorus is starting up again! Who'd think those bleating monsters were hardly alive this morning! Women of the household, rouse your drooping heads. When those little stomachs are full, let's go to bed.'

Elissa had a pleasant surprise when she entered her room. Logan had lit the fire in her tiny register grate. No doubt he'd done it for them all, but the flickering firelight spelt out a welcome. She dragged the knitting chair that had been her mother's across to the hearth, sat on the rug, rested her arm on the chair, and stared into the fire for a long time. No use to build dream castles in those flames . . . they didn't last. The children's words had made her realise how short her time was now. Hard to credit that soon she would know this no more. The heron would take its way unwatched round the rim of Treasure Island Bay; she wouldn't experience once more, as she had longed to do, Christmas in high summer, autumn in April, and next September someone else would help Logan to succour frail lambs if they came into an unwelcoming world. She didn't think it would be at Glen Airlie if it were Stacey by his side. It wouldn't be a high-country sheep-station. Stacey would wear down Logan's resistance. Women did, and her beauty was a powerful weapon. It had certainly triumphed for her. Logan hadn't seemed to care in the first days of their estrangement, but one glimpse of her and he had been lost.

But he certainly seemed to be trying her out, playing a cautious game, not being really lover-like. He hoped to get Stacey to opt for a high-country existence. But there was a hard core in her that wouldn't yield. These latter days, when Stacey had pulled her weight inside the house and out, Elissa herself had softened towards her, but tonight there had been steel in her insistence on Walter Airlie's guilt, something she was prepared to carry over into this era, four or so generations later.

She would hold out for reparation from Rupert for a long-ago injustice ... then Elissa knew what would happen. She'd get Logan to put the money in a down-country property where life was easier, and even the redoubtable Aunt Claudia had her limits, would be powerless to change things.

CHAPTER NINE

SEVEN days later it seemed scarcely possible that there had been a time of battle for survival, lamps instead of turning a switch, leaden skies and biting winds, frozen paths and blackened flowers.

Now daffodils ran in a wave under orchard trees that were breaking into diaphanous blossom, starlings were gathering straws from the hay-bales, thrushes pouring out ecstasies from every tree, and the *tuis* and bellbirds, the nectar lovers, were dipping brush-tipped tongues deep into the hearts of the flowering currants that made rosy patches in the shrubbery. But the best sight of all was the gambolling of fluffy white lambs in emerald pastures.

Bluey and Ben, despite the difference in their ages, were racing round as if Bluey too knew the abandon and sheer joy of puppyhood. It was remarkable how friendly they were, vying occasionally for Elissa's attention but never snarling at each other.

Isabel said, 'How I could've said goodbye to Ben if you hadn't been here, I don't know, Elissa, but he'll be all right with you.'

Logan and Elissa exchanged a startled glance. Isabel must have forgotten they might all leave together. Fortunately they said nothing. Logan said reflectively when Isabel had run off, 'Ben *is* going to be unhappy when you go.' When she didn't reply he added, 'That must have come out of Isabel's subconscious. She thinks you're right for here, and for Ben.' Elissa said, 'Oh, I think that's the phone,' and fled inside.

Later she made a pilgrimage, for her mother's sake, to Dingle Dell, behind the orchard where a long-ago Scots bride had planted her saplings of oaks, larches, beeches, leafing out now into green loveliness. Beneath them her

137

mother had planted the bluebell bulbs a cousin of hers had sent her from Surrey.

There it lay, a patch of blue as if dropped from the sky. Logan, a lamb in his arms, found her there, on the slope above, looking down on it.

He said, 'An unusual sight for here, isn't it?'

She said, 'Mother planted them. She saw them bloom only once.'

He looked up. 'The light's perfect. I'll drop this wee fellow in the shed and dash up for my camera. You could send her a photo then. Or do I mean take it?'

She didn't answer that last, just said, 'Mother would appreciate that.' Then, 'As you came along, you looked just like the first Airlie here—your lamb under one arm, your crook in your hand.'

He laughed. 'I daresay he still wore a kilt and a touree on his bonnet, but sometimes I feel more Walter than Torquil. Odd, isn't it? Torquil became a business man, and his sons and grandsons the same. But evidently I reverted to Torquil's own father and grandfather. I couldn't resist the pull of the land. Yet Douglas Airlie never wanted it. It's almost as if we weren't free to choose.'

Elissa, her eyes still on the bluebells, said, ' "No man is free in whom a thousand ancestors ride." '

'A quotation? from whom?'

'Oliver Wendell Holmes, I think.'

'Something else your mother taught you?'

'No. Something that was said about my mother by a great friend of ours, a barrister who lived not far away. He had known my grandfather. He was scolding my mother for letting someone believe *she* had repeated a nasty piece of gossip. Mother just laughed and said it wouldn't harm her as much as if this woman knew her daughter-in-law had said it about her. Mr Campeson said, "And being your father's daughter, you couldn't help yourself." Seemingly, my grandfather once took the blame for something much worse than mere gossip—covered up for a friend to save his marriage. My grandmother was dead by then and couldn't be hurt by it. Mr Campeson said, "History repeats itself,

Meg, but don't be too altruistic, you owe something to yourself", and he quoted that snippet. Logan, I'm keeping you from getting that camera, and I'd love a picture of this. You can send it on after me if you don't finish the film in time.'

'Can you possibly get all you promised Rupert done? Won't you need to prolong your stay?'

'Not if Sue sends for the children. I promised her and it would save her a terrific lot in fares. Anyway, this last two days I've got so much done by phone in the way of ordering materials. I couldn't have if Stacey hadn't pulled her weight and left me so free.'

· He said, 'Yes, but——' then cut off, and went off for his camera. Elissa decided not to wait for his return. She felt too aware of him today.

After lunch Olaf was to go into town to pick up some supplies for work on the stock, that otherwise would have to be delayed till the next visit by the launch. He took Stacey with him. Elissa went down with Logan to the mothering-shed, where they put in some good work persuading reluctant ewes who'd lost their own lambs, to adopt the orphans. Presently Logan excused himself. Elissa went in to wash up. Oh, Logan was on the phone. She heard him say, 'Thanks, Sue, you're a great sport. It means so much to me. I'm just playing it along, and maybe it'll come out all right. I'll see you don't lose by it. Goodbye for now.'

She closed the door quietly. He mightn't want to explain that conversation. You sometimes felt you must if someone had been within earshot. Play what along? And for what was he intending to reimburse his sister? She gave herself a shake for being so curious. After all, he'd had a letter from his mother yesterday. There might have been a message to pass on, and he might have been asking Sue to buy him something in England.

The next moment the phone pealed again. Logan came for her. 'Person-to-person call for you from Canada, Elissa —your mother. Take it in the office, there'll be no interruptions there. I'm here if you happen to want to ask me anything. Hope she doesn't want you to go over there sooner,' he added. 'I would like Rupert to get back first to check things with you.'

From Elissa's shining eyes, it was evident what a strong bond existed between this mother and daughter. Logan heard her voice go all choky and then steady as, no doubt, she reminded herself how much this was costing.

They had a few moments of ecstatic reunion per medium of a modern miracle that set leagues of air and ocean at naught, then Meg Montgomery said, 'I'd another ring from Rupert Airlie today, darling, and he said he felt rather mean keeping you from joining me here, but said that as no doubt I'd know from your letters, you had to help out with the lambing which has set you back, and he suggested I ring you at his expense to assure you I'll be here a few weeks yet and on no account to take off before he goes home.

'It was thoughtful of him to get me to do it, as that would convince you more if you heard direct from me, and it gave me the chance of a chat. So I would suggest, Elissa, that you should stay on at least another month or six weeks. He's so funny, Elissa, he seems more keen on the turret being redecorated than any other part of the house. He must have been very fond of his mother, who had that as her special domain. His own wife just used it as a lumber-room and playroom. By the way, have you heard from Judith and Elspeth? Oh, good. Pity they're both married to North Island farmers, or they'd probably have come to see you. I loved those girls. I suppose they can only get away in school holidays.

'Oh, by the way, re that turret room. Rupert said not to forget he wants the little davenport from his room up there. Oh, have you? Yes, I suppose it got a bit scratched through the years, but it was a lovely piece. Well, he told me that he'd found something of mine at Airlie House, but he wouldn't tell me what. Just liked being mysterious, I suppose, something that was in with some old papers he was going through. He meant to bring it to England with him, in case he could find our name in a directory, but he forgot it. He put it in a secret drawer in the davenport.

'He wants you to give it to me when you return. He said you're so *au fait* with antiques that you'd probably know where to look, but in case not, you pull the top drawer on the side out, feel upwards and you'll find a recessed finger-hole. Push it, and under the lip of the desk, a carved piece that's the front of the secret drawer shoots out. He said you'll easily see what belongs to me. Intriguing, isn't it? No, don't post it, keep it till you come. After what happened to Rupert's letter announcing your arrival, it's a bit risky.' They chatted on, then reluctantly said goodbye.

Elissa asked Logan to come with her to find the secret drawer. He said, 'It could be private. If you can't find it, call, but have a go on your own first.'

She shook her head. 'I think you should be there. Evidently there are family papers in it too, and I want you to be able to say I disturbed nothing else. It protects me.'

'All right.' He grinned, the blue eyes alight with laughter. 'I'll admit I'm glad you wouldn't take no for an answer. I'd feel like a kid being deprived of seeing pirates' treasure opened!'

They went to the davenport. Logan said, 'You're the expert, have first try.' He pulled open the top drawer.

Elissa got it almost immediately, and out came the shallow drawer, metal-lined, full of yellowed papers. Logan shuffled through them. 'They seem too old to belong to your mother—oh, could this be it? Looks newer.'

It was just one piece of thick blue writing paper with a gold deckle-edge. Elissa said, 'That'll be it. I remember Donsie giving Mother a box of that, one Christmas. She used it only for special letters. Oh!'

Logan's shoulder was against hers, looking over it on to the one sheet. Elissa said, after swallowing, 'It's Mother's writing. She wrote a lot of poems, many of them published. But this I've never seen.' Her voice tailed off.

Logan's hand came to steady hers. They read it in silence together. The title, *Lament for Angus*, had prepared them.

'Spring comes . . . and all my heart with gladness fills
 Though you, whom I so loved, are gone from earth,

And there is no one now to come to me
With daffodils.

High summer crowns the year with sapphire skies
Delighting me with beauty, day by day,
And I thank God that though you are not here
Your daughter has your eyes.

Autumn ... the trees we loved fling gold and flame
In matchless splendour to enthrall my heart
And every rustling leaf, it seems to me,
Whispers your name.

These comfort me ... so why should winter only
Withhold from me some compensating joy?
Dear one, without your chair beside my hearth
Winter is lonely.'

Elissa felt pierced with the poignancy of it. As she
finished her silent reading, her breath caught on a sob.
Logan turned her round to him, brought his hand up
against the back of her bright head, pressed her face into
the hollow of his shoulder.

The best sympathy of all ... wordless sympathy. He held
her till she stopped shaking with the tears she would not,
could not shed. He waited for her to speak, which was wise,
when at last she stirred. She turned her face sideways, but
still clung.

Her voice shook. 'It makes one realise how little children
know of adults' lives. If Mother wrote that when she was
here, then it was quite some time after my father died, and
I'd thought, with the casual acceptance of childhood, that it
had healed. She was so gay, so full of fun, made us all so
happy.'

Logan said slowly, 'I wonder if, in writing that poem, she
found it eased the longing, that it was all part of the healing
process. But you're right, Elissa. We don't know anything
of that sort of longing. In a good marriage, and your
parents' marriage must have been that, it must be a real

tearing apart when death intervenes. You live so closely—someone always there, day and night.

'I once heard Aunt Claudia say to Mother that the worst of all was when she was just coming up out of sleep and she would put her hand out and Dennis's wasn't there. And she added: "To think I was such a self-sufficient being for forty years! But it's something you can't regain. You find little compensations, and even enjoy life, but it's only a shadow of what it was before." ' Then he added, rather strangely, she thought, 'Some can cope with the loneliness, the night loneliness, more than others. And the ones who can't, ought to be understood.'

Perhaps he was thinking of someone who couldn't. She wouldn't pry. Suddenly she drew away from his arms. 'Logan, thank you very much for ... for this. Now we'd better put these papers back. I think I'm glad Mother said not to send it. Just imagine opening a letter and that staring up at you, your private anguish of a dozen years ago. I'll tell her it was a very lovely poem written to my father and that I'll keep it safe till I can bring it to her.'

Logan made a small sound, moved abruptly. She'd thought it a sound of protest. 'Don't you think I should say what it was? Just put it in an envelope and hand it to her, back home?'

But he said immediately, 'I think it would be all right to tell her. Elissa, I'm going to need you as a witness too. When I was leafing through those papers I saw my own forebear's name—Torquil's. I'm sure it wasn't his writing. Dad has some letters of his, carefully preserved because they were of the Coast and related to not only the mining era there, but to the intensely interesting period when "King" Dick Seddon was Premier. I feel a Paul Pry, but I'd love to peep.'

'Of course you would. You don't have to tell me if it's private.' She moved away a little.

He laid all the papers on the davenport, sorted through, found it. He looked at the signature. 'It's Walter Airlie's, writing to Torquil. Now how in the world did it get back here?' He turned it over. 'Oh, that explains it. Walter has asked him about the prices of commodities on the West Coast, in a sort of postscript, and Torquil had evidently just filled in the answers and posted it back.' Then he said, 'Listen to this, Elissa:

"Dear Torquil,

Yours of 25th November to hand. It was a fine letter, friend, and generous too, but in no way can I permit you to return that money I had paid into your bank account. That wasn't a business deal we made, and certainly I never expected any return from it, but suddenly more gold was found. You were too proud to take a loan to set yourself up in business, so I bought the claim from you. It was just a token gesture to save that mighty pride of yours. At the time I was getting good prices for wool and butter and many were the hours you'd put in, in the lean times, without pay, merely for your keep.

"When, finally, that vein was found running into your claim, I didn't regard it as mine. I took my purchase price out of it and arranged with the bank in Dunedin to deposit the balance in the Hokitika bank. Our friendship had survived many things, including your working without wages, something which helped me carry on during a slump. It has also survived distance, but it will *not* survive the hurt that would be mine if you jib at taking what is morally yours.

"Katherine is well and sends her love to your Marguerite. She was glad to know small Caroline is thriving, and pleased she will have a baby brother or sister soon. Let me know the baby's name in due course, and I will plant another lime-tree in its honour. Nice to think that the trees for your children and mine will still be here when we are dust and ashes. Ludwig Klausner is making me metal plaques for each one. It should be a magnificent avenue in its prime." '

With one accord Logan and Elissa swung to look out of the river at the avenue of limes. They knew that the plaque on the tree next to Caroline's bore the name of Walter

Airlie MacCorquodale.

Elissa's blue-green eyes were astar. 'What a day this has been! First to hear Mother's voice on the phone, just as if she'd been in the same room; to find that poem, and even though it was sad, it made me realise that even so, they had surely experienced the heights, and now there's this proof of a wonderful friendship that knew no breaking. Isn't rumour a cruel thing? Now Stacey will *have* to stop needling you about it!' Then she stopped, aghast. He and Stacey had become reconciled. How could she have blurted that out?

He shrugged. 'Well, nothing she might have said would have prevailed on me to mention any compensation to Rupert. He's been so good to me—let me buy in quite a bit of land, at a very generous discount. But Stacey got me worried. I was scared she'd come out with something to him. I shall show her this with the greatest satisfaction.'

Elissa said quickly, 'But not in front of anyone. No one likes to be put in the wrong in front of an audience. I mean, you don't want to provoke another scene. It's only just blown over. And she really has worked like a Trojan in circumstances out of her usual ken.'

He grinned at her, the well-cut mouth quirking up at one side. 'When you aren't blowing your top, Ginger, you're very tolerant. Don't worry, I don't want any more fireworks either.'

Elissa said, 'I must ring Trudi. I haven't for some time. Mother sent love to her. I've promised to go across some day. Next time Olaf goes in, I might make it. Trudi said that she'd have Theresa in for lunch too, with her little Emil and the baby Anna. Wasn't it marvellous that she and Murdoch Gunn married after all? Mother had a trip to Austria with a friend when Theresa was staying with her aunt in Salzburg and she told them the engagement had been broken. Now he's Rector of the High School, where his father was, in my days there. I'd love to meet them all again. Trudi said Murdoch's parents will be at the School Ball too. How I'm looking forward to it!'

Logan said slowly, 'You couldn't have a better partner

than Olaf, he's the best dancer I know. He's also expert in other things, so don't let him go to your head, little girl.'

Elissa blinked. 'Little girl? Me? Oh, I appreciate your brotherliness, Logan, but this little Red Riding Hood has had a lot of experience with would-be wolves ... you do these days ... and can cope very well.' She looked at the time. 'I must put the meat in, or Stacey will think I've not kept my promise to see to it.' He departed.

Stacey seemed distraite when she came back that night with Olaf. Logan noticed and Elissa heard him asking her what was wrong. They had no idea Elissa was in the pantry. She opened her mouth to call out some unimportant thing to let them know, but closed it again as Stacey said, 'Oh, Logan, it was so much worse than I'd thought it would be. I must be mad, mad.'

Logan said comfortingly, 'It's something you've got to get over, Stacey, and you will. Three months ago I wouldn't have thought you could, but now I feel you've got what it takes. We can't turn the clock back, my dear. But one thing we can control and that is how we allow these things to affect us. At the risk of sounding a prig, I'm going to quote that it's not what life does to us so much as what we *allow* it to do to us. Look, you've been a brick. This time last year you couldn't have faced up to this sort of life at all. Now you've proved you can. You're no longer a lily of the field. You've even earned Aunt Claudia's respect, and you know how anti *she* was.'

Stacey said, and it sounded wistful, 'Her respect, yes. But not her love, Elissa has that.'

Elissa felt a scalding sense of guilt and pity touch her.

Logan was at least honest with his lady-love. 'That's true, but then it just so happens they're two of a kind. Stacey, I can talk to you now as I couldn't once. There are more things ahead of all of us than we can dream now. In twelve months, you'll perhaps wonder why you agonised over it like this, because other things will have filled your life by then. Brace up, girl. The Ball isn't too far away, and once that's over you'll feel different. Who knows, you may even enjoy it!'

There was a murmur from Stacey, an answering one from Logan, then silence. Elissa thought Stacey was being comforted in the only way a man knew how. As he had comforted *her* this morning. So any hopes that had been raised then died. Presently the other two went away, together, to watch TV. Elissa hadn't been able to make much of it. But then she knew so little about their relationship, how they'd met, how long their attachment had lasted; there seemed to be more in their immediate past than she'd thought. It did sound as if Logan had put Stacey on probation. If that were so, then it seemed as if the waiting period, the time of testing, was nearly over. Elissa pulled herself together and went off to do some work on the job she'd been sent here to do.

It had its own poignancy. She was thrilled with the way her ideas were shaping, but the trouble was that she couldn't stop herself planning it round Logan. She could see nothing but Logan in the settings and furnishing she was creating. The room she thought ought to be a study as separate from the farm office which, inevitably, was cluttered ... it was never Rupert's silver-blond head she saw at that desk, it was Logan's dark one.

She must get on. In three days the carpet-layers for the turret would be here, and she wanted their samples and advice about the rest. The curtains and window squabs and cushions for the turret were being made at Alexandra and would come up with the men. The chairs were coming from Invercargill, ordered from a catalogue. Oh, yes, her task was really proceeding now. A spinning-wheel had been found in a loft and Logan was busy on that, sanding its scratched surface down to the bare wood and polishing it every spare moment at night.

The time to the Ball got shorter and shorter. Olaf was all pepped up about taking Elissa. Logan, annoyingly, was tickled about this. He said to Elissa, 'The dance-floor will be littered with his previous girl-friends, all looking daggers at you, the beautiful redhead from over the sea. Most amusing.'

She said icily, 'Not to me. Oddly enough I'm not the sort of female who enjoys a conquest like that. He's just a partner.'

'Wait till you see him all dressed up. It would be enough to make any girl's heart skip a beat. Just as well we're going in a party, otherwise you might succumb to his fatal fascination on the way home.'

Olaf came in on the heels of that, caught on, said, 'Boss, you're off beam. When I take a girl to a dance I don't come home in any party. And my new car's a beauty, being delivered next week. *You* can come home in your car with Stacey, I'll bring my own partner home, thank you.'

Elissa was only amused. She was human enough to be glad Logan wasn't at all pleased about that. Petty of her, but still ... She was grateful to Olaf. He was fun, often daringly outrageous at times, but with all the raillery and comradeship, it served to keep her from revealing her feelings for Logan.

She didn't feel she was so successful at concealing it from Trudi and Theresa the day she spent with them. Very little escaped Trudi's eighty-year-old eyes, anyway. Olaf took her in quite early one morning, but as he was staying overnight in Ludwigtown, she was to go back on the two-thirty launch. However, Logan rang to say the Campions from Twin Hills were calling at Glen Airlie for him in their launch, so he could come across to pick up his launch which was being refitted. The firm would like it taken away. 'So it will give you a longer day—you've got till four. Tell Trudi to have a cuppa ready for me and a large wedge of her apfelstrudel.'

Elissa had had a happy, happy day. Small Emil was a darling, engaging three-year-old, brimful of mischief, and Anna was so like her father, it was laughable. Trudi was happy to have beneath her roof again the schoolgirl who had fitted into her household so well a decade ago. She spoke so warmly of Meg Montgomery, it gladdened Elissa's heart. 'We were sorry to see her depart also, *Liebling*. She seemed one of the lake-folk. In time a newcomer, in our hearts she seemed to have been here for ever, the right calibre. Poor Rupert was so sad when she departed, I was sorry for him. He went in on himself. I think she had done so much to make him enjoy life again, he didn't know how to fill the gap. I'm sure he wanted her to marry him, and to us, it seemed ideal, but perhaps she didn't want to put anyone in her Angus's place. But I felt they could each have found much happiness with the other, an autumn even surpassing the spring, even as it was with my Emil and myself, who had both lost our first loves. And in some way, Meg was most unhappy too. And never wrote. As if she felt she must go back to her home, but did not want to be pulled by her friendships here. So I did not resent the silence. I loved her so much I felt her heart must have its reasons.'

Elissa had to restrain herself asking if there was any mystery about her mother's leaving, and remained silent. It seemed as if Trudi didn't know, and Elissa would rather wait till she rejoined her mother. She'd ask her outright.

Logan came in earlier than expected and spent a very happy time with them. Perhaps it was unreal, but Elissa felt as if a weight had lifted off her, solely due, she knew, to the fact that Stacey wasn't with them. Presently Murdoch Gunn came in, having managed for once to avoid the usual after-school-hours complications.

Theresa said, 'He's been late all this last fortnight. Peter Beaconsfield is here from the department. He's on a survey and Kotare High School was picked for the Central Otago one. Very interesting chap, but naturally it's made a lot of extra work for Murdo.'

'Not only for me,' said Murdoch, his reddish-brown eyes glancing in Theresa's direction. 'We've had him in most nights for the evening meal. He's in a motel because he likes to work in solitude with no noise from dining-rooms or bars or bands, so it suits him fine, but I feel it's been a lot for Theresa. Though he's very good with the children.'

Logan said, 'Seeing he's at a motel, it's a wonder he didn't bring his wife. Or have they a baby or something?'

Both Theresa and Murdoch looked astonished. Then

Theresa said, 'Peter? He's not married. He's still a bachelor.'

Logan looked astounded too. 'Is he? Someone told me he was married. In fact said they'd seen the account of the wedding—a year or two back—in some Christchurch paper.'

Murdoch said, 'He certainly lives there—is attached to Teachers' College there, but we think of him as a confirmed bachelor. I hear you're bringing a party over from the Glen for the Ball. Good show, we need the funds.'

Theresa said, 'Murdo, you sound horribly money-minded. Extending Kotare has gone to his head. As soon as the new gymnasium was finished and I thought fund-raising would take a rest, he wanted a new library. Are you coming across in the launch, Logan? I always think it's so romantic and old-timey to see lighted boats converging on Ludwig-town when there's a "do" like this on.'

'No. It would have been nice for Elissa to have had that experience, but I didn't think the *Kingfisher* would have been ready in time. I'll have another shot—I'd prefer that —but I think Olaf would think I was horning in on him. When I suggested one car he thought I was a real spoil-sport. He's taking Elissa. Trudi, when the turret room Elissa is doing up is finished, I'll come over the lake and take you back there for the day to see it. You'll love it. It's going to be a dream.'

Trudi's eyes sparkled. 'How that will please Rupert! I can imagine him wanting it to be restored to what it was in his mother's day. Letitia made it a sort of refuge. It got them away from the workaday atmosphere, and they seemed to get above—what is that modern phrase I like so much, Murdoch? They left their cares below and had views across the lake to make them feel less isolated and ... Murdoch?'

His brow cleared. 'Tru, I think you mean they seemed to get above worry level.'

'*Ja*. That is it—so expressive. We all need to do that at times. Letty was a wonderful woman, just a girl, a city girl at that when James married her, I believe, but in the end she loved the lake and the mountains as much as he did. It can happen, though not often.'

Elissa knew a stab of pure jealousy, an emotion new to her. Stacey would be the one to prove it could happen. Soon they rose, regretfully. Trudi had a box packed with a huge apfelstrudel for Logan and a big plummy fruitcake for Elissa, to help out the never-ending job of filling small tummies, she said.

As she kissed Elissa goodbye, she said wistfully, 'Give your mother my love when you write again. Tell her Canada is no longer too far for a visit. So why not, to please an old, old woman, fly over here before you have to go back? ... if go back you must. She could stay here at Cloudy Hill if she didn't want to be a self-asked guest at Airlie House.'

Elissa laughed lightly, said, 'I'll mention it, but she seems to want to stay on with Aunt Jean till I join them.'

'Ask her anyway,' said Logan, 'she might change her mind.'

The lines of the *Kingfisher* were superb, white with blue and green facings and a kingfisher painted beneath the name by a local artist. Logan got a peaked cap from a locker. It did things to his profile. He handled his boat—it was his, not Glen Airlie's—lovingly and expertly. Elissa felt moved at the sight of his tanned lean fingers on the wheel, the way he lifted his chin to gaze over the lake.

She said, 'Oh, Logan, you remind me very strongly of the boatman who took Mother and myself over the sea to Skye.'

He turned to grin at her. 'A clansman, perhaps, with the same beaky cast of features! Skye being the home of the MacCorquodales and the MacLeods. This is my element, Elissa ... hills and mountains for sheep, great craggy rocks and lochs cradled in those mountains. I could never live on an inland farm that wasn't near one of the great lakes.'

She said, faintly troubled, because this was the man she loved, and when he married, his happiness might be at stake if he couldn't compromise, 'How about a farm near the sea, Logan? In New Zealand coastal farms are always near the cities, because in the South Island, anyway, the main highway hugs the coast. So you could have the best of both worlds.'

He looked at her in amazement. 'The best? Not for me. My world is here, those ancestors you spoke of riding in me the other day.' His eyes roved over her. 'You fit the picture of the Skye boatman too, in your tartan skirt.'

'Not really.' She looked down at the blue tartan. 'This is a Montgomery one, and they were mainly Lowlanders.'

'It's the right colouring for this ... the blue and the green of it. A hand-knitted sweater too, clinging in all the right places.' He laughed as she coloured a little. The red-gold hair was blowing back from her small, exquisite ears. 'Pity we can't have figureheads on small craft. The lake is the exact colour of your eyes today. You're a Viking lass. Maybe a Montgomery married a lass from "Norway-over-the-foam". What a model you'd make for any ship, with that line of chin, and your full bosom.'

'You're so mad, Logan MacCorquodale.' Elissa was laughing now. 'Very good for my ego, though.'

'Surely you, above anybody, don't need your ego boosting?'

'Why surely me? A freckle-faced ginger-headed kid. That's what I was and what I've stayed.'

'Did you say *I* was mad? You *must* know you have something beyond the classical forms of beauty.'

Then he laughed because she really did look stunned. He seemed in a strange, exhilarated mood. 'Elissa, don't let's go home yet. It's been all work and no play till today. It's so long since I've had the wheel under my fingers, I can't bear to cut straight across Moana-Kotare.' He let her out.

He took the launch curving and swooping over the vast expanse of water until Elissa felt they were soaring like sea-birds above it, not on it. He said, 'That first night when you came back into the kitchen after your bath in that glam garment of my mama's, you really made me blink. Half an hour earlier you'd been a drowned rat, then suddenly you were a vision. I was going to say so, but I thought I shouldn't.'

Her laughter rang out again. 'You absolutely daft creature! I had a face like a boiled lobster because the bath had almost scalded me, my hair was still in witch-locks from the steam and the storm, and I really felt like something the cat had dragged in.'

'That colour suited you. What would you call it?'

'Apricot. The nearest to pink a redhead can wear.'

'And it had turquoise embroidery and ribbons. What are you wearing to the Ball? Have you anything like that?'

Warmth pervaded her. Had Stacey and Logan really made it up? Would a man with any sort of attachment to another, show this sort of interest in a girl? She said, 'Oddly enough I have. I was tossing up whether I'd wear a goldy-brown one I rather like, or a dress in just those colourings.'

'Then I'll choose for you. The apricot.'

'Then that's decided. It has bluey-green shadings merging all over it and lace cape sleeves in turquoise. Rupert bought it for me in Guildford when I consented to come. He insisted—took Victoria in, all unknown to me, made her try it on as she's exactly my size, height and all, then they brought it home on appro. He's a darling, was thoughtful enough to buy Victoria one of the others she tried on. He said it would do for a dance in Ludwigtown some time, even though I said I mightn't be here long enough, or even get asked to one.'

Logan said, 'That reminds me. I'm not very happy about you going with Olaf, in a new car that will probably go to his head, though on a road like that, he can't very well try out its capacity. But I've told him that if I see him drinking too much, I'll kidnap you and bring you home with Stacey and me.'

That brought Stacey back into the forefront of their minds. But not for long ... whose thoughts could dwell on people when in front of them, westward, the sky was putting on a show of unparalleled splendour? Above the purple shadows and contours of the mountains that bordered on their own lake, the jagged rims of the Remarkables were taking on their copper-rose colouring.

The sun was raying up lances of purest and palest gold from the skyline of even more distant peaks, and turning every cloud in a green sky to islands of coral, flame and rose. As one peak cut off some rays, others seemed intensified and for a few enchanted moments Logan seemed to be setting his course directly into the sunset path on the lake waters, so they were bathed in light.

He said, 'Do you ever feel when you experience a sunset like that, that it's impossible not to believe in eternity? As if God wouldn't create beauty like this, if He hadn't meant it to be for ever? No wonder some song writers speak of the next world as the sunset land.'

One lean hand left the wheel to hold Elissa's. She saw the whimsical mouth tilt at the corners, the laughter lines crease at the side of his eyes. 'I never talked like this to anyone in my life. So don't come back at me, Elissa, the way you did in the hen-house. It would be quite out of keeping with all this.'

She did not withdraw her hand, but neither did she answer. She couldn't. Happiness was breaking over her like a wave . . . this could only mean——

He continued, 'It's been a strange time, all fouled up with difficult relationships, rumours of past strife and misunderstandings, isolated by snow, weary to the point of exhaustion with the lambing, but I'm daring to hope everything's coming out right now. I'm not by nature a patient man, but I've had to be.'

She waited hopefully for him to be more explicit, but he seemed to think he'd said enough. What did this mean? Had Stacey asked for things to return to their old footing, and had he, understandably, said they'd better mark time, find out if they were really suited? And had Logan decided they weren't? Did he want to wait till Stacey had gone from Glen Airlie before saying anything more? That would be it. Logan was a compassionate man, careful of other people's feelings. Not a man to be on with the new before he was quite off with the old. What he had said that morning of her first disastrous meeting with Stacey must be right. He'd decided not to marry her. A wave of pity engulfed her then, for Stacey, who'd fouled things up for herself, when she'd sought to make capital out of something that had happened long ago.

They skimmed along the far shoreline, coming close to inlets and arms of the lake Elissa had known in her childhood, lovely lonely places where only birds called. Logan looked longingly at the far end of the lake, deepening now into twilight as the sun sank behind the gigantic westward peaks, 'I'd love to drop in at Twin Hills, but it's too late. We must visit them soon now we've our own water-transport back.'

He took a wide arc out into the lake, then curved back on the homeward run. Other duties, other people awaited them there. He had relinquished her hand to do this. The warmth of his still lingered.

They came into the warmth and light of the house. Stacey was setting the table. Elissa thought she looked at them rather apprehensively as they entered. Elissa felt there must be a little of that sunset glow about her still and felt guilty. If only she knew what had transpired between Logan and Stacey that first night of Stacey's return!

CHAPTER TEN

SHE knew soon enough. It was after the children had gone to bed. They were all watching television. Aunt Claudia had fallen asleep in her chair. Logan answered the phone, said to Stacey, 'It's for you. Like to take it in the office?' He replaced the receiver as soon as he knew she'd picked up the other one.

Elissa was knitting a blue jacket for the boy twin for six months hence. Gwyneth, of course, had prepared only for one, and so many tiny garments had flooded in as presents, it hadn't been a problem right away, but she'd need help knitting for the coming months. Elissa hunted in her knitting-bag for her stitch-holder, remembered she'd left it in her bedroom and went to get it.

The office was opposite her room and Stacey hadn't bothered to shut the door. The stitch-holder had fallen behind the dressing-table, so Elissa got down on her knees to try to reach it. Stacey's voice was attractive, but carrying. Elissa felt that it fell with devastating clearness on to the mirror of her mind and shattered it. 'Oh, yes, Peter, everything's cut and dried. Even the date of the wedding, though we've not announced the engagement. I don't happen to believe in long engagements ... with reason, as I'm sure you'll agree. What did you say? Do I mind the isolation? Why, no. Yes, I used to be fond of the gay life, but one changes, matures. Logan has been very good for me, has taught me a different set of values.

'He has his Aunt Claudia here. She's acting as governess to his brother's children temporarily till their parents find a house in Cambridge and send for them. So Aunt Claudia brought me here to housekeep. I've been here right through the lambing—and what a lambing! You'll remember that late snowfall? Well, that was the day the lambing started. Even the girl who's here redecorating Airlie House for us had to pitch in. The power was cut off ... we really did work hard against great odds, but it was somehow great fun. Yes, we are coming to the Ball. It'll be nice to see you then. Peter, I *must* go—Logan is calling me. See you Saturday night, bye-bye.'

Logan wasn't calling, but it was evident Stacey hadn't wanted to keep chatting. Elissa crouched on the floor, numbed. To think she'd actually thought, in that enchanted hour on the lake, that things had been changing. It was quite some time before she went back to the lounge.

It was a good thing the men arrived with the curtains next day. Elissa spent most of her time in the turret. It gave her more of a pang than ever. She could see Logan and Stacey sitting here in the delightful intimacy of a room isolated above the others, reached by what she and Judith and Elspeth had always called the Secret Stair. Would Stacey make Logan happy? No, Elissa, keep your mind off that. Logan's happiness is no longer anything to do with you. Get on with your work, dance merrily at the Ball with Olaf, be ready to take off soon after Rupert comes home. Keep your mind off Trudi's suggestion of a visit from Mother. That suggestion Logan had backed up.

She almost hated herself for wishing a disastrous storm would sweep up the lake, causing slips on the road, putting paid to any chance of taking water-transport to the Ball. Good job anyway, that no one could manipulate the weather.

They had been invited to a pre-dance dinner-party given by the Rector and his wife at the little town's largest hotel, The Forty-niner. Under other conditions, Elissa would have loved it. There were small tables, and Elissa and Olaf, very handsome in his Viking style, even in formal dress, were at a table with Logan and Stacey who looked a dream in a fuchsia gown of shot silk, giving out glints of blue and magenta and silver and reminding Elissa unbearably of the fuchsia-draped master bedroom that would some day be hers and Logan's. Purple was a colour Elissa couldn't wear; these apricot and turquoise shades suited her far better, but she felt insipid, even if as Logan had caught sight of her before she and Olaf had left, he'd given her the sort of look she might have delighted in, had he not been engaged to Stacey.

Trudi was at the table too, in black, with touches of red and green, very much an Austrian still, one of the best-loved figures in Ludwigtown. Peter Beaconsfield was her smiling partner. Elissa felt drawn to him immediately, because of the way he looked after Trudi. Trudi did too. She gave his hand an affectionate pat as it lay on the table. 'Me, I had thought to give up functions like this long since, but I have been a very fortunate old woman, in that I can still find gallantry among the young of today.'

Peter's grey eyes smiled down on the little nutcracker face with sheer affection. 'Trudi, you bring out the best in us. You demand that gallantry and we count ourselves fortunate to be in your company.'

This time Trudi smacked his hand. 'You are wasting your talents and compliments on me. You should have a wife here to appreciate these touches. I would not mind eating partnerless, or sitting on the dowager line, if you had a wife at your side.'

Stacey, on Peter's other side, turned to him and said, 'What a pity your wife couldn't be here, Peter. This is such a scenic place it would have made a lovely holiday for you both, even if you had to combine it with work. How is Merle?'

Elissa herself felt startled, because on her visit to Trudi, mention had been made of Peter as not being married. Pity Logan hadn't told Stacey.

But if Elissa felt startled, it was nothing to the effect this had on Peter. He just gaped at Stacey, a forkful of sweetbreads halfway to his mouth. He finally said, still staring at her. 'My wife? Merle? What—why——'

Logan came in, after a watchful moment, 'Oh, did you too think Peter was married, Stacey? So did I. Someone told me he was. But at Trudi's the other day, I heard he wasn't.'

Stacey swallowed, dabbed her lips, turned to him. 'You might have told me! After all, I was the one who told you he was married. You could have prevented me making such a *faux pas*.'

'Slipped my mind entirely,' he said cheerfully, 'Meant to, but never thought of it again till now.'

Why should Stacey give him such a disbelieving look?

Peter said, 'Never mind, Stacey. But why Merle? I——'

Stacey took a sip of wine, said, 'I saw the account of what I thought was your wedding in a Christchurch paper. It's not a very common name, Beaconsfield, and it was at St Barnabas's Church. The bride's name was Merle.'

He nodded. 'My cousin is also Peter. It's been confused before, mainly with mail. I had an invitation a month or so ago that was meant for them. Just as well that we're nothing alike. He's as fair as I'm dark, so if we're at the same party, there's no confusion, once folk get the idea there are two Peter Beaconsfields.'

Elissa wondered if anyone else noticed Stacey's continuing pallor, or that her efforts to join in the conversation were very forced and staccato. When they went to the powder-room before the dance, she asked Stacey if she felt well.

All Stacey's aplomb seemed to have deserted her. She looked like any uncertain girl, rushed to the mirror, said, 'Goodness, I *am* pasty!' she began hunting feverishly in her bag for make-up and succeeded in spilling it all over the floor.

Elissa helped her gather it all up, went to look at her own reflection so Stacey wouldn't feel under regard. Elissa said, 'I'm feeling a bit washed out myself, haven't slept so well the last night or two. Could be we're feeling the strain of the last few hectic weeks.'

She was surprised to see Stacey bite her lip and thought she was going to cry. She said, 'Wait here for me, Stacey, I'll be back.' She slipped along to the kitchens, tapped on a door, and then asked if they could give her some aspirin, as someone had a headache. She took them and a glass back and Stacey accepted them gratefully.

Then she wiped her lips, applied more lipstick and rouge, and said, 'I'm all right, Elissa, and thank you.' She hesitated, added, 'We got off to a bad start, didn't we? But somehow, it came right—due far more to you than to me. I've seen my faults lately and haven't liked myself very much. I was always thinking the worst of everybody, even of Rupert Airlie's ancestor, and trying to turn it to my own advantage. But not any more.'

Elissa felt the tears start in her own eyes. 'Oh, Stacey, don't—please. That was an easy conclusion to jump to the morning you arrived with Aunt Claudia.' She giggled. 'It had such an effect on me, being branded that way, out of the blue, that probably now I'd refuse to believe the most blatant example and excuse the very devil himself.'

Stacey burst out laughing and gave Elissa a hug. 'Come on, let's see the funny side of things and enjoy ourselves, the other stupid sex notwithstanding.'

All puzzling to Elissa, but at least they were more in the mood for dancing now. Olaf was a delightful partner, and, as Logan had said, a superb dancer. But it was heaven to dance with Logan. To be in his arms but not feel guilty, because he really belonged to someone else. As he released her at the end of the dance he said, 'Elissa, don't say too much about Stacey and myself to Peter—in any way—if he asks you for a dance.'

She turned an astonished face up to him. 'What *could* I say?'

'What indeed? But I'd rather he didn't know too much about our dealings—our spats and so on.'

Elissa said coldly, 'I can just imagine pouring out the whole thing from A to Z, Stacey catching us alone in the house, for instance, as we do a stately old-world waltz, and tangoing madly while I tell about her coming back to apologise, It's a habit of mine to pour out any old gossip to strange partners. I hope I won't be dancing with him, if you've got funny ideas like this. Though I can scarcely be rude enough to turn him down if he does ask me. But I'll keep clear of him if I can.'

She couldn't. He asked her as Logan escorted her back to the group. She liked Peter so much that her fury against Logan subsided. Unfortunately Peter didn't keep the conversation to the usual trifles. He said, 'Tell me, Elissa, you've been at Glen Airlie the whole time Stacey's been there, according to Trudi. Where do you figure in this set-up?'

She laughed lightly. 'It will sound odd,' and acquainted him with Rupert Airlie's plans to do up Airlie House and her connection with it as a child.

'I like it,' he said. 'I like to think of someone like Rupert Airlie who has spent his whole life in what some would term a backwater, suddenly upping and offing to Europe and Canada, and engaging someone from the other side of the world to restore Airlie House to its former glory. My parents used to be connected with this part of the world and told me it was a wonderful place, very hospitable, too, in Rupert's mother's time. Oddly enough, I can't imagine Stacey there. How has she been?' He felt her stiffen in his arms and said, 'That's another odd thing, Elissa, but it's important to me. We were very good ... friends three years ago, and I'd like to think of her being happy. I'm afraid I didn't deal with her very kindly. I thought her extremely fascinating but spoiled and arrogant. Tonight, I felt she was different, and the very fact that she seems about to—oh, sorry, that was said to me in confidence—let's just say, the fact that she was keeping house over there during lambing made me lift my eyebrows a little. Do I sound insufferable? Am I on the right track?'

Elissa's blue-green eyes searched his, 'I think you really want to know, that you'd be glad for her sake, Peter. I thought as you did when I first met her, but living under the conditions we lived in, with the road impassable, and no electricity, she proved a brick. She even delivered lambs in the snow. She never blanched from any task. I think suddenly she wanted to prove herself, and she certainly has.'

What Logan would say she knew not. He'd passed close to her, dancing with Theresa, several times, and could have heard enough to guess they were engaged in serious conversation. She was taking no chances on his seeking her out and accusing her of gossip. When Peter took her back, she said to Logan, 'This time I'm asking you for a dance, but I want us to slip away for a few moments. I've something to say to you.'

They passed old Trudi's chair, and Logan picked up a fleecy green stole from the back of it. 'You're much too hot to want this, aren't you, Tru? Elissa's need is far, far greater. We're going out for a breath of air,' and he winked audaciously.

It was too chilly for many couples to have taken advantage of the leafy balconies that leaned out almost over the lake waters, and Logan seemed to know the place very well, so he found a small one screened from the others by pot-plants and creepers. Only the lamps in the grounds and the stars over the lake illumined them faintly. 'What do you want to tell me, Elissa?'

'That to my surprise Peter swung into asking questions about Stacey immediately. I'm sure it was his sole reason for asking me to dance. I'm not going to have you think I gossiped madly about her. But even though I knew I'd incur your displeasure, I found him so refreshingly direct and candid, without any of the reserve you males so often stupidly display, I answered his questions as he asked them. He asked me how Stacey had been during this time overlake. Said he used to think of her as spoiled and arrogant. But he thought she'd changed. I liked it when he said he hoped I'd not think of him as insufferable.

'I didn't. He impressed me. I told him she'd been a brick during lambing, hadn't flinched from any task, horrible though some were; that I thought her upbringing had made her what she seemed like at first. It seemed to make him glad. Don't look at me like that, Logan! I've been aboveboard with you. Evasion doesn't come easily to me. You can think what you like. It *wasn't* gossip. I just gave him the truth and now I'm going downstairs to enjoy myself with Olaf,' and she turned and ran away before he could grab at her to stay.

Olaf was looking for her, his handsome face creased with displeasure for once. 'Fine thing when you take a girl to a dance and she goes to sit out in a secluded corner with another chap, night like this, too, in only a flimsy dress and stole ... and snow still on them thar mountains. Though there are more ways of keeping warm than putting on a fur coat.'

'Oh, Olaf, don't be absurd. I hope no one else thought that. I took Logan away to have a little tiff with him, not sit out. I left him flat when he would have lectured me. I'm fed up with Logan. I said I'd come to enjoy myself, and enjoy myself I will. I've never known anyone so high-and-mighty. He even thought he could dictate to us about going home in a party, didn't he? Come on!' She was whirled off immediately.

There were little things she noticed. Stacey dancing with Peter, not speaking at all, but looking as if she'd regained her poise. Logan dancing with Stacey and talking to her all the time, intimately, his cheek close to hers, his mouth at her ear. Then, some time before the last dance, she couldn't see any of them, and didn't care.

Suddenly it was over and she was heading round the lake home on the thirty-mile drive. Maybe Logan and Stacey had gone ahead. Their car had been gone from the parking space, anyway. Olaf had expressed satisfaction over that. This car was the last word in comfort. Of course Olaf's father's estate was one of the largest on the lake. Meanwhile he was an amusing companion, quite undemanding emotionally. There were no awkward corners about Olaf. You couldn't imagine arguing with *him*. He was a frivolous lad, yes, but a harmless one, not expecting anyone to take him seriously, she thought. Mind you, it would be easy for a young, inexperienced girl to mistake his attentions, think he was falling seriously in love with her. She disengaged her hand for the third time, said, 'Olaf, on a road like this, and at this hour when you must be tired, it's not wise to drive with only one hand.'

He laughed, 'There are few roads in the whole area that don't twist and turn or wind uphill and down, so I'm an experienced driver. But I agree that Central Otago isn't exactly a paradise for motoring lovers! Maybe you'll like me better out of the car some time.'

Suddenly Elissa longed to be by herself, tucked up in her

bed, the long day over. Day? Well, it must be three in the morning by now. Her head was aching, her feet tired, her heart heavy. The lights of Ludwigtown opposite began to run into each other, her lids drooped ... then suddenly, she was wide awake, aware that the Jaguar had stopped. She looked straight ahead for one uncomprehending moment. There was no glimmer of starlit waters, no faint outline of mountains beyond them, no lights ringing the far shore. There was only, in front of them, the dense shadows of a patch of native forest, with a track ending close to the trees. And she was with Olaf, rather an unknown quantity. Oh, how silly to panic all of a sudden. Hadn't she said she'd had a bit of experience with would-be wolves? Olaf was just after a little light dalliance. Only she wasn't in the mood for kissing, much less anyone she hadn't an atom of feeling for.

Olaf's arms came about her, his face bent towards hers, he tilted her chin. She put up a protesting hand, 'No, Olaf. I dozed off. I hadn't realised you'd turned off the road. It's late ... too late.'

He laughed, his face coming nearer. 'It's never too late for this. Look, I'm not a man to trespass on another chap's ground, and I admit you and Logan had me foxed for a bit, but it looks as if it's all on with Stacey again, with him, and if you didn't want a spot of parking in the dell, why didn't you say you preferred to be in a party? That's cheating.'

'Good heavens, I wouldn't be likely to take you up on that note of light banter. Olaf, let go of me immediately and drive on.' She felt his hand come to her throat, move against it caressingly, then slip downward.

She said, suffocatingly, 'Stop it this moment! I've no taste for this sort of thing. Okay, it's a lax society, but no man had the right to expect that because he takes a girl to a ball, she's going to permit petting.'

'Well, you *do* sound a little Puritan! How very surprising. But what fun. Who'd have thought it of your mother's daughter?'

Elissa got such a shock she stopped struggling and

found herself being very thoroughly kissed. And she hated it. How different from—She struck out at his face, with her evening bag, and it had a gold metal rim. She hurt him. In that moment of recoil she had the door open, got out into the night, her slender-heeled shoes digging into great ruts and almost throwing her to the ground. Olaf swore and lunged after her. She swung the door back, not caring if she got his hand in it, but he drew back in time, and turned for his own door.

She knew full well she couldn't outdistance him. Olaf was built like a giant and had huge strides. She turned to face him, slim, shaking, but game.

She said, 'Olaf, you've had more to drink than I thought. I've been warned about you, but I thought you were better than your reputation. Don't come a step nearer.'

Surprisingly he didn't. Then he said, 'Elissa, I thought you were just playing hard to get. Some girls do. I didn't mean to go *too* far, only . . .'

Her voice, like an icy wind, stopped him in mid-utterance. 'I'm not interested in how far you meant to go. Any distance was too far for me. *But*,' and something gave her the courage to go on, 'you are going to tell me exactly what you meant about my mother. Why you thought my mother's daughter would be an easy mark. Tell me!'

Suddenly he turned sulky, malicious. She guessed it was because she'd made him look a fool. He said, 'All right, I'll let you have it. How was I to know you had any illusions about your mother? That she'd brought you up strictly despite her own way of life? I thought she'd probably have carried on after she left here, much the same as she had then.'

Elissa's voice was incredulous. 'As she carried on here? What *can* you mean? What wild untruth is this about my mother?'

He said, 'While Rupert thought her the soul of virtue, she used to slip out at night to one of the fellows in the single quarters. That's why he sent her packing. So now you know and maybe you'll not be as smug and righteous.'

For a moment she rocked, shivered, pulled her loose

white coat about her, said through stiff lips, 'But how could *you* know?'

He laughed shortly. 'How could *I* know? Because it was my Uncle Hamar she was visiting at nights.'

She was finding it very difficult to even frame her words. 'I still don't believe you. I *know* my mother. You don't. There's some mistake.'

Suddenly Olaf became more normal, not so hostile. 'Elissa, don't take on so. Every family tree has its black sheep, and Uncle Hamar was ours. And perhaps I bid fair to be the one in this generation. It *was* caddish of me to behave like this and blurt that out. Not everybody's mother and father are pillars of rectitude, you know, and it's hard for their children to recognise this. I had one drink too many, I think. I'll grovel. I can't take back what I said, because it was true, but I'll grovel.'

Her teeth were chattering now. 'It's too ridiculous for anything! It's a piece of unsubstantiated gossip. I suppose Mother took one of her night-time prowls when she couldn't face going to bed early, she missed Dad so much.'

He said, reluctantly enough, 'I'm afraid it was anything but unsubstantiated. Even the police came into it. They paid a surprise visit by launch, looking for someone. You know how it is, you get some pretty rough chaps in the shearing quarters at times. They took Rupert with them, after they'd called at the house to get permission for the search. They found her in Uncle Hamar's quarters—the ones I'm in now—undressed. There was no mistake. Rupert sent her away the next day.'

Elissa turned away, a cry like a wounded animal bursting from her, and stumbled up the track to the road. She gained the last stretch and was out on the stony surface, almost running. She had to get away from the scene of her humiliation, be alone.

She buttoned her coat around her as she went, the now cold wind blowing off the high tops, sending tears streaming out of the corners of her eyes. She heard Olaf start the car up, reverse, turn, and knew from the skid of tyres on shingle just when he regained the road. He drew level with her, passed, stopped, got out.

'Come on, Elissa. You'll get pneumonia if you don't get in the car. I won't lay a finger on you.'

She didn't think she'd ever looked at another fellow-being like that before. 'Oh, *that*!' There was utter contempt in her voice. 'I know you wouldn't. You're not a monster. You're only a bit tipsy, but I wouldn't risk my life with you on this road for anything. Anyway, apart from that I wouldn't ride an inch with a man who just told me that about my lovely mother. Olaf . . . do you know what? . . . I'm *still* proud of my mother. It makes me realise what a wonderful comeback she made. I'm not foolish enough to suppose she *couldn't* err, but it makes no difference to the way I love her. I'm glad you told me, because Trudi wanted me to ask Mother to come for a visit. I know so well now why she never wanted to return. I won't be tempted to stay now, either, because it would make her unhappy. I'll never let her guess how much I longed to stay. Olaf, Logan and I found a poem recently written by my mother to my father's memory. The last two lines were:

"Dear one, without your chair beside my hearth
  Winter is lonely."

'What if, in some weak moment, she *did* find the winter *too* lonely? How could *I* blame her?'

Olaf caught her hands and she didn't even flinch away. He said, 'I could cut my tongue out.'

She gave her head a little shake, said, almost absently as if her mind was back in her mother's lonely past, 'I do hope your Uncle Hamar was kind to her, understanding, that's all.'

She thought he was reflecting too. She looked at him and Olaf said, 'He once said she was the finest woman he'd ever known. I've said sorry, Elissa. Will you get back in now?'

'No. This road is a death-trap, stone-sober. I'm all my mother has and I think now I may have hurt her deeply by coming here. She'll be afraid it will stir up the mud. I'll walk.'

He groaned. 'It's a good two miles yet. Logan will have my blood.'

'Don't worry. By the time I walk it he and Stacey will be in bed, asleep. I'd rather sneak in than meet anyone tonight.'

'I'll wait a bit, then catch you up, you may feel more like riding then. This has sobered me up, and I wasn't really tight to begin with.' It was no use. Elissa walked away from him even though she knew it would test her endurance to the full.

She stumbled on, trying to avoid most of the rocks that were continually falling on to this road, stepping over the rivulets that had cut into the roadway when the watertable or the culverts were blocked. Olaf caught her up four times, was turned down four times.

She thought she'd never be warm again, never be able to think of anything but her mother shamed and confronted by Rupert and the police, having to leave Glen Airlie, having to cope with a broken-hearted child. Once she pitched clean over a boulder brought down in a recent rain and landed up to her knees in a drain-hole where a sizeable stream trickled down the rocks. Accident-prone in an aquatic way to the very last, that was her. She tried to laugh at herself, failed. These light shoes were murder! Though she'd be lucky if they lasted the two miles. The fall had ripped one, and her left foot was torn and bleeding. She limped on, thankful this was one of the times Olaf was ahead, waiting, and so hadn't witnessed her downfall.

Suddenly a light streak hurtled along the rough surface and in an instant she recognised Ben. He flung himself on her, leaping up and bumping her chin, yelping ecstatically. She bent over him, trying to curb his exuberance. He began to subside, still uttering pleased but diminishing sounds. She felt his neck. He'd actually slipped his collar. Oh, the darling, darling dog! It was as if he knew she needed his company. Protection too, perhaps, but she didn't think she needed that any longer. They reached the car.

Olaf was standing beside it. 'I knew it was Ben. That fool dog! Passed me like a streak of lightning. He'll give us away when we get in, he'll bark his head off when we chain him up. Elissa, you'll be okay now with your guardian angel beside you. Heaven knows my head is more than clear now.

Wish my conscience was.' He looked at her so ruefully, she burst out laughing.

'It's all right, Olaf. I've made too much of it, I know. It took me off balance. No hard feelings. And nothing to be said to anyone else. How's that?' She held out her hand.

Olaf shook it with fervour. 'You're a fine woman, not petty. I'm mighty relieved we're pals again. Get in, and that great lump of a dog with you. Wish I could gag him. What on earth will the boss say to me? ... look at you. Mud up to the knees and bleeding!'

'If, by ill-luck, he's up, we'll say we thought we had a puncture, got out to look and I fell in a culvert. Logan knows water has a dangerous attraction for me.'

'You've a fine imagination too,' said Olaf admiringly.

'You really mean I'm an accomplished liar ... when the need is desperate. I'll sneak Ben into my room,' and on that laughing note they came quietly on. Elissa, holding Ben by an ear, slipped across the back yard and into the house. She'd have loved a hot bath, but didn't dare leave Ben for any time alone. She was grateful to find her room bright with firelight and the electric blanket on. Ben looked round him, decided he'd never had it as good, curled round three times and fell asleep on the hearth rug.

It was a surprise next morning to find Stacey not here. Aunt Claudia seemed to know all about it, so she must have heard Logan last night, or rather early this morning, and been put in the picture. Logan had a set look to his face. Had he and Stacey quarrelled again? Fortunately the children had no inhibitions about asking questions.

He said to them, 'Oh, old Trudi thought she'd like company for the night, Isabel, so Stacey offered to stay.'

Isabel sliced the top off her egg at one fell swoop. 'See that! Even Rennie can't do it with one go.'

Her unimpressed uncle said, 'Neither does Rennie get yolk all over the table-mat.'

Isabel persisted, 'Why'd she want company? I thought Martha Thingamy lived with Trudi.'

'So she does. She must have been away somewhere.'

Bess giggled. 'I wonder what Stacey'll wear. One of Trudi's nightgowns, perhaps.' The thought of it made them all laugh.

Presently they filed off for the bathroom drill and school-room. Aunt Claudia, on the same track, looked back at the door. 'I think you should tell Elissa the truth about Stacey, Logan. It won't take long to be all over Ludwigtown.'

He said drily, 'She ought to have guessed most of it. She was the one who started the ball rolling.'

Elissa was still toying with her toast. Olaf hadn't come in; Elissa guessed he'd not felt like facing her this morning.

She pushed back the red-gold strands that last night had been caught up in a glamorous topknot, leaned her chin on her hands, elbows on table and said, 'What do you mean, Logan?'

'You told Peter Beaconsfield how much Stacey had changed. Sold her to him, in fact. That she was no longer spoiled and arrogant, that she'd tackle anything now. They used to be engaged—did he tell you that? That encouraged him to take her aside . . . in the same corner where you gave me a piece of your mind . . . and he found out then that Stacey had never stopped caring for him, but she thought he'd married. Well, the upshot was that he and I and Stacey went away from the Ball for some straight talking. Trudi offered us Cloudy Hill. And the result is that everything in the garden is now lovely, for Stacey and Peter.'

She said thinly, 'For Stacey and Peter? But not for you, Logan. Oh, what have I done?'

She couldn't read his expression. She said, 'That's twice I've brought your world crashing down upon you. I wonder why I didn't just say to Peter he'd better find out from Stacey herself. Talk about life and death in the power of the tongue!'

He said brusquely, 'Don't whip yourself. If he'd done just that it'd have come to the same thing. They *really* love each other. I was just a stop-gap to Stacey. He once told her she was a beautiful idiot, that if he shook her she'd rattle. Oh, it all came out, that was some talk we had. It ought never to have been a three-cornered one, but Peter insisted I stay for it.'

'How could they? They must have thought only of themselves.'

His tone was crisp, hard. 'Not a bit of it. It took me to convince Peter that Stacey would never have married me.'

There was a pause, during which Elissa looked searchingly, even hopefully, at Logan. He gave nothing away.

Then he said deliberately, 'Ever since you arrived it's been nothing but excursions and alarms. I can hardly remember what an uneventful existence we had till then. But Rupert will soon be home, you'll depart, and Sue will come for the children. The shouting and the tumult will die.' He walked off, leaving her.

Elissa felt numb. Everything she did was done with precision, automatically. She kept to housework, knowing any work done on the decorating would have lacked inspiration this morning. She'd seen Logan go up the hill, Olaf on to the jetty to unload and store drums. Poor Olaf! He didn't know how to meet her again. He might try to skip morning tea too, so she'd better make it easy for him. She went down.

He looked up, reddened. 'Don't look like that, Olaf. I took you too seriously. I went on like a Victorian maiden repelling the villain's advances and it wasn't like that at all. It was just you, a man I've worked with and liked. I was upset about something else; I told you Logan and I had had a tiff, and I was in no mood for kissing, and it made me too dramatic. Let's forget it.'

Olaf said slowly, 'That's mighty generous of you, Elissa. But I can't forgive myself for letting out what I did about your mother. That was a case of ignorance being bliss. Elissa, you must never tell her.'

She raised her beautiful eyes to his. 'I worked that out for myself in the early hours, then I did manage to get a couple of hours' sleep.'

'But what did you do with your dress, your shoes? You must let me replace them. Pick what you want next time you go to Ludwigtown and I'll reimburse you.'

'No need. I dropped the shoes in the tip. They weren't by

any means new. The dress, surprisingly, washed. It looks such a fragile material, but must be a tough synthetic. I did it with a lot more, so it'd not be too noticeable on the line. If the kids ask why I'll say someone tipped wine over me at supper.'

'Like I said last night, I admire your imagination, but I'll certainly buy you some shoes.' He rolled a drum over.

Elissa laughed, turning another over and rolling it. 'I'll put last night down to experience, Olaf, and experience always has to be paid for. I wasn't entirely blameless.'

At that moment Olaf hissed at her. 'Look out, here's the boss.'

They both stopped rolling, straightened themselves, turned to face him. The penthouse brows were down, the lines in the lean cheeks deeply grooved. If she hadn't loved him Elissa would have described him as hatchet-faced. He said, 'Since when has stowing the fuel been part of your duties, Elissa?'

Stung, she replied, 'Nobody has ever defined my duties. You yourself didn't keep me to either decorating or house-keeping when you wanted me up on the hill in the snow.'

'That's absurd and you know it. That was sheer necessity. This is just wasting time—my time. You had your fun last night. Don't try to carry it over into the working day.'

Elissa felt as if every strand of her ginger crest stood upright. 'I'll just tell you, Logan MacCorquodale, Lord-of-the-Isles and what-have-you, that if I want to walk down and have a little private conversation with Olaf, I will! This isn't a kingdom. It isn't even your sheep-station, it's Uncle Rupert's. If I take ten minutes off to see Olaf about something, I will, because there's been times here when I've put in a sixteen-hour working day and never as much as thought of asking overtime pay. I've never even moaned about being tired. And that's that!'

She turned and as she sped off the jetty heard Olaf say, 'Now look, Logan, you aren't to take it out of Elissa. She's a brick, and you're damned lucky to have her here. I won't have her spoken to like that. She's worth a dozen of that Stacey, so——'

Elissa spun round, to try to stop them fighting, tripped as she went to step on to the jetty again, caught her foot in a steel band off one of the drums and pitched neatly into the lake head first.

The resultant splash was followed only seconds later by two more, almost synchronised. Elissa bobbed up, gasping, and was amazed to find each elbow grasped and a man each side of her, propelling her towards the first lot of steps. They thrust her on to them, then scrambled up beside her. She looked down on them wrathfully. 'You silly fools!' she said with a shocking lack of gratitude, 'I swim like a fish, and it wasn't even deep. Now we're *all* wet, and what will the children think?'

Logan said, 'You went in head first, and it's not diving depth. You could've struck your head.'

Olaf added, 'Besides, it was automatic, sheer reflex action. Modern girls!' he said gloomily, 'I bet that damsel St George rescued didn't tell him she could have choked it herself!'

They became overcome with laughter. Elissa had to hang on to the steps. It did them all good. When they sobered up Olaf said, 'We're all like bears with sore heads. Night-life doesn't suit us.'

Logan relaxed, said, 'Obviously. Well, I've heard of chaps breaking up dog-fights by turning the hoses on the combatants, but never expected to have it happen to me. Sorry, Elissa.'

Elissa said, 'No apology needed. I brought it all on, coming down here in the first place, then tipping into the lake, and you're entitled to feel low this morning, Logan, after last night's events. I suppose you've told Olaf?'

'Told me what?' Olaf's voice held a lack of knowledge.

She said, miserably, 'I've said the wrong thing again. But as you'd told Claudia and me, Logan, I thought——'

Logan said, 'Okay. Tell him then.'

She said reluctantly, 'That Peter Beaconsfield and Stacey were engaged long ago. She thought he'd married someone else on the rebound.'

Olaf said, 'Oh, was that what was happening at the table

last night? I thought she was upset about her mistake. Go on.'

She looked at Logan, but he wouldn't help her out. She continued. 'Logan straightened it out for them. They left the Ball and went up to Cloudy Hill. And—and Logan let Stacey go.'

Logan positively barked. 'Let her go? What in hell are you talking about? You know damned well Stacey and I were finished from the day you arrived here. You must be mad? We had that blazing row in front of you. Why——'

'But she came back. She apologised. And Uncle Rupert's letter turned up.'

The brows were up, his eyes blazingly blue. 'Has there been one single thing to make you imagine we'd made it up? Come on ... cross your i's and dot your t's. What has there been?'

She said, her dander up, 'I'll tell you. Every i was dotted, every t crossed. The night you got the *Kingfisher* back, Peter rang. You told Stacey to take it in the office. I went to my room for something and heard Stacey say, "Oh, yes, Peter, everything's cut and dried, even the date of the wedding, though we've not actually announced the engagement yet." So there! You can't get any more dots and crosses than that.'

Logan's face was a study. Then he said, 'Poor Stacey, more face-saving. She didn't want him to find her still unattached. None of it was true. Sorry I bawled at you, Elissa.'

She said hesitantly, 'But I'd wondered before that. You took her off on a moonlit ramble the night she came back.'

He nodded, 'But not with the idea of murmuring sweet nothings in her ear. I ripped her off. Peter may have told her she was a beautiful idiot, but that was nothing to what I told her! Then coming back to the house that night she confessed to me, quite frankly, why she'd come back. She'd heard Peter was coming for this survey, and she wanted to go to the Ball with a partner. It was as simple as that. She was very grateful. But I said if I allowed her to stay, she could damn well pull her weight.'

'Another thing, though. You said you wanted her to apologise. What was I to make of that?' (She just couldn't bring herself to mention the gladness on his face when he saw Stacey again ... he wouldn't want to be reminded of that. Men liked to save their faces too.)

'Couldn't you guess? I was worried for your sake that Stacey would spread a garbled story of the night you spent here, round the district. If she apologised, she wouldn't go on doing that. I thought letting her stay on would put paid to any rumours.'

Elissa felt a gladness at that reason. 'Now look, that lake isn't exactly tropical in midsummer. I think we'd better away up to change. Oh, look at that!'

The side door had burst open and out came three flying figures, the leading one bat in hand. They didn't see their wet adults till they were nearly on them. Aunt Claudia appeared behind them. Four pairs of eyes went round.

'Elissa fell in the lake off the jetty and we both followed,' said Logan. 'And believe it or not, she hasn't as much as thanked us. Said she could've got out herself! We're going up to have hot showers. Will you make the morning coffee, Aunt Claudia?'

The day from then proceeded amicably enough, though after that brief period of laughter Logan seemed very taciturn. For some reason it made Elissa feel guilty. By half-past eight that night she was yawning her head off.

Logan looked across at her. His voice was impatient. 'Why not turn in? After all, you and Olaf were certainly in last after the Ball.'

She felt the colour run up her face and recede. Aunt Claudia looked up and said, 'I meant to ask you what happened to your dress, Elissa. I saw you'd had to wash it.'

Elissa had an inspiration. This would answer Logan's accusation about her lateness as well as provide a reason for washing the dress. 'It was that stupid Ben,' she said in a tone so natural, she was proud of it.

'Ben?' They spoke as one.

'Yes. He slipped his collar, and came loping along past

Crenellated Bluff. It took Olaf and me quite a time to get hold of him and he not only muddied my dress, but he tipped me into a drain.'

Logan had a strange look. 'How come he submitted so quietly to being tied up again?'

'He wasn't tied up. I smuggled him into my bedroom to avoid waking everyone.'

Logan said, 'Was that all that delayed you?'

'Yes. Ben's not the most obedient yet. What else could have?'

'What indeed?' said Logan smoothly, and picked up his book. He'd sounded sarcastic, disbelieving. Why?

Elissa rose. 'Well, an early night sounds like heaven. Goodnight.'

She thought of something. What if Logan mentioned Ben's escapade to Olaf? She'd better let him know how she had manipulated that incident. That she'd given catching him as the reason for their lateness. She slipped out, sped across the yard and tapped on his door. Olaf had a book in his hand. 'Oh, come on in, Elissa.'

'No fear! But I must tell you this.' She did. He nodded, 'Thanks for letting me know. Goodnight.'

She slept exhaustedly, but was not revitalised by it next day. She felt lethargic, heavy-spirited. It was one of those days. The egg-and-bacon pie for lunch lacked her usual light touch. Perhaps a heavy heart didn't agree with pastry-making. The soup boiled over and the resultant smell was hard to banish from the kitchen. A handkerchief worked over the rim of the automatic washing-machine and gummed up the works. It took Logan half an hour to put to rights. It took time he could ill afford.

Something went wrong with the supply launch so they were short of milk and had to use dried, which nobody liked. When Elissa took afternoon tea to the men, Ben ran madly ahead of the farm truck she was driving, looking back constantly to see if his idol was still coming, and he ran into the lime-tree at the end of the avenue and knocked himself clean out. His body shot up in the air and he fell senseless into the dust.

Elissa braked with a horrible screech, leapt out, and was bending over the big yellow dog uttering squeaks of dismay when Logan and Olaf and Hew reached her. They turned Ben over. His eyelids quivered, his eyes opened and fixed themselves on Elissa's face in a glazed sort of way. He made a feeble effort to lick the face so close above his own, and staggered to his feet, wagging his great pow from side to side and looking bewildered. He soon recovered, Elissa helped him into the truck and took him into the kitchen with her to keep an anxious eye on him for further signs of concussion. Ben was the only one happy about this and managed to delay all the dinner preparations.

The children fought over who was to wash the evening meal dishes and who would dry, and in so doing smashed two plates, and Aunt Claudia got a bit of ash in her eye, and it took some time to get it out.

Elissa decided she'd have an hour of the lengthening twilight to herself. Perhaps some balm would strike into her soul from the beauty of lake and mountain. She showered, changed into a turquoise dress with a matching jacket. She was tired of working garb. She brushed back her coppery hair, feeling every stroke helped to lift the nerve strain from her temples, dabbed her ears and wrists with purple lilac perfume and for once used a little colour on her high cheekbones. She went out into the scented garden, saw a kingfisher in a flash of blue and green dive from one of the larch branches into the tiny stream below and fly off to its nest to feed its young.

She mightn't have felt a return of her old serenity had she seen Logan making his way down to Olaf's quarters. She made for a spot loved long ago, an octagonal seat built round a poplar, for Letitia Airlie, by Rupert's father. It had a background of rhododendrons and camellias at this time of year, burgeoning into their October liberality of bloom.

She wondered if she could bear staying here much longer. How could she, loving Logan as she did, hide her feelings? There hadn't been much sorrow in his parting from Stacey, but he hadn't turned to Elissa as she had hoped so foolishly, the night the *Kingfisher* had taken them into that sunset realm.

She was so deep in thought she jumped when suddenly Logan appeared before her. There was a purposeful air about him. She said, 'Oh, do you want me back at the house?'

'No.' He put one foot upon the seat beside her. She felt he loomed over her. She settled back a little nervously against the bole of the tree, hoping she looked more at ease than she felt.

He said, 'I've been down to see Olaf. He told me about last night.'

She drew in a deep breath, defensively. 'Logan, it might have sounded bad, but it wasn't really. I reacted rather stupidly, handled it badly. And he wasn't quite himself and blurted that out about my mother. He had no idea I didn't know why she left here all those years ago.' She looked up, misread his expression and said sharply, '*You are not to say one word against her*. You read that poem too. Without my father she found the winter lonely.' Her voice broke with the intensity of her feelings. 'I hated finding that out, but I understand. So don't look like that.'

He bent over her, took her hands in his, said quite gently, 'You're at it again, trying to read my thoughts. That's just all wrong. It so happens, Elissa, *that I don't believe that of your mother*. And *you've* no right to believe it of her, either,'

She gazed up at him in utter astonishment. 'But, Logan, I think it has to be true. I don't think she ever denied it. Olaf said Rupert and the police found her there ... in her night-attire, in his Uncle Hamar's quarters. How could she deny it? It's something I've got to live with.'

He shook his head. 'I think you've been in a state of shock ever since. Get your mind off a sense of her guilt, Elissa, and bring sweet reason to bear on all you know of your mother. I knew about this, and wondered. But gradually, all you told me of your mother made me doubt the truth of it. At first, I was just making excuses for her.

Didn't I say once to you that the little devil of loneliness drives hard?

'Then it began to add up to something. Her integrity about the tax fiddle of a firm she was working for. She lost her job rather than turn a blind eye. Then what the solicitor said about her father, when she too took the blame for something someone else had said. I thought about history repeating itself, and wondered if it had been repeated again here. Can't you see Meg Montgomery shielding whoever it was the police had come for? If she believed him innocent, or perhaps a victim of circumstance. I don't think she would have otherwise. She'd respect the police, be law-abiding. But an illicit affair with Hamar Haraldsen? No. Olaf told me his uncle once said she was the finest woman he'd ever known.

'We've got to get to the bottom of it. I'll have to be discreet, because Hamar married late in life and is a model husband now. I'll go over to Queenstown and see if I can get him to meet me on his own. You *must* know. Otherwise it might affect your whole future relationship with your mother, no matter how much you tried not to let it matter.'

Elissa's eyes were shining. 'Oh, if only you could be right! I want so much to believe it, but——'

He pulled her to her feet, held her hands against him.

'Elissa, it's too fatally easy to believe the wrong thing. *I* was in a stinking, disbelieving mood yesterday, wasn't I? I was all churned up, eaten up with jealousy, ready to believe the worst of you, because I'd seen Olaf's car parked in Calamity Gully on the way home from the Ball. It was even worse when I overheard you say to Olaf you were putting the night before down to experience, that it had to be paid for, that you weren't entirely blameless. Imagine what I thought! I softened up a bit when you told me about Ben, but was furious when you said that was all that had delayed you. And all the time you were just covering up for Olaf, just as I feel your mother did for someone. Tonight I decided to go down and ask Olaf what that overheard conversation meant, not to torture myself any more. When Olaf told me—what's the matter?'

She'd clutched him. 'Logan, you didn't hit him? Olaf said you'd kill him if you knew. It wasn't as bad as it sounds. I'm afraid I was too dramatic. I've heard of girls who walked home rather than finish a journey with a chap who expected too much, but it wasn't as bad as that. It was only that he was a *little* too—too amorous. And he had had one too many.

'That was why I walked most of the way home. I was scared of driving with him. But most of all, I was mad clean through about what he said about my mother. I think I really was in a state of shock. Oh, poor Olaf, I'd better tell you what happened, or you'll think it more lurid than it was. I'd dozed off and came up out of sleep, to find us parked in the gully. I didn't like the way he kissed me, and lashed out with my evening bag—You might have noticed the mark on his cheek. I was in an awful temper when he said he'd not expected me to be such a puritan because of my mother. It's a miracle I didn't take his fingers off in the door. Poor Olaf! He kept following me and passing me, imploring me to get back in the car. I tripped into the drain. Then Ben came along like a comet. I felt different and got back in the car for the last half-mile so it wouldn't be too awkward for Olaf. Logan, you *didn't* clock him, did you? Oh, you're laughing!'

'I can't help it. No, don't worry, love, I was so darned relieved you hadn't wanted to park, I didn't even think of hitting him. And I've got to hand it to him, he didn't try to lie his way out of it. I just told him I had to know because I loved you and wanted to marry you. Elissa darling, will you—oh, hell and damnation, who's coming?'

There was a crashing of bushes and into the circle round the poplar bounded Ben. He had something in his mouth—a shoe. A golden foolish dance shoe, ripped and stained with mud and blood. He laid it triumphantly at their feet, looked up for approval.

Logan picked it up, said, 'Good dog. Good dog! The proof of the pudding. Benjamin, you're a daft dog, but I think you knew my lady-love wanted you last night. More than *I* knew. But you've stopped the fine flow of my proposal. For Pete's sake, Elissa, tell him he's a good boy and he'll lie down and let me get on with it.' She did. Ben subsided but kept an eye on them.

Logan said, 'He's unnerving me, sweetheart. Elissa, I know we've been at sixes and sevens, especially with you hearing Stacey declare we were engaged. I ought to have sneaked you out to tell you she wanted me to play it along while Peter was here ... she saw him in the street one day and threw a wobbly that night ... but I thought you'd think I was no sooner off with the old than I was on with the new. But I purposely didn't tell her he was unwed, to shock her into revealing her feelings. She did. I thought I could then wait till she'd gone and I could really set myself out to do a spot of courting. You've been cheated of all that——'

She held a hand up. 'No courting? What about that time you kissed me in the glade? How you held my hand in the *Kingfisher*? But I loved you long before that. Right from the start, I think, when you told me I was to have the room with the key.'

She was caught, held, kissed thoroughly, triumphantly. Ben jumped up, barking madly, flung himself against them. Logan, really incensed this time, tried to push him down. 'Stop it, you idiot! You'll bring everyone rushing. Don't you see that now the idol of your heart can stay here with you? Lie down or I'll haul you away and tie you up.'

Ben wasn't half the idiot most people thought him. It made sense to him. He lay down, panting, tongue lolling out. Elissa was laughing helplessly.

Logan took hold of her, drew her down with him on to the seat. 'This way I hope he won't think I'm wrestling with you. It was meant to be so romantic, love, and it's turned into farce.'

She looked up at him, gave a comprehensive wave that took in the entire scene set before them ... the rustling trees, the scented garden, the pure turquoise of the lake that so shortly was going to deepen to purple, the curve of the headlands, the nearness of the native forest, the lap-lap of gentle waters, the whistling of mating thrushes from the orchard ... 'How can you say not romantic? All this ... *and you.*'

It was quite some time before she could say anything else, then she raised her head from his shoulder to say, 'But why, oh, why did you look so glad when you saw Stacey had come back?'

'Oh, that? I was so glad that we'd come out of the bush like that, hand in hand. Thought if she'd come with any ideas about having a reconciliation, she'd know it was no go.'

Then Elissa said, reproachfully, 'It took you much longer than me ... I loved you from that first night.'

The dark blue eyes glinted, 'Oho, did it, bonnie lass? I beat you by quite a few minutes. I loved you from the moment you swam into my view in Mother's négligé. I told you once I thought you were a vision of beauty then.'

She turned her head into his shoulder again. 'Don't ever tell anyone that. It sounds most irregular!'

He laughed. 'I'll tell Mother. She's a born romantic, she'll love it. They can hurry back now. I told them not to return too soon. And also, I even rang Sue one day to say on no account was she to ring up and ask you to bring the children over. I said I was hoping to give her for a sister-in-law, the most wonderful girl she could imagine. That the children already adored you and so did Aunt Claudia. That I'd gladly pay her fare over to get the kids. Hope she doesn't make it too soon; I expect it will take a few weeks to arrange everything, and I'd like her at the wedding.'

That did it. Elissa sat up with a jerk. 'Logan, what will this do to Mother? She won't want to come back here. How could she? Mother was born long before the permissive age, and will still regard this shadow on her name—even if undeserved—as a barrier. But Trudi never suspected that. She thought Rupert had perhaps wanted to marry Mother, that she didn't want to marry again.'

They gazed at each other. Then Logan said, 'He probably did. Remember Aunt Claudia saying he was disillusioned about someone he loved dearly? Elissa, don't look like that. Let's get back to our belief that she might have been shielding someone. Don't let your mother know we're engaged till I've seen Hamar. I'll ring him tomorrow and get him to meet me on the lake-front at Queenstown. I've a feeling that's it, and if it is, I'll see everyone who thinks that of her and put it right. Darling, the world's ours tonight. I'll tie this animal up and we'll take the Secret Path to that little glade. We'll face tomorrow's problems when tomorrow comes!'

Another twenty-four hours had come and gone. Logan hadn't been able to see Hamar, who was away—at some dog-trials, his little boy had said. He'd try again.

They had told Aunt Claudia, who was so happy for them, and they would let the children know soon. Now night had fallen. The launch today had brought not only milk, but books from England for the youngsters, so they all opted for an early bedtime, to read. Aunt Claudia had vowed there was nothing but trash on television tonight and she'd read her whodunit before the kitchen fire. She said, 'That lovely turret room Elissa has re-created hasn't been given a house-warming yet. The two of you haven't had much of a courting, with Logan's ex-girl-friend here, to say nothing of you both behaving like morons. You don't want to be with me all the time. I won't even call you for the phone unless it's urgent. Off with you!'

They felt the loveliness of the room that was presided over by Mount Serenity give them a sense of well-being. They planned their future, talked of years to come, even picked names for the children they hoped to have, decided to write very soon to Judith and Elspeth to ask them to the wedding. What a reunion that would be. Logan told Elissa of his inner anguish every time she'd mentioned returning. How he thought she would never love him enough to place twelve thousand miles between herself and the mother who would be lonely without her. That made them remember the last shadow that lay across their happiness. They pinned their hopes on Hamar.

The night turned a little chilly, so Logan lit the fire in the tiny grate for the first time for many years. He was in a deep chair in front of it, Elissa on a stool beside him, her arm across his knees, just within kissing-distance.

He linked his fingers in hers. 'Something to be said for living at the back of beyond, Elissa. Short of some real emergency, good old Aunt won't let us be disturbed even by the telephone.'

At that very moment they heard movement outside, and Aunt Claudia's voice demanding, 'May we come in? We've got visitors.'

Logan said something under his breath that was unprintable. Elissa scrambled to her feet, the door swung open and they both stood staring. Logan saw Rupert Airlie and a strange woman. Elissa saw Rupert Airlie and her mother. Behind them, beaming, were Aunt Claudia and ... Trudi!

Elissa flew across the room, said dazedly, '*Mother!* Oh, Mother darling, how wonderful, how unbelievable ... Logan, this is my mother.'

Logan held out both his hands to this slim dark woman with serene eyes and said, 'I can't believe it. Welcome back to Airlie House, Mrs Montgomery.'

It was only then that a smiling Rupert spoke. 'You've got your lines crossed, Logan. It's Mrs Airlie, Mrs Rupert Airlie.' The pride and love in his voice were unmistakable.

Elissa put a hand out to steady herself. Logan clutched her, 'Steady, my love.' She grasped him in turn.

Claudia's voice said from the little landing outside, 'Trudi and I will fall backwards if you don't move in soon.'

It brought them to their senses. They moved in, made room. Logan said, 'But how did you get here?'

Trudi answered. 'In Murdoch's car. They flew in this afternoon and very wisely came straight to me. It seems a lot of people got their wires crossed a long time ago. Marguerite and Rupert have wasted ten years of their lives, but it's all been put right now. Now, Marguerite, go easy with the telling. Elissa will probably wax indignant to know anyone ever thought anything but good of her mother, as well she might. Me, I never knew about it till today. I was astounded. I'd suspected a quarrel between her and Rupert, but never anything like this.' She looked at Rupert and

Meg. 'My dears, would it be easier if I, not too closely involved, told this story to your daughter? Yes, Logan, what is it?'

Logan said, his hand covering Elissa's, 'May I tell you what we worked out last night? Well, Elissa found out the night of the Ball why her mother had left here. She was grieving over it for her mother's sake, for her suffering at that time. But she had told me so much about you, Meg, of you taking the blame for some gossip, and a few other things, I was sure there must be some other explanation, that you must have been shielding the person the police were looking for. So I made an appointment to see Hamar Haraldsen tomorrow. He couldn't see me today. Olaf, his nephew, who works here, had told me Hamar had said you were the finest woman he'd ever known. Perhaps I don't need to see him. I have a feeling the truth is out and that's why you're here as Rupert's wife. Is it?'

Marguerite's dark eyes were shining. 'Yes, but the loveliest thing of all was that Rupert asked me to marry him in spite of what he still believed about me. He'd found a poem of mine here, written to Angus, and he felt he could understand how lonely I'd been, how desperate. I still didn't know what to do, felt I should tell him it hadn't been like that, but—anyway, we went to tell Douglas we were going to marry, and before I could stop him, Doug came out with the whole story.'

Rupert took it up. 'You know my son went wild when he went to Varsity. Got in with the wrong crowd, but had no idea they were pushing drugs. He found a lad in desperate straits—had been hooked on hard stuff supplied by this lot. He informed on them. They were out to get him, and the leader, a vicious type, vowed to get Douglas. He actually went in fear of being maimed, if not killed.

'He managed to get away, but was followed through the gorges, so dared not take our one-way lake-route. He shook them off. He knew the hills at the back of here, of course, so came that way in, fording rivers, climbing bluffs, taking one of the old gold-mining tracks, nearly starved, fell down a working and injured himself. Finally, not daring to come to the house in case the gang-leader had turned up, he stumbled into Hamar's quarters. Hamar knew it would break me up, saw Doug needed nursing, and came for Marguerite. She tended him for days, creeping from the house when all was dark. The night she was caught out, Doug had haemorrhaged badly. Hamar had tapped on her window in the early hours and she'd gone straight over.

'The police launch arrived, and naturally enough weren't giving much away to me, the boy's father, so I didn't know they had a fair idea he'd given the tip-off and was wanted mainly as a witness. When Meg and Hamar saw, from a darkened window, police uniforms, she acted quickly, in conspiracy with Hamar. They pretended to be confused, caught in an illicit affair.

'They saved my boy. When the police launch had gone, Hamar took Doug in our launch, secretly, by night of course, to old Tin-pan Dan, the hermit on Bluecliff Island. Later he asked for time off, hired a launch, when Doug was well enough, and got him through the hills again and up to Christchurch Airport. No passports needed for Australia. When Hamar got back here I'd got rid of Meg, in my bitterness. The rest you know. He made good. She did it as much for me as for Doug.' He looked across at Elissa's mother. 'Because she loved me,' he added softly.

He looked about the turret. 'It is well, Elissa. This is how I planned it long ago when I hoped to ask your mother to marry me. Meg, this is your parlour. Your very own.'

She smiled back at him. 'Not mine, ours, Rupert. For a refuge from those boisterous grandchildren Logan and Elissa will no doubt present us with in time.' Her eyes sparkled mischievously. 'First Trudi prophesied it when we got to Cloudy Hill this afternoon, and Claudia confirmed it when we came into the kitchen half an hour ago. Yes, my darlings, we've been here as long as that, being put in the picture. You poor pets, you've probably been planning a *ménage* for two and wonder how you can take all this! That's why Rupert and I had just a short honeymoon in Tahiti. We thought if we dallied too long, the redecorating might have gone a bit far to start dividing up Airlie House.

We had strong suspicions from what Elissa *didn't* say in her letters that she was falling for him, and as that crafty Rupert had hoped for it, he said let's be on our way. That was his idea in sending you out, darling, to provide an antidote to Stacey. Ever since Walter and Katherine's day, with their brood of eleven, this house has been too large. This wing is to be ours, the rest yours.'

Trudi was unashamedly wiping away tears, as was to be expected, but to see Aunt Claudia at it was really something. Of a sudden Rupert took a look at his wife and stepdaughter and burst out laughing. 'What active tear-ducts! Come on, let's lighten the situation. What about the fatted calf? I'm starving.'

Aunt Claudia rose, 'Thank goodness that ham's not been cut into, and that Logan brought in some button mushrooms today from the far paddock. Nothing like eating to get things back to normal.'

They went downstairs, Trudi and Claudia in the lead, two hand-in-hand pairs following, but as the others entered the kitchen, Logan detached Elissa from them. He took her out on the pillared front terrace, with its railings festooned with the frail stars of pink clematis. Spicy stocks scented the air.

Across the dark waters the lights of Ludwigtown sparkled in its half-circle, and those of Twin Hills gleamed in paler gold. They heard from the lagoon, as once before, the bittern boom.

'Gone all the bitternesses of the gold-rush days,' said Logan, 'the acrid quarrels, the drunkenness, the brawls. It's as if it was given back to God when the gold ran out.'

Elisa turned to him. 'Yes,' she said softly, 'why seek for El Dorado when there's Eden close at hand?'

Harlequin

COLLECTION
EDITIONS OF 1978

**50 great stories
of special beauty
and significance**

$1.25
each novel

In 1976 we introduced the first 100 Harlequin Collections—a selection of titles chosen from our best sellers of the past 20 years. This series, a trip down memory lane, proved how great romantic fiction can be timeless and appealing from generation to generation. The theme of love and romance is eternal, and, when placed in the hands of talented, creative, authors whose true gift lies in their ability to write from the heart, the stories reach a special level of brilliance that the passage of time cannot dim. Like a treasured heirloom, an antique of superb craftsmanship, a beautiful gift from someone loved—these stories too, have a special significance that transcends the ordinary. **$1.25 each novel**

Here are your 1978
Harlequin Collection Editions...

Original Harlequin Romance numbers in brackets

ORDER FORM
Harlequin Reader Service

In U.S.A.
MPO Box 707
Niagara Falls, N.Y. 14302

In Canada
649 Ontario St.,
Stratford, Ontario, N5A 6W2

Please send me the following Harlequin Collection novels. I am enclosing my check or money order for $1.25 for each novel ordered, plus 25¢ to cover postage and handling.

☐ 102	☐ 115	☐ 128	☐ 140
☐ 103	☐ 116	☐ 129	☐ 141
☐ 104	☐ 117	☐ 130	☐ 142
☐ 105	☐ 118	☐ 131	☐ 143
☐ 106	☐ 119	☐ 132	☐ 144
☐ 107	☐ 120	☐ 133	☐ 145
☐ 108	☐ 121	☐ 134	☐ 146
☐ 109	☐ 122	☐ 135	☐ 147
☐ 110	☐ 123	☐ 136	☐ 148
☐ 111	☐ 124	☐ 137	☐ 149
☐ 112	☐ 125	☐ 138	☐ 150
☐ 113	☐ 126	☐ 139	☐ 151
☐ 114	☐ 127		

Number of novels checked @
$1.25 each = $ _____

N.Y. and N.J. residents add
appropriate sales tax $ _____

Postage and handling $ ____.25

TOTAL $ _____

NAME _____

(Please Print)

ADDRESS _____

CITY _____

STATE/PROV. _____

ZIP/POSTAL CODE _____

AB ROM 2239

Offer expires June 30, 1979

And there's still *more* love in

Harlequin Presents...

Yes!

Four more spellbinding
romantic stories every month
by your favorite authors.
Elegant and sophisticated tales of
love and love's conflicts.

Let your imagination be swept away to
exotic places in search of adventure,
intrigue and romance. Get to
know the warm, true-to-life
characters. Share the special
kind of miracle that
love can be.

Don't miss out. Buy now and discover
the world of HARLEQUIN PRESENTS...

Harlequin Presents...

The beauty of true romance...

The excitement of world travel...

The splendor of first love...

unique love stories for today's woman

Harlequin Presents...
novels of honest,
twentieth-century love,
with characters who
are interesting, vibrant
and alive.

The elegance of love...
The warmth of romance...
The lure of faraway places...

Four new novels, every
month — wherever
paperbacks are sold.